T0374317

The Alpha of My Eye

BLESSILDA CHEONG

PARTRIDGE
A Penguin Random House Company

To order additional copies of this book, contact
Toll Free 800 101 2657 (Singapore)
Toll Free 1 800 81 7340 (Malaysia)
orders.singapore@partridgepublishing.com

www.partridgepublishing.com/singapore

For my mother, Precious Benemerito—Here's to dreaming and fighting for my dreams. To, having all these crazy imaginations and being able to do something with them. For teaching me to listen to my heart instead of my head. For believing that I could start something and finish it. For. Everything!

I have found the paradox, that if you love
until it hurts, there can be no more
hurt, only more love.
—Mother Teresa.

❧ ACKNOWLEDGEMENT ❧

First of all I would like to thank my sister, Pauline Cheong, for literally pulling my arse off the floor and saying, 'You can do this, just don't give up.' Thank you.

I would also love to thank both my godmothers Elizabeth Puno and Yolanda Muyot for every help and support they have given me, it means a lot to me.

An enormous thanks to these amazing people that are in my life Aqilah Suhaimi, Haifa Jafar, Hanna Awang, Hariz Zulfaqar, Hazirah Jahari, Kamaliah Ishak, Mia Krecu, Najwatul Karim, Shami Abdullah and Qamarina Doming. Thank you so much for standing by me and for all the help and support you all have given me, you are all incredible.

To my new amazing friends in LCB for supporting me in this. To Janine Perez and Sydney Felicio, for helping me, guiding me in this. Thank you very much.

And lastly to all my fans on Wattpad, thanks for all the support, you guys are amazing.

❧ PROLOGUE ❧

D id you ever love someone so much that you were willing to change fate? Because I did. Have you ever wished you had something so big, that you can never have? Because I have.

Do you know that everyone has a mate? Do you know that you only get them once in a life time? That once you let them out of your sight, then it's gone forever? Unfortunately, I have gotten four chances to redo my mistakes over and over again. I guess, it's either a 'do it until you get it right' thing or fate just wants me to suffer more than others, but why me? I will never understand.

To feel that kind of pain, it's just awful. Just thinking about it alone could make anyone shiver. Being rejected by your mate? It feels as if you are living in a body whose soul has already gone, waking up every day wishing for death.

As for the ones that have lost their mates to death? They literally die soon after, because living without a mate is as good as trying to live without air.

I know the feeling, I really do. The butterflies in your tummy? Or the spark that runs through your body when you come in contact with them and even the crazy smile on your face when you think of them, it must be nice, huh? That your heart skips a beat or for that moment alone you suddenly realize, it isn't air that you need any more to live.

I have felt all of that and more. I know what it's like to lose them too, so listen to me when I say, 'when you have them, don't let go. They may slip up or you may slip up but there is a reason why fate has chosen them.'

And what if you want to go against fate? Be a 'badass' for once, you know you only live once, right? But what happens if it ends up with fate asking you to choose? Would you choose your kind? Or the one fate has destined for you? Would you stand your ground and fight? Or cower and run? I have lived for more than five hundred years and I have witnessed as my parents lived every day with pain in their eyes, the same pain I have lived with as well.

My father is King Balthazar Claw, the king of Werewolves and our dear old fate, has given him Queen Isabella Claw, queen of vampires as a mate. They had it hard of course, being two different creatures. What's worse is that, the two kinds had been at war for thousands of years and my parents were forced to live separate lives.

The only amazing thing that they got out of this hell on earth is me, Princess Katherine Rose Claw. I guess that's what happens when life gives you lemons, huh?

I'm the one and only hybrid princess, I don't know why, I just am. Creatures have always been given mates of the same kind, but I don't get why fate had decided to change things and of all the thousands of people out there, I got to be the lucky winner. Yay me! I will never get who I am? Or what I have done to deserve all this crap fate throws at me. Well, not that being the strongest creature alive and dead is crappy or anything.

It's just that my father? He isn't immortal. Werewolves, they can stop aging when they want to. That's what my father did, he stopped ageing, to keep up with me. He, being the king got to live more years than normal wolves would.

And my mother? She could die as well. Yes vampires get to live forever, but everyone has their weaknesses and for my mother is a stake carved from a very rare tree, the Mpingo Tree. So basically what I'm saying is that, I'm going to lose them someday because that's just how life is, you lose one to gain one.

But here's the click, what happens when you can't die? You're going to have to see your love ones die one by one of course. So object me if I'm wrong but I believe that if there is such a competition to see whose life sucks the most? I'd win hands down. Don't you guys see? Being powerful isn't everything anymore and getting to live forever? Just doesn't sound as cool as it used to.

In my five hundred years of moving back and forth between my parents, I've grown to meet new people, learned to love them and let them in, only to watch them die later on. Every century I move between my mother and father, it's obvious that they can't live together with their situation.

And for this next century, I'm going to live with my father. Not knowing that I might lose him, but I know very well that I will always gain another.

So if it isn't obvious then let me put it this way. Fate? Always wins! But fate? Is just the tip of an iceberg.

❧ Chapter One ❧

'Being deeply loved by someone gives you strength, while loving someone deeply gives you courage.'

—Lao Tzu.

TWO CENTURIES AGO

"Katherine!" I turned to see a group of my men making their way to me. They all bowed in respect before they started reporting about the distress alarm from earlier made by one pack at the Far East.

"Rogues again?" I guessed knowing that I would be right. They nodded causing me to growl as they took a step back as a response of their fear. I walked passed them into the mansion, busted the front door open and slammed it shut as I made my way towards my father's office, shoving any wolves that were in my way.

"*These rogues have been causing chaos and it has to end, today!*" My wolf growled. I knocked on the door but couldn't wait for any response as I just went in and was met with a few high rank warriors discussing with my father about the matter at hand.

I growled causing them to jerk and made their way out as fast as they could. My father got up from his seat shaking his head in disapproval of my actions before meeting me and planting a kiss on my forehead to make me calm.

"Another rogue attack, father. Five times in a week, do you not think that it is time we intervene?" I've spoken with full confidence, always have ever since I came back.

"Very well, what do you suggest we do, Princess?" I growled at the pet name he called me earning myself a glare. He knew how much I hate being called 'Princess' yet he still chooses to call me that.

"Extinction. We wipe out all the rogues, they are nothing but extra baggage. Isn't that right, Father?"

"That is no way for a princess to talk, especially about their people. You can't just wipe out all the rogues, they aren't a pack. You wiping them all out, doesn't mean that in the future, others will choose to be rejected by their packs and go rogue."

"Says the man that did not know anything about a particular rogue but still kills him anyway." I said with annoyance. "Fine then, we hunt down all rogues, make them submit to a pack and if not then they will be punished by death. The death of a few rogues for the lives of a million packs, is it not worth it?"

"It is never worth it, Princess. We will feel their death. We will grieve. You are a princess, it's not in your place to kill."

"So what father? Being a king does? Can't you see? We are giving them a choice. A choice you didn't give Lucas and so I think that's enough, don't you?" I know my words were harsh but how can I ever really forgive him for his biggest mistake towards me? I watch as he sighed meaning that he was going to let me have my way, wasn't my wanting reasonable? The lives of a few rogues for a million packs, is it not worth it? And now even more, if these rogues would agree to submit.

"Alright, have it your way. We will gather every man tonight."

What? No! Nowhere near hell am I allowing Victor to be a part of this, it's too dangerous. I growled to myself.

"Father, the men aren't ready. We need others, how about Alphas? And Betas? With all of them combine, we could take out a few rogues."

"It looks like you have everything planned. Very well, I'll contact all the packs here in England. We will meet up tomorrow." I nodded and made my way out but before I could even reach the door, my father stopped me. "Princess, it's not too late to change your mind. There are other ways to deal with this."

"You know me well, father. I am not the kind to change my decision once it's made."

He signed one last time, "very well." I nodded and shimmered out back to the yard and watched as Victor and a few men were training with Albert and James.

As I put on my attire, I smelled the different scent of the alphas and betas that has finally arrived. I tied up my hair in a pony tail before grabbing my red hood. I walked down the stairs only to meet Victor at the other end. "Morning, Katherine. Did you have a nice sleep?" I nodded with a smile.

"Morning, Victor. You had breakfast?" I walked over to him as he held out a hand for me to take. I gripped it, wishing that I never have to let go.

"Yes. What's happening today? A lot of alphas and betas are arriving, you know how dominating they could be," I nodded with a smile. I guess being best friends weren't enough anymore for me. I looked passed him as his wife walked over causing me to growl. Every time Victor brightens up my day, that mate stealer of his would always find a way to ruin it.

"Morning, Katherine." I nodded at her greeting still not used to her. Victor let my hand go to take hers, and as he kisses her hand. I felt my heart shattered into pieces. It was hard to hold the sharp pain I felt in my chest, but she didn't know about me and Victor so I forced on a smile and just walked ahead of them but the thing she said made me stand my ground, "be home by dinner."

I turned to look at them as he held her in his arm. It was hard not to glare at the sight of them as much as it was hard to hold my wolf from coming out and ripping her off of what's mine, "what do you mean? Be back by dinner?" I growled.

"Balthazar asked me and a few men to accompany the alphas." Victor answered making my blood boil at the request of my father. Rogues are much stronger than they seem, when combine with others they are able to wipe out a pack. This is because rogues go for the kill whereas packs must only capture them and are only allowed to kill when there isn't any other choice. Rogues don't live with rules, unlike packs and killing another wolf is a crime. This is too dangerous for him because rogues won't think twice when their lives are on the line.

"You are not going anywhere, you stay here!" Was the last thing I said before I shimmered towards my father.

"Father!" I called busting into every room I thought he would be in only to find nothing "Father!" I screamed with pure anger.

"Princess! Keep it down, werewolf voice. Use your werewolf voice we have heightened hearing, you are killing some of us here," I glared at him.

"Why is Victor coming? The reason why I am asking the alphas and betas to do this is because I want Victor out of this he isn't ready, I thought I made myself clear last night! Isn't what you've done to Lucas not enough that you have to take Victor as well? Rogues are dangerous," I said with pure hate.

"But still, you manage to snog one?" I was taken aback by his words, how dare he? Say that to my face. "Honey, I—" I raised my hand to stop him before it gets to a point where I am going to regret the words that my mouth could utter.

"I never thought you would stoop so low, father. But then again the apple doesn't fall far from the tree, does it now?" With that I left, only with hopes that everything will go as planned. That Victor will come home safe.

"If only my father knew how much more dangerous he is than those rogues." I muttered to myself as I walked to the field. Wondering to the sky I remembered the story that my father told me centuries back before finding my mother. He fancied a rogue, a rogue that only wanted the crown and not his heart. He fell so deep and so hard, that when he found out about her true intention, she was exiled. I wonder what it must have felt like. To put death on the shoulders of your first love?

"Alright, first of all I would like to thank all you alphas and betas for taking the week off to help with the problem we are having at hand. We will be divided into four, it wouldn't be wise to put all alphas in a group but we have to make exceptions. I would like the rogues to be dealt with before any 'submissive wanting' to happen. My daughter and I will take east, alphas from the West and east take west. Betas of the west and east take the South, with the warriors and the others take North." The nerve of him, he knows how much I hated that Victor is here and now he dares to keep him with a different group, with weak betas nevertheless.

This is wrong, I should stop him. *Come on, Katherine. Suck it up and go tell him not to go.* My wolf begged. "Breathe," I murmured and started walking towards

him only to have my father stop me, "it's time to leave."
I nodded and looked back at Victor one last time before
walking away.

"It's alright. You'll see him in a week and if we finish
early you would be home waiting for him to come home,
trust me the feeling of seeing him coming home to you
will be worth it. I've been away from your mother too
many times and at every time I come home, the smile on
her face was worth leaving." I smiled at the attempt of my
father to calm me down because I knew my smile wouldn't
be the one worth leaving.

With one last word from my father, we all parted. "Shift!"

❧ Chapter Two ❧

'I'm coming home,'
                                          —Skylar Grey.

I was looking out the window, into the woods. My heightened sense helped me hear the laughter of children playing outside a few yards away. Someone knocked on the door and I turned to see who it was. I opened it to find my mother and her guards, I motioned for them to enter before walking back to the window side and watch a few guards spar.

I wasn't like any other princesses, I could fight but I wasn't always like this I used to be shy and quiet. I didn't know how to throw a punch. Hell! I didn't even know how to 'bitch-talk' even if it would save my life but after what happened between me and my father centuries ago. I didn't want to be a weakling I wanted to be strong, to fight for myself and protect the ones that I love. Sometimes after school I would hang out with some of the warriors and do a little sparring.

"Are you ready to leave, Katherine?" The sweet voice of my mother asked. She is from Romania and so she had that accent that could make you cower. She is the granddaughter of count Dracula. I didn't believe her at first until count Dracula himself came to visit me on my eighteenth birthday when I first shifted and grew my fangs.

"Why yes, Mother. It's not as if I have to pack or anything, it's the same-old-same-old." I had everything I needed at my father's mansion so I never had to pack every time I moved, "When will he be here? And where is it this time? New York? Las Vegas? Malaysia? Brunei? Last I heard he was in California."

"Well my darling, I've spoken with your father. Your new personal guards will arrive shortly to take you and this time it will still be here in New Zealand. I have a little business over in Australia. You know, rogue vampires and all."

"Alright then, so who might my new personal guards be? You both do know that I am much stronger than them and it will be me that would protect them not the other way around, right?" My mother laughed. I tilted my head a bit to see the two bodyguards behind her, Henry and Jake trying very hard to hold their laughter in. "Yeah, keep laughing, boys. I am also much stronger than the both of you. In fact, I am stronger than anyone, period!" Cocky I know, but you can't argue with facts, now can you?

My mother turned and laughed at them. She maybe a dozen centuries old, but she will always be eighteen by heart. The warriors and royals, we're all a family. They know when to get serious and when to have fun. "Why, darling, your new guards are Alex Fox and Isaac Zink. Do you know of them?"

Zink and Fox? Might they be the sons of James and Camellia Zink, and Albert and Bethany Fox? "I think I might know of their parents or grandparents. After all it's been a century since I've last seen the wolves."

"It's such a pity that they aren't immortals like us, you have to see some of them die. I wonder how I would live if it is your father's time. I might as well find that damn tree and—"

"My queen," one of her guards stopped her from finishing what she was about to say. My mother turned to the guard who bowed his head. "Oh Henry. I was just joking and if I do die, Katherine will be here to take care of all of you. Maybe by the time Balthazar and I are no longer in existence the world of vampires and werewolves would learn to play nice."

Another knock was heard on the door, I nodded to one of the two guards to open it. He was talking to another guard, it looks like my ride was here. I know I have heightened senses and I can hear the werewolves in my head no matter where the packs are. I just choose to shut them out because you wouldn't believe the things I've heard.

The guard closed the door and came back to us, "The mutts are here to take you, my princess."

"My princess? Seriously? It's Katherine, call me that alright? It's my name and F.Y.I I'm half mutt, thank you very much." I glared at him before turning to grab my purse and walked out the door with my mother by my side and the guards behind.

I could smell the fear out of the guard who called my people mutts. I stopped and turned to him, "Jake, keep your shirt on, ok? I'm not going to stake you. You're allowed to talk freely you do know that right?" He nodded, "so stop freaking out." I gave him a friendly smile which he returned and we continued our walk to the entrance door.

"Now, darling. You stay with your father alright and your personal guards. These are bad times right now, the rogues are attacking not only vampires but also the werewolves, a few mermaids and fairies here and there."

I didn't answer her, I was too lazy to open my mouth. These rogue problems have been going on for centuries but nowadays it has gotten worse. I guess my father was right, it doesn't mean that getting all the alphas and betas to try and wipe out any rogues that wouldn't submit into packs that more won't arise. Being a rogue isn't always a choice. "Are you listening, Katherine?" This time I nodded, "Very good. You're my only child and I have to take good care of you. You might be five hundred years old but for a vampire that is still a young age and to me and your father, you'll always be our baby girl."

I fight off the urge to whine 'Mom, not in front of the boys' but managed a smile before looking away from her, feeling nothing but guilt. I have been hiding something from my parents and I was hoping I could tell them together on this day but since my father isn't coming to pick me then it'll just have to wait for another century for my mother to come pick me up from my father's. I won't like repeating what I was about to tell them, I rather tell them both at the same time and let hell have its way with it.

11

"Is something bothering you, darling? You seem distracted." I turned to her once again and shook my head.

Finally we have reached the entrance. The guards opened the door and I could smell the scent of the two werewolves outside, a few miles away. They soon came into view, both in their early twenties. Hair as dark as the ground, eyes in the colour of my favourite shades of blue. They were both around six feet tall, both wearing simple jeans and a fitted shirt that made their eyes stand out, making them look smoking hot.

"Princess Katherine, my name is Alex Fox and this is Isaac Zink. My cousin and I, are your new personal guards. Your father has asked us to escort you back to the mansion." He let out his hand for me to take but in a split second my mother who was once beside me was now strangling the two guards one with each hand, both their feet off the ground, choking.

"You two pretty boys better get my baby girl safe to her father, you hear? Or I will see to it that I have both your heads, personally!" They nodded and I could feel the smirk on every guard's face as they watched their queen took on two royal werewolf guards.

"Mother, put them down!" I scream causing her to let go of them, once they hit the ground I walked towards them to help them up. "Sorry about that, love. My mother, she likes to show off around her guards. You don't have to be scared. Now where is the car? Or bike, my father is fond of bikes. Did he shipped all his bikes here from California? Or did he waste money and bought new ones of the same design and model?"

The two men looked at each other, Isaac nodded and Alec spoke. "We ran here, your father thought it'd be nice to have a bonding moment with you, Princess." I hated it very much when people call me 'Princess'. For the first few years, it'd sound special or something but it gets annoying sooner or later. Especially when you are so used of being known as the only hybrid but unfortunately not the only princess, it makes me feel not unique so I'd rather people call me by my name at least if I couldn't be unique I'd be original.

I nodded and walked past them until I was a few feet away to turn to see them still standing where I last left them, the front entrance. "It's Katherine, you call me Katherine not 'princess' now come on. We could walk, I'd like to get to know you too. Now hurry up boys, we have some bonding to do. Even though being in the same god damned car and driving home could also be bonding. Seriously my father doesn't think sometimes, the older you get the wiser you become they say. Well, that's a load of bull crap." I threw my hands up in the air in frustration and continued to walk away.

A few seconds later I was sandwiched between them. We walked home where ever home was. I did want to get to know them, after all I will be spending a century with them.

"So, how old are you really?" Alec asked a bit ashamed.

"What? They didn't teach you my age in werewolf history class?" I laughed at my joke and stopped when I realized I was the only one laughing and Isaac hadn't joined me. "Of today I'm five hundred, Pup." I said poking his chest, he looked shocked.

"But but but—" he stuttered. "But you look like you're only ten," he continued.

I nodded before I willed myself to age into twenty one which I thought was his age. His jaw dropped at my appearance and I turned to see that Isaac had the same expression on his face, which made me laugh.

"I can change my age, love. That's what helps me adapt, vampires usually have to move every decade of years for the humans not to notice they haven't aged. But I don't, I can change my age, my mother moved here ten years ago so now I look like how I was when I was ten because I have to attend school like normal kids." They both nodded and I turned back into my ten year old self.

I could feel that he was ready to ask me another crazy question, "why is it that I sense that there is something else bothering you, love?"

"I get that the queen has a Romanian accent and that Balthazar has an American accent but I don't get how you ended up with an English accent?" I burst into laughters at his remark. There is no way near hell was I going to explain my accent to him. I was born and had lived my first century in Britain, therefore the English accent which is a plus on my side. If you're a six foot two with long curly hair running down your back and fit at least a size 2, who is also naturally tanned then you're hot but if you're all that and with an English accent then you're burning.

"Do any of you have mates?" They both shook their heads, "Good then, we'll be having fun." They looked shocked, as if I would bite them with my fangs. "I like to have fun, hang out and train and if you have mates then you guys would have to be dismissed earlier than you are supposed to. I don't know if my father has told you but for the next hundred years, you two will be my best friends like your grandparents were. The males of the Zink and Fox families have always been my guards. James Zink and Albert Fox? Ring a bell?"

"James is my father and Albert is Alec's." Isaac spoke.

"Where are they? I've missed them, they must be too old to be my guards now. Which is why they have sent you two handsome ones instead, huh? After all they know how much I love fresh blood." I joked but Isaac bowed his head and I didn't get him so I turned to Alec for answers, "They're dead, Katherine. Murdered."

What?" My wolf howled, it was going crazy inside of me on the news. She wanted to know who killed them. She wanted names and she wanted them now. Why hadn't my father said anything? Did he not think that it is important information? I walked two steps further and stopped to turn back at them, fangs showing off, I had to stay far just in case I couldn't control my wolf and shifted. "I want names!" I growled, my eyes must have turned red because Alec and Isaac took several steps back. "I said Names!"

"Ah ah ah-ke-Kevin and his followers." Alec answered.

"Whoever this Kevin is, if he and his followers are alive I will torture them to death! But wait—followers? Doesn't he mean pack?" I growled at the thought of Kevin being a rogue.

"What happened to them? Did they escape?" Both nodded and I let out another loud growl. "I'll kill them, them bastards! That freaking rogue just barked up the wrong tree! You two shouldn't be scared of me, we are a family now, we protect each other. If I ever lay eyes on that damn rogue, he won't know what's coming for him!"

I finally calmed myself down and we continued walking back to the mansion. "I want to know more about this rogue."

"Well, he is the reason all the rogues are going crazy. He had gathered up the other rogues and has planned on attacking every pack. Exterminating the Alphas and their families along with their Betas, but we aren't sure why though." Isaac explained.

"Last we heard, he was in California, there are still two packs that haven't been attacked and the royal guards in the area are now standing by the two packs. There was a rumour going around that his next location is here, when he is done with Cali. That's why the king has moved here, to New Zealand."

We have finally passed by my elementary school, could the mansion be any farther? We have been walking for half an hour and we had faster speed than humans. A half an hour walk by us is an hour and a half in human speed.

"How old is this dude? There is an estimation of more than thirty packs in California and I'm sure it'll take a few years before attacking one pack and then another, right? And if there are only two more packs, what happened to the alphas and betas from the packs he had already attacked, are they dead?"

"Well, Kevin takes up the appearance of a man in his late twenties. He might have stopped his aging, so we don't know how old he really is. As for the packs, sometimes we are able to reach the packs before both alpha and betas are killed and other times we're just not lucky enough, it's always one of the two that will be gone by the time we arrived."

I'd noticed that Isaac was the quiet one, since Alec was the one who has answered most of my questions and actually committing to this supposed to be bonding moment. "Is the mansion close yet?" I turned to ask Isaac. I wanted him to answer me, but all he did was shake his head.

"What is my father planning to do about Kevin?" I turned to Alec this time. Knowing Isaac wasn't going to answer and shaking his head from side to side or up and down and even raising his shoulders isn't a real answer, but to my surprise I heard a voice answering but Alec's mouth wasn't moving. I turned to look at Isaac, and stared at his moving lips.

"The king doesn't know what to do, that's why he is waiting for you. He wants to discuss this matter with you, plus he has high hopes that the guards at California will be able to stop him. So, from now on all we're going to do is wait and train to be prepared."

"When do you think the next attack will be? Is it any time soon?" Isaac shook his head and I thought that, that was his answer but he continued explaining, "Their last attack was just a few weeks ago, they attacked two packs at once. It was too late when we got the other packs call for help. Every single warrior and your father went to the far east where the first attacked happened and once we reached there, we got another call of an attack on the far west. We split and went to save the other pack but by the time we reached there, everything was gone. Kevin wiped out the whole pack leaving us to bury every female and children, the sight was horrible. The alpha and beta were ripped into pieces, their families were beheaded. We all howled for the fallen that night." That explains the pain

I felt, it was as if someone had shoved their hands in my chest and gripped my heart really tight ready to tear it out. "Usually it takes them two to three years to attack again, to regroup and find more rogues, you know the drill." I nodded.

"The mansion is five minutes away, if we shift and run." Isaac spoke again.

"Alright then, let's walk into the woods." We walked into the woods, a few meters from the road to keep off of any human that might be jogging by.

I nodded and the two men walked to the back of a tree to strip before appearing again only with their clothes in their mouths, "drop your clothes boys, I'll carry them."

Isaac looked at Alec and tilted his head, Alec nodded in response and they both dropped their clothes. I went to grab them, folding them nicely, "alright, let's go." I ordered but they only stood their ground and look confusedly at me, "Just go! Run!" I spoke in my alpha voice and they both started to run.

I started to run myself and to my surprise I was shocked to see that the boys were no longer in front of me. They must have run faster than me that was what I thought until I heard growls coming from behind me and turned my head to see two wolves.

After five minutes of running I finally saw the roof of a house and soon the walls of the house came to view. Alec growled as to say, "This is it."

Alec's wolf was brown and so was Isaac's, it's just that Isaac's fur was more of a golden brown and Alec's was a dark chocolate shade of brown. They both bear the sign of the 'Warrior', on their right shoulders which only the Zink and Fox family have always borne. It's a birthmark, a crescent moon. We stood in front of the back gate and I handed them their clothes back, which they both took with their mouths before disappearing once more into the woods only to come back fully dressed. We went in through the back door and guards bowed their heads as I passed. I remembered some of them as the kids I used to know and played with. They are now old, well not older than me of course.

"Where is my father?" I asked.

"Over here, Princess." I turned to see my father, he looked exactly like he did when I left. I ran to him and hugged him as tight as I could. "Princess, I-I-I can't breathe!" I let him go and he kissed my forehead. "Stop calling me that, father. You know how much I hate being called 'Princess'."

He let out a faded laugh and took my hand, "I missed you, Princess." I glared at him for his stubbornness. "How do you find your new guards?"

I turned to look at them and nodded, and as a response they walked away to let me be alone with my father. "They are great. They told me about James and Albert, father. I want vengeance. Whoever this Kevin is I want his head! On a silver platter!"

My father chuckled at my words, "we are trying to deal with it, Princess."

"Father, if you'd let me I want to spend this next century differently. I want Kevin." I stated.

"Well that's one thing we can agree on." He replied causing me to glare.

"Father, I want it to be me! Who takes him down. Another thing is that, I want to continue going to school like I did with mother. When I come home, I could train with your men, I could also train any new recruit, if you'd like."

"If that's all then I think we could work something out."

"That's not all, there is one more thing. Six years from now when I turned sixteen, I want to follow you on your outings. You know, when you visit packs or if there is any rogue sightings."

"Princess, if that is all then, there isn't a problem. You used to come with me on my outings."

"I want you to introduce me as your personal warrior, father. I don't want to hide behind a red hood. Do you not think that it is time that my people finally know who their princess is?" I wasn't sure why but no one other than my parents and the royal guards were allowed to see me. Packs only know me by name and visualize how I look like using their imaginations.

I remembered a boy once back in Italy. He was the son of an alpha, a very nice young lad. He came with his father, who had to discuss with my father about a problem that their pack was having. I remember him running up to me when I was walking around the garden, he pulled on my hood asking if I was the princess.

"You are the princess, aren't you?" He spoke in Italian and although my Italian was a little rusty I understood him.

"Yes, my boy." I answered causing him to pull on my hand just to plant a kiss, his actions made me smile. "What a gentleman you are, how old are you, my boy?"

"I am only five, Princess."

"And what is your name? If I may ask."

"Antoni, son of the alpha of the Sea Wolf Pack. The second largest pack in Italy." I managed a smile knowing he could see them. The hood couldn't fully cover my face but only partially, wolves that have seen me could see as high as my nose. No-one has ever met my eyes before.

"Princess, is it not hard to see where you are going with that hood?"

"We are werewolves, my boy. We have heightened senses, it helps me to understand my surroundings more. For example, look up at the tree on your right on the middle branch there's about three to five little birds." I look at him as he stared at the direction that I have said, I saw the smile on his face indicating that I was correct. "I don't need all my senses to know things. It's the same as a blind man, it doesn't mean that he is blind that he can't see, remember that child."

I never questioned my father about the hood so every time I go out, I had to wear my red hood. In fact, I find it amazing how years ago a human man saw me shift by accident. When I was trying to help this elderly woman from being killed by rogues, he started telling people about it, he sounded crazy that nobody believed him but with that craziness and a little bit of imagination that humans are well gifted with that I found amazement at how he did a story about me, about a little girl in a red hood and a vicious wolf of course.

It might not have been as popular as it used to be nowadays, but I am well sure that every little girl has heard of me. The story was used to scare little girls who would wander off in the forest centuries ago and now, it's used to put little girls to sleep.

"As much as I am against this, my wolf has agreed that you are right. Since, we have been waiting for Kevin to attack in California. The warriors here will just keep training and if he still makes it out then we will make a plan to protect the packs here." It brings joy to me and my wolf that my father has agreed to my wanting without starting a fight.

"But Princess tell me this, why wait six years? Why not now?"

"I'm only ten if you haven't realized, father. I go to school, what do you expect me to do? I went to school yesterday looking like a ten-year old and what? Aged six years in two days?" I glared at him before giving him a tight hug and kissed his cheeks before walking out of the living room to find Alec and Isaac.

❧ Chapter Three ❧

'Gravitation is not responsible for people
falling in love.'
—*Albert Einstein.*

SIX YEARS LATER

"Father!" I called out looking for my father, it was the first day of school again, and usually he would be the one to personally send me off. "In here!" My father called back from his library. I knocked before entering, I may be a princess but I have respect for my father's privacy but that's only when I'm not pissed at him.

"I have to leave for school now or I'll be late and I don't want to be late on my first day." I saw my father looking through some papers about Kevin. I hate that man and I want to see him dead personally.

"Father, it has been six years. He hasn't even attacked California. Stop obsessing about catching him, he might be dead or something. We don't know his real age, he might have been a hundred when he last attacked."

My father got up from his chair and walked towards me, "I'm just being—" I cut his sentence by raising a finger because I knew what he was going to say, he has been saying the same thing over and over every time I try to get him away from his table.

"I know, father. Now come on! You have to send me to school, like you always do," he nodded and we walked side by side. "The car is ready, I've told Alec to get it ready."

As we walked to the entrance I felt the guilt eating me from the inside, I have been dying to tell my parents about the secret I was holding from them because I don't think I can hold it in any longer.

The drive to school was about half an hour, I saw my friends standing near the entrance as we reached the drive off zone. I saw Uriel getting out of his car and my heart started beating fast, and sometimes it skips a beat too.

"Have you found your mate, Princess? Your heart is beating like crazy."

"Crap! Could he hear it? Stupid! Stupid! Stupid! Of course he could." I have to control my heart next time my father is around and my crush is within eyesight.

"No, Father. It's just the boy I fancy, I haven't met my mate for this century yet. There he is." I pointed out the window which was tinted of course, towards Uriel.

"He's cute I guess, how old is he?"

"Why the sudden curiosity? It's not like he is a wolf, but we won't know for sure since he's only sixteen." My wolf stated.

"He is only sixteen, by the end of the year he'll be seventeen. His little sister Saraquel is in the same class with me and she is one of my best friends." If he was a wolf he would change when he turns eighteen or when he meets his mate.

I heard Alec laughed in the back seat. "Got a problem, pup?" I like calling them 'pup' because I am after all much stronger than them and a fully grown she-wolf. Although men are more dominant, they wouldn't have a chance with me.

"Nothing, Katherine. It's just typical that you fancy your best friend's brother, that's all." I glared at him. I shouldn't have minded him.

"What is his name? I'd like to meet him someday." He isn't my boyfriend yet and my father is starting to interrogate him through me. "His name is Uriel Spike, his sister is Saraquel Spike. They are named after Archangels, Saraquel's mother died a few years ago and his father is Raphael Spike."

"Are you planning on dating him, Katherine?" There it is! He just said my name. He only does that if he doesn't want me to do something, I thought of doing (a.k.a he's pissed). "You do know you're going to have a mate? And when your mate finds out you have another man, he might not want to approach you."

"You know what father? I'm sixteen and I am at the right age to date and yes I might date him because I like him and when my mate comes then I might leave him for my mate. That is if I do even get him. But as of now I'm single, so loosen up." The bell rang right after I finished my sentences and I thanked the spirits to have cut this long argument short. I opened the door and ran out to catch my friends.

"We will continue this argument when you get home, Katherine. I might be busy and so I have asked Alec and Isaac to fetch you when you're out."

My father was the only person that could get through my head even when I shut people out. It's because he is still my Alpha, he is still king. I growled in reply and my father growled louder. I caught up to my friends and let the thought of my father fade away.

⟪⟪⟪ |BALTHAZAR| ⟫⟫⟫⟫⟫

I could hear my daughter's heart beating faster all of a sudden. God! The only time it beats this fast is when she meets her mate! I just got her back, I won't lose her to her mate. Every single time she meets her mate, she leaves me and I know I sound needy but at this time I need her more than anything. How am I supposed to let her know that this might be my last century with her?

I have lived for more than six hundred years and it had killed me to be away from my queen. I chose death when she was forced to be queen, meaning we had to be apart. I just wanted to kill myself, but then who would teach Katherine of my kind? Mates just can't be away from one another because it literally kills them.

"Have you found your mate, Princess? Your heart is beating like crazy." The sound of my darling Katherine was no where far from her mother, she might as well be a mermaid with a voice like that.

"No, Father. It's just the boy I fancy, I haven't met my mate of this century. There he is!" Did I hear right? She fancies a boy? I looked out as she pointed out towards one of the boys, dark haired, blue eyes, muscular built, just like Lucas.

I wondered how old is he? He might be a werewolf. Unfortunately I could only smell a werewolf when they have reached the age of seventeen, I should teach my daughter that one day as well. "He's cute I guess, how old is he?"

"He is only sixteen, by the end of the year he'll be seventeen. His little sister Saraquel is in the same class with me and she is one of my best friends." Alec chuckled in the back as to hold his laughter. My daughter turned to him before speaking, "Got a problem, pup?"

It puts a smile on my face every time my daughter calls her guards 'pup'. Well they are of course for her and me but to normal wolves they are of high ranks, even higher than an Alpha.

"Nothing, Katherine. It's just typical that you fancy your best friend's brother, that's all." I agreed with Alec, it was typical, so this might just be a phrase.

"What is his name? I'd like to meet him someday." I didn't like the thought of Katherine dating a human, she could only mate with her kind. I won't allow her to mate with a weak human or any other creatures, maybe shifters or nihilism since they're strong.

"His name is Uriel Spike, his sister is Saraquel Spike. They are named after Archangels, Saraquel's mother died a few years ago and his father is Raphael Spike." Where have

I heard that name before, Raphael. It's a common name but I didn't know many people with the name Raphael.

"Are you planning on dating him, Katherine? You do know you're going to have a mate? And when your mate finds out you have another man, he might not want to approach you."

"You know what father? I'm sixteen and I am at the right age to date and yes I might date him because I like him and when my mate comes and I might leave him for my mate. That is if I do even get him. But as of now I'm single, so loosen up."

Before I could protest the bell rang and my daughter was out of the car and a few feet from her friends in a blink of an eye.

"We will continue this argument when you get home, Katherine. I might be busy and so I have asked Alec and Isaac to fetch you when you're out." I said through my mind, I am the only one that could get into her head, I am the only one she couldn't block.

❧ CHAPTER FOUR ❧

'Whenever I think of the past, it brings back
so many memories.'
—Steven Wright.

((((|ALEC|))))

I didn't get why Isaac and I had to move rooms? The princess is strong enough to protect herself, not that I mind being close to her but did Balthazar have to give her the top room? She is the freaking little red riding hood, not Rapunzel. My cousin Isaac and I used to have our rooms on the ground floor back in California. All the guards' rooms are supposed to be on the ground up to the second floor. But ever since the princess came back, Isaac and I were appointed to move to the chambers next to Katherine's. Her room is between mine and Isaac.

I got into my room exhausted. After dropping off Katherine, the king had ordered me and Isaac to train with him. The word of Katherine earlier fancying a boy just sends my blood boiling, every time I think of it.

I lay on my bed forcing my eyes to rest, I was too tired to take off my shoes and I dozed off in a second.

Why is it getting hard to breathe in here? I got up to see smoke, thick black smoke entering from under the door. I got out of bed, the floor was warm, so warm. What is going on? There's a fire. The mansion is on fire.

"Alec!" Mother! I ran out the room, I ran to find my mother and the first place I thought she would be in was her chamber and I was right. When I found her, half her body was buried under the wooden drawer that had tumbled over, what is going on?

"Son, don't. You have to get out of here! Go find your father, you have to help him. He is with James, the rogues have come." Tears were falling making my vision blurry, "I'm not leaving you mother, I can't. I know how to fight now I can save you!"

"Just go, son. The house is going to collapse, this drawer is too heavy, Alec. You haven't shifted yet, you won't have the strength, now go please! And remember that I love you and your father." She kissed my forehead.

"I can! I can shift!" I close my eyes and willed myself to change but nothing happen, I open my eyes and tears fell. I couldn't save my mother, "you have to go son, it's alright. I love you, so much."

"I love you too, mom." She wiped off my tears, "go, now!" And with that I ran out of the house.

Isaac came running towards me. "Cousin, we have to find our fathers. We have to help them!" I nodded and we ran through the village to find our fathers. The rogues were everywhere, the pack was fighting, the children were all grouped in one place crying as they saw what was happening. I heard a boom and I turned to see that my house had finally collapsed and a few seconds later I heard a very loud howl and I knew it was my father, he must have felt the loss of my mother.

Isaac and I ran towards the howl to find my father and James fought side by side fending off five wolves. One of them was a grey wolf with a scar on his right eye. "Kevin," I whispered. "I know him," I muttered. My father must have sensed me nearby, "Son, hide in the bushes and don't come out, Isaac is with you, take care of him. Don't come out no matter what happens!" He said through a mind link.

The grey wolf shifted back into human form and spoke, "You two must be Fox and Zink. I have heard of your family. You are very important to the royals, I can tell but why are you here instead of being beside the princess? Oh yeah. She's with her mother am I right? Your king isn't coming to protect this village, let's just say he is having his hands full at the moment and I guess he left two royal guards to protect a very large pack?" He laughed.

One of the wolves behind him shifted into human form, rogues couldn't communicate through their minds because they aren't in a pack. "Guards are coming, the royal guards, dozens of them with the king too." Kevin growled and my father attacked him and so did James.

I had realized that more rogues appeared from nowhere and they attacked my father and James and in the end it was

Kevin who bit down on James before turning to my father. He nodded his head towards the rouges and they all ran away in retreat.

I ran to my father's side as did Isaac to his. "Father!" He isn't dead. He is weak but he hasn't shifted yet, "Son, listen to me." He said through our mind link, "when the king comes, introduce yourself and Isaac. You will both live with him and train. You will protect the princess. I'm sure you will like her, she is a nice person and she will be your new family, you protect each other."

I nodded as tears came again and I knew what he meant, I knew he wouldn't survive this. "I love you son! Remember that, mummy and I love you."

"I love you too, Father." I said, wanting him to hear my words, then he shifted, he laid down their naked and dead. I hugged his body to me, "No!"

"No!" I woke up in a cold sweat. *"It was just a dream, a nightmare!"* I can never forget what happened that night and I never will. After my father passed away, a few seconds later I heard the small growl from Isaac. I turned to him, he was hugging his father's shifted form as well. His mother was also a guard unlike mine and she had died that night before he came looking for me. That is why they didn't fight harder, my father and James. They couldn't fight harder because they have already lost their mates and maybe Isaac and I wasn't enough of a reason to keep them fighting.

A little later the royal guards came forth and fought off the remaining rogues and when it was all finished the king came up, front and centre asking for my father and James.

I walked up to him dragging Isaac with me, I introduced myself and Isaac and he told us to follow him. Once we were at the mansion, we told him what had happened.

I was having a headache, thanks to that stupid nightmare. I turned to my side desk to check the time, there was a few more hours before Katherine got off, I might as well take a shower and find Isaac.

⟪⟪⟪ |ISAAC| ⟫⟫⟫⟫

My back hurts! Training today was tiring. After sending Katherine off, I went straight for training. Now I was just walking around the garden for some relaxation and silence. I often come here to think. I plucked a red rose and smelled it.

"Where are the Fox and Zink?" The king asked after the attack, Alec walked up to the king dragging me with him.

"I'm Alec Fox and this is my cousin Isaac Zink we are both the only son of Fox and Zink, our fathers have been killed during the attack."

The king bowed his head towards us and put his hands on our shoulders. "You two boys will follow me, you will live in the mansion and will train with the guards. You two have an important job that has been given to your family which began from the time of your ancestors."

Alec nodded his head and we followed the king home that night.

I smiled as I remember these things, I used to be quiet and I liked being alone. I hated fighting and I was never good at it. Before being a guard I was a loner, I would spend every day alone reading my books. That was my everyday life and I think my father was disappointed in me, I never liked training with him, and we Zink were suppose to be known for our strength.

"Isaac, come on it's time to train. The king will be waiting for us to train with him." Alec said as he walked into my chambers. I was just a few months younger than him but he takes care of me like I'm a five year old child.

"I don't want to, Alec. I can't do it, I'm not good at it. Never was and never will be."

"You don't have a choice, Isaac. We have to, now come on. I'll have your back. You don't have to worry," as usual every time I reject Alec he would start dragging me by the collar, he was stronger than me then.

Every afternoon we would train till it was dark, sometimes we would over train and the longer I trained the better I knew how to defend myself. It hurt when I started, but soon the pain faded away and I became numb.

The first time I came home, with a lot of cuts and bruises. The daughter of a beta from a nearby pack saw me while visiting her cousin at the mansion.

Heather was her name. Long, beautiful brown locks, grey eyes with rosy cheeks and pale red lips, "Boy, are you alright? What happened to you?" I turned to her and at first I thought that she might be my mate but no, it was just a crush because I didn't shift that night.

"I came from my first day of training, that's all. It doesn't hurt as much as it looks," she giggled and came closer to help me.

"Come on, let me tend to your wounds. I'm Heather, daughter of the Beta from the Wolf Spring pack. Are you new here?"

I nodded before speaking again, "I'm Isaac, Isaac Zink. I'm from the Moon Dark pack." She looked shocked and I didn't know why though.

"Zink? As in the warrior Zink? Your father must be James Zink? I heard that he is the princess' personal guard, I've never met the princess before."

"Yes, my father was James Zink and he just passed a few days ago. I was appointed as the new guard."

All of a sudden her face changed, her beautiful smile faded, "I'm sorry I didn't know. Come on now let me help you." She helped me get to the mansion and into my chamber before leaving to grab a medical kit. She came a few minutes later and tended to me.

Heather, her scent was like roses, I remember. I felt a tear run down my cheeks thinking about her. She is dead now, a few months from meeting her I finally got the courage to ask her out and I was relieved when she said yes, and then he came back. Kevin came back and . . .

"Wolf Spring. Attack. Kevin. Move!"

I was with Alec playing cards when the words came through mind link, Alec and I were finally guards by the time. We threw the cards into the air and ran out the door, we didn't wait for anyone and ran straight to the Wolf Spring pack. All I could think of was Heather.

"It's going to be alright, Isaac." Alec spoke through our mind link. He was a player like most of the male wolves, but being called a player was an understatement, he and most male wolves are 'man whores' the term she-wolves use. "Heather, I hope we will make it in time." On our way there we met up with a few guards. The fight had already begun between the rogues, the guards and the fighters of the pack.

Alec and I were always told to fight Kevin, the king told us that it was our right for what he did to our fathers. We tried covering the whole area and at the end we found the beta and alpha fighting side by side and joined them, they were holding back over a dozen rogues, the beta and alpha were both injured. Alec and I fought off the rogues in just a matter of minutes.

I shifted back into human form and so did Alec and the beta. "Where is Heather? I can't find her." I spoke with authority.

"She must be fighting alongside a few men."

"Fighting! Why is she fighting?" I hissed with pure anger towards the beta for letting his only daughter fight a dangerous battle. A growl rumbled out and we all turned to the noise.

The beta and Alec shifted back. A man came out from the back of a tree with a few dozen wolves. There was a girl with him, he was pulling her by the hair to make her follow him. The girl was Heather.

"Heather! Let her go! You are hurting her! Let her go or I'll—"

"Or you'll kill me? Is that it? You must be Isaac Zink," he laughed. "I killed your father, James Zink but you know that, if my memory serves right, you and the Fox kid were hiding somewhere in the bushes. Front row seat, huh?" He laughed again and this time Alec growled. It wasn't funny, I didn't find the humour in his words.

"Now. Now, watch it, pup. I'm not talking to you. This girl," he pulled on her hair again and this time I growled before shifting, "hold it, mutt! What is she to you? A lover? Or may be a mate?" He smirked.

A howl came forth, wiping the smirk of Kevin's face because it was to announce that the King has arrived. "It's time to go boys, the big daddy is here." He winked before shifting into a wolf and bit down on Heather, I growled and attacked him, but still it wouldn't have changed a thing.

Every time I see roses, I would remember her. She might not have been my mate but she was my lover and now she is gone and it was my entire fault, I couldn't protect her.

The night before the attack Heather had asked me to dinner and I said no because I had to stay on guard. If I had just brought her to the mansion with me, we could have had dinner while I stayed guard, she would still be alive.

Kevin has taken everything from me, he has taken everyone I love and because of that I have never tried accepting another person again, other than the king and Alec of course. They were my only family.

I saw two children playing in the garden a boy and a girl, I called the boy over and gave him the rose before walking away. I came into view of a mother with two children, both boys with one of the guards, their father, he was teaching the boys how to fight.

I was playing with Alec out in the garden when the king spoke to us, through our mind.

"Alec, Isaac, meet me by the bush of roses." We stopped playing and raced towards the king, we bowed our heads

once we were standing in front of the king. "Let's take a walk, boys."

The king started walking and we walked together with him between us, "Do any of you know why, the Zink and Fox are always to be the princesses' guards?" We both shook our heads no, "So I see your fathers hadn't told any of you of your family's history. Isaac, you read books. Have you heard of a book called Warrior Wolves? I'm sure it must have been in your father's library." I shook my head no and he laughed, "oh, well let me tell you then, boys."

"Since the world had been made and werewolves have existed, the royals have always been giving birth to boys but in the year 1505 the first princess was born. Right away rogues tried to come after her and mate with her because if they mated with her than would mean that a rogue would be king after the king at the time died."

"Rogues would control the wolves and we all know it wouldn't be good. The king and queen gave out words for all males of each family to meet up at the field to find the fastest and strongest wolf to protect the princess and at the end of it all it was down to two men Adam Fox and Mabbit Zink, both cousins."

A little girl came towards the king and gave him a bunch of flowers of different types after thanking the girl he went back into his story.

"Adam Fox had speed, he was faster than any male wolf, even an alpha though he was just an omega. They say that his speed could be at the same rate as a prince and Mabbit Zink had strength. Strength of like Hercules and so instead of one guard the royals appointed two, Mabbit and Adam. Adam was taught to fight while Mabbit was trained to heighten his speed."

We were walking around the back garden which then lead to the werewolf village pack, people started greeting us by bowing their heads. "Now where was I? Ah! The princess found her mate and they bore a child, a girl again and two boys. They needed new guards to be appointed to the new princess and at that time Adam and Mabbit were old and the Queen wouldn't trust anyone with the princess other than Fox and Zink."

"So what did they do, my king?" Alec spoke, I almost thought he wasn't there. We were silent throughout the whole walk, "they called a witch," the king replied.

"A witch? That is barbaric! To have us work with one of them," Alec said with disgust. Witches were horrible people because of which they were burned.

"If I may," the King asked to which Alec nod and the king continued, "They called upon one witch. She was the strongest witch of the century and they made her bless—or was it a curse, it depends on the Zink and Fox family I guess, whether it was a curse or a blessing."

"Well the blessing was that, every Zink and Fox will always bear a child. Only one and that it would be a male, with it comes the strength of Mabbit to the Zink family and the speed of Adam to the Fox family and ever since then the Zink and the Fox have always borne a male child and that male child has always been chosen to be the personal guards of the princess."

"That would explain, my speed I guess," Alec said out loud and the king nodded. "And that explains, your strength, Isaac. You are strong Isaac you just need to know how to fight to use your strength."

"Isaac!" I turned towards the voice that spoke out my name. Alec he was jogging towards me, "Want to play some cards? A few more hours and we have to get Katherine." I nodded before speaking, "alright, come on let's play by the lake then."

❧ CHAPTER FIVE ❧

'Our dead is never dead to us, until we have forgotten them.'

—George Eliot.

"**R**ight left, right left. Double left kick. Punch-punch, kick." I repeated the words in my head over and over again as I was throwing all my anger towards a dummy I made with Isaac and Alec a few years back that mirrored the image of Kevin, I let out a growl just thinking of him, "Stupid, rogue." I murmured.

Thinking of him alone burned the blood that runs through my veins, making me more worked up. 'Right-left, right left. Double left kick. Punch-punch, kick.' I picked up my speed and strength repeating my movements over and over.

'Katherine,' I heard my name being called but I just shove it to the back of my head, 'Katherine!' the voice called again making me more pissed, 'Katherine!' my name echoed making me lay my last punch on the dummy with my full strength, causing it to burst. Leaving the bits of sand in it scattered all over the floor.

I turned around ready to burst a tantrum on whoever that was calling me only to see my mother, arms crossed, leaning on one leg while the other tapping on the ground out of annoyance. My facial expression relaxed, so I attempted a smile to lessen the tension that I've just created.

"What are you doing here, Mother? Aren't you supposed to be in Australia?" I unwrapped the band that covered my fist. My mother finally loosened up, she walked over to me to kiss both my cheeks.

"I am in Australia, darling." All of a sudden a towel materialize on my mother's hands, she handed it to me. I grabbed it without hesitation.

"So I'm dreaming?" I asked, I find it cool how vampires are able to get through a person's head. Not all vampires though, every vampires are either born or made with a special gift but for royals, especially the soon to be princess or prince, he or she is born with an extra rare ability. One of my favourites is my ability to change my age, which I mastered only a year from when I grew my fangs.

"Let's take a walk." I nodded and followed as the environment around me changes from day to night, I wasn't shocked though. I was fully aware that in dream land, we could change things to our likings but I still don't know how to on my own volition, so my feelings change it for me. "How are you? How is school?"

"I'm fine. Everything is fine and dandy. Wait—why are you here? In my dreams? Is something wrong? Did something happen? Do you need me to fly over? Isn't Australia like a million hours earlier than New Zealand? Aren't you supposed to be awake? Because trust me if you sleep more than you are supposed to you are going to wake up feeling exactly like your age, no kidding."

"Just so you know it's only two hours apart and Australia is the two hours time back, so it's you that has overslept." She said with a smirk on her face making me feel stupid at some point, some mother she is but then she frowned. "It's that time of the year again, Katherine." That time of the year? What is the date today? Oh damn! It's their anniversary.

"Happy anniversary, mother. Sorry I am just so caught up in school and training." I let out a deep sigh because not only was it my parents' anniversary it was also Lucas' death day.

"Thank you, darling. Are you going to leave today? To go to the grave land?" I shook my head.

"I can't, Mother. I have school but don't worry, I'll find time." I managed a smile so that she wouldn't worry.

"Well, darling I am only here to check up on you, to see if everything is going alright. I have to leave now, apparently the rogues here don't sleep till five in the morning." I nodded, she pulled me in for a hug. I willed myself to hug her back, my arms started hurting from the training earlier.

"Goodbye, Mother." I whispered as I held her tight, eyes shut willing the tears to hold back. When I opened them back, my mother was gone and I was alone. Just like when he passed, leaving me alone in a world. A dark cold world, he left me alone and scared, taking my heart with him.

I shut my eyes once more as the wind blew, the cold air it brought was the exact coldness I was left with. "Lucas." I whispered his name.

I opened my eyes and I was back in my room, I sat up on the bed and just stayed like that till I saw the ray of sunlight, brightening up my dim room. I stood up to walk to the window and stared out as the animals finally awaken and came out of their homes to play.

School this pass few weeks has been hard, I spent most of my time thinking of Uriel and the other time I was either snoozing or talking nonsense with my friends. I didn't get a single word in my head for three weeks, it was crazy and if I leave now? I'd miss another one to two weeks of school.

What was I thinking? There is no use of school anyway, not for me. I have forever to live, I could go back to school any time I want. It wasn't like this was my first time, every time I got to live with my mother, it's either I go to elementary or secondary school.

I unlocked the lock to my window and opened it for fresh air, I needed it. I looked out into the woods, it was beautiful, so beautiful. I closed my eyes again trying my best to hold the tears but there was only so much I could hold on to, so I let a few tears slipped away, running down my cheeks, "Lucas, I-I—I miss you so much." I called out to the wind hoping that it could carry the message even six feet under.

I opened my eyes only to have my vision blurry, "I—" I took a deep breath and let it out, "I'll be there soon, love. Wait for me, I'll be there, I-I—" I shut my eyes again letting more tears fall only because I couldn't hold it anymore, "I promise." The last two words echoed back to me.

I pulled myself away from the window, walked over to the closet to grab a baffle bag from the top of the closet and laid it on the bed as I started shoving in my clothes. There was a knock on the door but it didn't cause me to stop what I was doing, instead I picked up my paste moving faster, the sound of the knock became louder and louder, making me panic.

"Katherine!" He called out my name, causing me to stop this time.

"Come in," I replied. Isaac and Alec came in, I looked at them in a busted expression, as if I have done something bad, as if I was caught red handed doing something horrible.

"Katherine, are you alright?" I willed myself to shake my head but it seemed as if it was really hard to move, like cement finally hardening up. "I think we should call Balthazar, Isaac. Something is wrong with her." I watched as Isaac nodded before leaving to go get my father, making me panic even more.

I grabbed my bag not waiting any longer and shimmered out to the garage, grabbing the keys on the key holder that was nailed to the wall. I picked up my helmet and got on my bike roaring it to life the same time my father reached the garage door, "Katherine! It's alright, it's alright." He said, but it wasn't.

He wasn't going to stop me and I won't let him not again. I positioned myself and rode off leaving my father. I was so deep in my thoughts that I almost missed the turn to the entrance of the Auckland Airport.

I took my phone from my bag and as I walked to the counter, I dialed Isaac's number, it rang twice before he answered. "Katherine, are you alright? Where are you?"

"I, I have to go Isaac. The bike, I'll leave it at the airport, come pick it up later, alright? I have to leave."

"Where are you going, Katherine? Alec and I need to know where you are going. Your father, he-he won't talk to us. He locks himself in his room, Katherine. His room not his office."

"I'm going to him, Isaac. I'm going to Lucas. I'll be back in a few weeks, don't worry. I'm a big girl, I can take care of myself. You just watch over my father, ok. Bye." I cut the line before he could say anything else.

"Hello, good morning. How may I help you?"

"A ticket to Italy please, back and forth." The woman assisting me handed out a form for me to fill my details and I gave it back after a few minutes later. Isaac knew where I was, he and Alec might stop me. I needed to cross the checking field fast or they might literally drag me back by my tail.

I grabbed my ticket off the counter with a smile before walking off. Got my bags checked in and wasted no time and went to the waiting area where people without a ticket couldn't pass. I sat beside an elderly woman reading the newspaper. A 23 hour flight, I hope I don't have a freaking seat buddy.

The flight only consists of me looking out the window day till night, from when I boarded on till I got my arse off the flight. My father tried getting through my head a couple of times but all I did was push him away. It was hard but I tried to keep him out of my head, he might have finally taken a hint and stopped. I knew he didn't deserve this, the way I was treating him but I didn't deserve my first heart break either.

I knew that he was sorry, and always will be but it still won't change the fact that Lucas was gone and it certainly won't change the fact that it was because of my father's act of stupid pride that I will forever grieve Lucas' death.

The past six years I was really into training that I forgot about this day. My father must have thought that I have gotten over it, but how could I? He was my mate, and not only my mate but my first mate, the first guy that I ever really opened up to, the first I cried for and forever cry for.

I stretched all my muscle before shimmering off to the grave land. A piece of land that belonged to Lucas five centuries ago by the seaside on the cliff, a land I once dreamt of calling home.

I stopped just right in front of the border of the grave land. I raised my hand feeling the air I felt the force field that I've compelled a little light witch to do around the land of Lucas to keep away supernatural creatures that wanted to piss me off.

I took a step forward going through the field. I closed my eyes and took a deep breath as the breeze from the sea below passed me, sending shivers of colds to my body. I saw the four tombstones at the edge of the cliff equally spaced from one another.

It has been six years, it's been long. I walked over to the first tombstone at the end, I dropped to the ground kneeling and again having myself holding in my tears, "Lucas, I'm here just like I promised, love. Just like I promised." I managed a smile before wiping off the dust that covered his name from his tombstone.

I leaned down to kiss the ground where he lays in forever, "I'm here. I'm here, Lucas." The wind blew against my face again and with it I heard my name being called. It puts a smile to my face, as I heard his voice calling me I shut my eyes.

"Father, where are you?" I called out from the front porch, I had this uneasy feeling to find my father "Father?"

"Over here, Princess." I turned around to see my father both his arms around two of his men as they helped him back into the house. I ran to him worried, "I'm alright, Princess. Just a few rogues, they got away though but I'll be fine, can't say the same for my pride." Seriously, at times like this you'd think a man would learn to shut up, but no, not my father.

"King, I'll round up more men and head out to track them," my father nodded.

"Wait, I want to follow. I'll teach those nasty rogues a lesson or two!" I called after him. I was already dressed for the occasion. I started training just a week ago and was sure as hell I could take out one or two rogues, maybe not a million but yeah, one or two.

"No you are not going any—" but father tried to reason with me but I didn't wait for him to finish what he had to say. I shimmered out of the house and mind linked the two men that I'd go ahead before blocking back my thoughts.

I sniffed the air taking in all the different scent still I find many unfamiliar scents mixes with one that smelled like the forest, the scent was so nice so mesmerizing. I shimmered following where the scent took me.

And only stop when I hit something hard. I fell on the ground butt first, got up and met face to face with a very handsome male wolf. His deep grey eyes stared into my chocolate brown ones "compagno" he murmured snapping me out of the state.

"What did you say?" I asked, for I had thought he said mate in Italian and with an Italian accent making him sound hotter than he already was.

"Mate, you're my mate. Your scent it smells of the breeze from the sea." I managed a smile before looking away blushing. He took a step closer to me, "you don't have to be shy mate, what are you doing here? Out in the woods, it's dangerous, there are rogues out here."

"I have never seen you before, are you one of the royal guards?"

"No, are you? You haven't answered my question mate, what are you doing here?" He took hold of my hand, making me blush even more. It was the first time I ever let a man held me with so much care.

"I-I—" What am I supposed to answer him? He isn't one of the guards I can't tell him that I am the princess, "I-I um—"

"It's alright, mate. There is nothing you should be scared of, I'm here I'll take care of you, protect you—" He couldn't finish his words because the sound of the guards from behind me screamed saying that 'he is near'.

"No." I whispered. It can't be, my mate is a rogue and before I could do anything, he carried me over his shoulder and

ran away from the guards. I was still stunned to do anything about it.

He finally stopped letting me down on the ground, I turned around to see that I didn't know my environment. "Where is this place?"

"My home." He answered pointing to the cottage just near the end of the cliff, "Come on." He grabbed my hands once more but I pulled it back.

"No!" I screamed, "I am not going anywhere with you!" He frowned looking hurt, the sight of him hurt made my wolf whimper. It was hard to hold the urge to hold him close. To tell him 'it's ok' that I didn't mean it. To kiss those lips of his and to do all the things my mind wants to do to him.

"Why not, mate? Have I hurt you?" He took a step towards me but I mirrored it by taking a step back not reducing or increasing any space between us. It was hard being close to him without wanting to jump him as well as it was hard to be far from him.

"You!" I pointed at him, "You're a rogue!" He nodded. "I—I can't mate with a rogue my father would kill me."

"Your father, doesn't have a say in your relationship. We are mates, he won't be able to do anything till hell freezes over. You don't have to worry, mate. Now, come on." He let out his hand but I wasn't going to take it, I wasn't going to betray my father.

"I-I'm Princess Katherine!" I blurted out, he was taken aback from my outburst. "My father, won't accept us, he won't accept you!"

"Like I said, princess or not. He won't be able to do anything till hell freezes over! You are my mate and I will take *care of you whether you like it or not! Now it's either you come willingly or I'll make you." Unbelievable this man has the same attitude as my father.*

"You will have to make me!" I hissed crossing my arms, and standing my ground. He closed the gap between us and I thought he was going to kiss me but instead he squatted over and tried to carry me over his shoulder like earlier but I meant what I said, he was going to have to make me.

"What the hell have you been eating, mate? A barn full of cows?" He said finally giving up at attempting to get my feet off the ground. I actually laughed at his joke, "now that is a true diamond right there, your smile is priceless, mate."

"What is your name, stranger?"

"Lucas Sontoro." He let out his hand for me to take and I did only to have him plant a kiss on it making me shiver as the sparks ran through my body.

I suddenly giggled after snobs as I remember the day we first met. In time we fell in love, so in love, we had that Romeo and Juliet vibe going on between us. I remembered running away in the middle of the nights compelling guards that caught me to forget ever seeing me.

We were happy, we have planned everything. To run away, to get married and have children, tell them stories of our crazy love life. I looked down at my ring finger so cold and empty, we were going to get married even when supernaturals didn't have to get married.

I remember asking my mother once when we were going on our usual walk around the park, we stumbled on a wedding ceremony. So beautiful, so pure of life.

"What is going on, Mother?" I asked pointing to the group of people. I watched as the group of people made way for a couple to pass as they threw petals. The man wore his best suit as for the lady with the most beautiful bouquet of roses, wore one of the most stunning white dresses I've ever seen.

"It's a wedding, Katherine. Beautiful isn't it?" I nodded, "unfortunately, creatures like us don't have those kinds of ceremonies."

"Why not?" I asked because I was too young to understand. I had too many questions, not many answers but in time my mother had reminded me. I'd know things as I get older, I'd understand more. I'd understand life. I'd learn to be grateful for it, for love, death and even fate.

"We are born with mates, darling. Supernatural creatures are born with mates. A very long time ago before I was even born, man was made with two faces, four arms and legs. Zeus, the king of the skies feared of their power and therefore before anything could happen. He split these creatures in two. Making it have a single face, with a pair of hands and feet while the other half of this male creature was a female image of him. All of us, even the humans are born to have their own mates but unlike us, they were given a stronger task before they could be with their mates but that story is for another day, as for creatures like us. We would know our mate by either scent or when you first meet each other. For werewolves and vampires the moment you both mark each other, it could be called a marriage because when you are marked. Your souls become one again, you don't have to get married. It's not part of our culture, Katherine. One day you will find your mate, and then you will understand what I mean."

My mother showed me her mark that day. She even told me what happened to the marks of mates who have died. Werewolves and any other creature could reject their mates and only once rejected can another male or female mark him or her but it would never be as strong as their true mates' because once their mate realizes their errors in their ways and gets it through their thick head that there is a reason why fate matches them, they would come back and when they do they would claim their mate, the mark that was made by the other creature would be gone.

These marks are to show other creatures, that they are taken and if your mate dies, the mark vanishes because the bond you share is broken. Just like fate, death too, screws us over. When a female is marked her scent mixes with her mates', that's how other male wolves would know she is taken. As for vampires, female are to mark their mate first before the male is to mark his brides.

"How are you, under there?" I joked. "I'm fine here, but how I wish I could be with you. How I wished you took me with you, instead of leaving me here. You promised, Lucas. You promised me things, things that I crave for. Things I will never be able to have. We shouldn't have run, Lucas. We should have stayed and fought. We should have done so many things that we didn't do. You should have kept your promise, instead you dragged it down with you. Leaving me to wonder what could have been."

"Katherine, we have to leave." He begged as I pasted around my room. It was going good, everything was good. The men that knew about Lucas being a rogue was sent out for a mission to track down the rogues Lucas was with the day I met

53

him, that was where I got the idea to ask Lucas to post as one of the guards, to make it easier for us to be together.

I didn't know he was back, he saw him. He saw Lucas with me and ran to get my father. My father's men back then were more loyal to him than me since I am a hybrid and to them I have no loyalty for I am broken between two kinds and unfortunately the other kind is the kind they have been at war with for centuries, add that I wasn't strong and confident, the position I had then was near to nothing. My father was out fighting a few rogues when his men went to get him, giving me time to think of what to do. "I can't, Lucas. I can't leave my father," I started crying, "But I can't let you go."

He walked over to me, grabbed my cheeks in his hands. "We have to, Katherine. Or we will lose each other forever. I'll take you away now, like I promised, we will get married like you planned. Have a family, kids. Come with me now, you don't have to pack. You don't want your title and I don't want the crown, we must leave, there is nothing for us here."

"Katherine!" I heard someone called my name from outside my door before a loud bang was heard but by the time they got the door open, I was jumping out of the window with Lucas. I was going to leave my family, it was going to be worth it. He was my mate, it was right to run away with him. It was how fate planned it, right?

"Find them! And kill him!" My father's order echoed in my head forcing myself to run faster. We were both so focus in running we didn't think about shifting till we were circled by the dozen of the guards. Lucas shifted and started fighting, I shifted as well and started fighting alongside with my mate, but I wasn't as good of a fighter as they were.

Then everything happened so fast, five of my father's best warriors held me down as the others held Lucas. "Shift," my father ordered as he materialized from behind one of the trees. Both Lucas and I were obliged only because he was using his alpha tone.

"Father, please!" I cried out. "Let me go!" I hissed towards the guards. "Please father, I love him!"

"No!" My father's words echoed. "No daughter of mine! A princess nevertheless will be with a rogue of all ranks! I don't know what this mutt has stuffed your head with Katherine, you should know better than to defy me! Rogues want nothing more than just the crown! I will not let you make the same mistake I did, Katherine." With one nod the guards bit down Lucas' neck, taking away his life, right in front of my eyes.

"No!" I screamed as the sharp pain in my chest was unbearable, the guards finally let go of me and I dropped to the ground. I turned to look at my father with tears in my eyes, "why?" I cried. "Why? My mate," I whispered "Lucas."

"What?" The words left my father's lips, "what did you call him?"

I stood up from the ground, for the very first time feeling angry. Nothing but anger in me. I felt the life in me being sucked out the second I felt the sharp pain in my chest. I shimmered to the wolf that bit down on Lucas and shove my hands in his chest, grabbing his heart and ripping it out. The anger I felt wasn't helping in keeping my wolf at bay, I was out for bloodlust.

I turned to my father, "I will never forgive you! For killing my mate!" The word mate echoed and I watched as the fear grew in my father's eyes as he finally realized his mistake. "Lucas isn't like any of your whores before you met my mother

55

and he certainly wasn't like that slut who had her eyes on the crown. Lucas was my mate! He didn't want the crown! He deserved it!"

"Katherine, I-I—" before he could finish, I carried Lucas' body and shimmered away. To the grave land, it was raining heavily and I was left cold and alone to bury my mate.

"If I wasn't so stubborn and just left when you asked me too, we could have had forever, couldn't we?" I laughed at my stupid question, trying to lighten up the mood. "I could have had that ring on my finger? I could have worn a beautiful white dress. I could—" I let out a deep sigh. "We could have been in each other's arms at this moment looking at our children with their mates as our grandchildren ran around playing. I could have done so many things, you could have done so many things. We could have done all of the things we dreamt of, planned, but right now all I am left with is with what I could have. I love you, always have and always will, Lucas Sontoro."

I laid my hands on his tombstone feeling the words I engraved on it as I read them out, "Lucas Sontoro, loving mate and rogue." I wasn't ashamed of him being a rogue, never was but because of my father's reputation, Lucas was known as one of his warriors.

"Always have always will." I repeated those four words.

"Mate! I am coming for you," he teased as we played a little game of hide and seek. "Come out, come out where ever you are." His teasing voice just sent shivers all over me.

I was hiding behind one of the trees, the only reason he couldn't find me right away was because I hid my scent, but I knew he could still smell me, but couldn't find me because the sea wasn't far away and to him I smelt like the morning sea breeze.

I watched as he searched everywhere but got distracted by some squirrels. I shimmered to them but before I could feed off them, I felt arms crawling around my waist and the warm breath on my neck near my mark. "Got you, mate," he whispered into my ears.

He turned me to face him, he made a funny face when he saw the squirrel I was holding, "you're hungry?" I nodded a bit ashamed. Ever since I tasted his blood, I just kept wanting more but I had to keep myself in check or I might kill him. "Oh, mate. Have anyone ever told you? You look cute when you're hungry."

"Oh, please Lucas, everything I do is always cute to you." He started tickling me, taking away my breath.

"You think so huh?" I nodded to answer. "Oh, mate. I love you, always have always will"

"Always have always will." I mimicked him before sticking out my tongue.

And like that those four words have always been our words 'Always have always will' I smiled.

❧ CHAPTER SIX ❧

'Love is what we are born with.
Fear is what we learned here.'
—Marianne Williamson.

I finally got the strength to stand up and walked over to the grave beside Lucas'. "Hello, Victor, old pal." I sat on the ground beside his grave, leaning on his tombstone. "Miss me?" I forced a laugh, "because I miss you."

"Alright, I am going to say this and I am going to say this once. My training is tough and if you can't handle tough, you are welcome to leave." I heard my father giving the full on so-called 'scary pep talk' as usual every time it's time to call in the new recruit werewolves who are to be potential guards as I was making my way to him.

My father did that walk where he had this hands behind his back, body a bit arch walking back and forth like a man waiting in a hospital for a doctor to give news on whether his baby is a girl or boy. "If you think you are the best of the best, then—"

"Think again." I finished his words for him smirking as I walked to my father's side, "Hello, father." He looked at me with wide eyes and his body stiffen. "Miss me?" I said, holding in the smile that wanted to creep out at his facial expression, it was as if he saw a ghost. But then again it has been more than a century from when I last saw him, after what he did to Lucas I ran away and stayed in Lucas' cottage and when I was done morning, I went to live with my mother where I met Benjamin.

"Katherine, I—I wasn't expecting you." He admitted.

I lean towards him to whisper into his ears, "Yes I know, the past is past. So why not just move the hell on? It's not as if I could stay in a frozen time, cursing to myself for not being as strong and confident as I am now, right? It's not as if I could right the things that you have wrong, now can I?" I pulled back, shooting a wink towards my father while I was at it before I turned to the recruited men. The air had a different scent, a mesmerizing scent. A scent I was so familiar to, the scent of the forest.

I walked around the group trying to find the source of the scent, till I have come across with a tall dark and handsome guy. He was very mysterious, eyes as green as the leaves on the trees. "Mate," I murmured, but all he did was bowed his head.

"Victor!" I turned to the cause of noise to see a woman carrying her child. The woman walked towards me, "sorry, warrior. My husband left his fighting equipment."

"Husband?" I repeated her words causing her to nod at the same time I felt the sharp pain in my chest. It was hard to hold the urge of slapping the smile off her face. How dare she? Call my mate her husband and how the hell is she even having a child? Supernatural creatures are only able to bear a child with their mates.

I gathered back all my pride and smiled back at her before walking back to my father, "Mrs." I called out to the woman who was still there beside my mate. "Homes," she replied. I managed a smile before bitching her, "well, Mrs. Homes. As you can see this is a recruit and unless you are part of it please." I paused only to look at my mate for a moment and back at her, "get the hell away!" I continued with a straight face causing her to jump a bit before running along.

"So boys, I hope my father hasn't been hard for any of you?" I said only to hear gaps and whispers of them asking the person beside them if I was the princess. "Yes, people. I am Katherine Claw in the flesh and I will be the one to train you and trust me, it won't be easy."

"I still don't get why the spirits do the things they do, like how men are to mark the women and not the other way around, it's sexist. I hate that creatures like us, no wait. I hate that every creature on earth has all these special powers of strength and speed and all that such. But still they let the weakest of the weak, they let the humans nevertheless, possess the most powerful power anyone has ever dreamed of. A power that we can't see nor touch, I can't believe they get to love who they want, to have a family with whom they choose. I hate that when werewolves and vampires watch their mates with another, a sharp pain stabs them in the heart, literally. When you are with her? When you held her the way you should only hold me, my heart felt like it was being ripped out. When you said the words that were supposed to be only for my ears to hear, I felt my heart stop but you know what, Victor? Even when my heart was only for Lucas, I did love you or I thought I did because of the pain, and even when you were married to her, I was jealous but who was I to show any kind of weakness? And because of my stupidity I lost you. I should have tried and loved you, I should have fought for what was mine but I was so full of pride. I was still so lost with the hope that Lucas might come back from the dead."

I started pulling off some of the grass from the ground to keep myself from getting bored, "I couldn't have you as a mate, but I had you as a best friend. That should have counted for something, right? Sometimes I wonder—I wonder if you ever regret choosing her over me. If you regret rejecting me for her?" I picked up a stone from the ground and threw it into the air.

"I don't get it, how you could have chosen her over me? I was your mate, given by fate herself but you went against her. Something I have been trying to do for years, go against fate but I just can't seem to win with her!"

I let out a smirk that crept out from the corner of my lips, "And they told me not to take it personally because fate, screws us all over, ha!"

"Princess!" The guard called just as I was about to take my shower. I got dressed and shimmered out. "Princess Katherine." He bowed and the others with him did as well.

"What is going on?" I asked in confusion.

"Princess, I am sorry to have to be a carrier of bad news, Victor Homes was killed in action." His words echoed in my head. The pain I felt in my chest earlier, it was him. No wonder the feeling was so familiar. My mate is dead, the mate I never had.

"No!" I cried before dropping to the ground only to have my men catch me. "He should still be alive, I could have prevented it from happening. I should have forced him to stay, I should have kept him safe!" I cried, "But I still let him go with those betas to wipe out the rogues, this is—this is my fault!" The men tried to calm me down, put reason in my head. It wasn't supposed to be like this I came home a few days earlier to be waiting for him to come home not his body, the anger towards my father grew more, he said the feeling of him coming home would have been great but here I am once again being left to bury another mate.

I took a deep breath "I must be crazy huh? Here I am the great and powerful hybrid Princess Katherine Rose Claw, leaning over one of her dead mates' tombstones talking to herself. How pathetic am I? You, Lucas, Benjamin and Dylan have already moved on while here I am. Crying my heart out bitching at you guys for not taking me with you."

"Because of my father's doing, I lost two mates. Losing Lucas wasn't enough, he had to take you too." I let out a loud laugh, "you don't know how much I'd rather be six feet under than here. I guess we can't have everything we want huh, Victor? Or at least I can't have everything I want. I couldn't have Lucas. I couldn't have you, Benjamin or even Dylan and I am sure fate is about to hit me in the arse again and take whoever my next mate might be and that there is the reason why I never even try." I got up from the ground as I pretend to hold a class up in the air.

"Here's to me, and my messed up life. Here's to fate for messing up my life and here's to all of you! For leaving me behind!" I screamed at the same time a thunder erupt startling me, making me stumble to the ground where I just laid there as the rain started pouring.

I just stayed like that on the ground for two days straight, thinking why? Why was fate so cruel to me? What did I do to deserve this? People say that you are born with crap because you are going to be destined for greatness, how can I be destined for great if I can't even handle a few boys? What am I supposed to be destined for? Destined to be the girl who can live forever from one heartbreak to another? That's pathetic.

I got up from the ground feeling weak, I dragged my legs to Benjamin's grave. "Hi there, Mi Amor. Sorry for being late, I did some heavy thinking there. Shocker, huh?" I laughed at my own words, the laughter soon changed into tears as I again dropped to the ground because I wasn't strong enough to hold myself.

"I know, I know I finally lost it. Your crazy little mate, right?" I said laughing once again but this time tears came with my laughter, I suddenly stopped everything as I stared into the air.

"Come on, Katherine. Let's have a little friendly race, at the same time catch any small animals with you and we will see who is faster as well as good in hunting. What you say, Mi Amor?" Benjamin gave me his signature smirk, I nodded and positioned myself.

"Don't start crying, if I end up beating you again," I said winking. "On three, Mi Amour." He started counting in Spanish and on three I shimmered trying my best to move as fast as I could, hunting for animals. This was the way Benjamin taught me to hunt. After that we got to drink the blood of the animals we hunted.

I managed to capture eight squirrels and was the first one at the meeting point. I sat there on the ground waiting for my mate, as he finally showed up I smirked at him. "I got six!" He called out.

"Well, my love. Looks like I won, I got eight and I was here first." I said shimmering to him stopping just inches from his face. I gave him a little kiss before grabbing one of his squirrels and sucking the life out of it.

Benjamin laughed at my act of hunger. "Oh, looks like my crazy little mate is hungry," he said trying to take my food from me I growled at him causing him to jerk back his hands.

After mourning the death of Lucas I went to live with my mother where I found Benjamin, he taught me almost everything I know, the perfect punch, the deadly kick. He taught me to fight so that the next time I won't be just watching as my mate gets killed. "It's almost time for me to go, Benjamin. I got to check on Dylan and I'll be on my way, take care, Benjamin." As I stood up the cold breeze covered my body, the first time Lucas took me here, I knew right away why he chose this as home or the reason why he liked the scent of the morning sea breeze.

I was feeling really uncomfortable with my clothes. Who wouldn't be if you have been wearing the same thing for almost four days? "Hello, Dylan." I spoke formally, Dylan wasn't just any warrior for my mother. He was the head warrior, my mother's right hand man.

"How is everything, General?" I asked doing a salute like I always did to make fun of him. "Well my life sucks, if you wanted to know. I won't say long, Dylan. I stayed here long enough, my body aches, Alec and Isaac must be looking for me now. I just, I just came to say hello. I know we aren't close but you were my mate and I did care for you, you know what? If only you weren't so hard all the time, or maybe if I weren't so stupid and just move on, there could have been us."

"Katherine, you are here! Just in time, I am about to go to a meeting, come with me? I'll introduce you to my men, you can get to know them." I nodded and held my hand out for her to link her arm with mine.

"Good morning, boys. Please take a seat, I have a surprise for you. My daughter is back and I would like to introduce you all to her." I was hiding behind the door waiting for her to give the signal for me to enter. The room had a smell, a scent so mesmerizing. A scent that I thought Benjamin would only have, the scent of blood. "This is my daughter, Katherine Rose Claw." I managed a smile, as her men stood up one by one to salute me while announcing their names and rank, but the one at the end was the one I was waiting for.

He finally stood up, his black coal eyes burned through me, "Dylan Meath, General." He saluted, I nodded and he sat back down.

I wiped the dust away from his tombstone like I did with Lucas', "Dylan Meath, the great general and mate." I read out as I stood up straight and salute one last time, "till next time, General."

I walked away trying not to turn back to Lucas' grave and as I was about to step my foot through the field the wind blew strong stopping me. "Katherine," I heard my name being called like a whisper. I turned around and there he was.

"Lucas!" I called, looking at him with wide eyes, trying to process what I was seeing. "What, what?" The words couldn't come out, the air in me was almost gone.

"Breathe, Katherine. It's alright." He took a step closer and I wanted to mirror his movement but I couldn't move, "it's alright, mate. Breathe, you need to breathe." I finally sucked in air, but my vision blurred.

"How am I seeing you?" I asked, when I felt a tear ran down my cheeks. He held his cold hands on my cheeks as an attempt to wipe off my tear but couldn't. He couldn't touch me, but how I craved for his touch again.

"Let's take a walk, mate." I nodded and went to his side as we walked around his land, "I like what you did here, the plants you grew, they are beautiful," he motioned to the bushes of flowers.

"Thanks," I smiled. "I—I miss you," I finally burst out. I stopped to look at him, taking all the time I could to look at him. "I—I—" I attempted the same thing he did, I held my hands up to hold him but only went through him, leaving me disappointed.

"I miss you too, mate." He smiled that perfect smile, I remember I used to see on his lips. "Everything is going to be alright."

"What do you mean?" He let out his hand, giving me way to the edge of the cliff where we sat letting our legs dangle in the air as we watch the waves coming in.

"I have been watching over you, mate. I know how you have been and I am sorry I really am, for leaving you here but you need not worry anymore, Katherine. Everything will change, my death wasn't your fault, I need you to know that. I love you, Katherine. I really do, always have and always will," he said the words we always said before 'always have always will'.

"You have been blaming yourself and your father—" he continued but I stopped him.

"I blame him because it's his fault, you know what? I remember a few centuries back, we had a family dinner, me, mother and him. He was so full of himself, he thought I had forgiven him that I've forgotten. You know what I said to make sure he remembers that it is his fault, I will never love again?" I didn't let him answer and just went on with it, "I said that 'how do you expect to forgive and forget, father? I haven't god damn forgiven you, so how the hell was I supposed to forget?'" I said shaking my head in disbelief that my father would think that his action was just something minor, as if something that I could just brush off my shoulders and move on.

"But it was neither your fault nor his, it was mine for choosing to be a rogue. It was mine because I tried to bring you away instead of staying, to settle things like men. Mate, look at me." I looked away from the ocean and turned to stare at his dead grey eyes, "it's alright, Katherine. It has always been alright, to let me go. To move on because you deserve it, you of all people deserve it, look around," he motioned behind at the three graves.

"They were all your mates, you could have had a life with them. I knew you could but you were so scared to open up, because of that you lost them. No, you didn't lose them because you never had them, but I want you to. I want you to feel it again, the love you had for me. I want you to feel that again, for someone who is alive, not dead. Someone you could hold and not just see, for someone who would love you the same way, not just partially. Katherine, voglio tante cose per voi. No, I want everything for you, everything I couldn't give, he will."

"He? Who? Who are you talking about, Lucas?" I asked in a confused tone.

"Katherine, I have to go." He said but I wasn't ready to see him go again. I need him here with me.

"No, please don't! Please!" I begged as I covered my face letting tears run down.

"Don't cry, mate. Don't ever cry because of me, I am not worth a single tear, but he is and when he comes Katherine, accept him. Accept him even when it hurts." I wiped my tears and looked back at him again, he leaned forward and as he tried to kiss my forehead I shut my eyes, only to see him gone the moment I opened them back.

I stayed there, just sat there looking out to the ocean for another three days just thinking about what Lucas said. *How could he just leave like that? How could he? Who was I supposed to accept? There can never be anyone, anyone better than him. There can never be any creature, night or day that can ever make me happy they way he did."* I asked my wolf but she didn't say anything.

I finally found the strength to stand up, I started walking the first few miles before shimmering straight to the motel I was going to stay in. I needed rest, my body ached everywhere and the worst part wasn't that but my heart, my heart that was broken centuries ago. My heart that I mended back together by time was now falling apart again.

But I had to do this, I had to do this for Lucas. I owed him that much, after what my father did to him, I owed him this much because I couldn't save him. *"Whoever this 'he' is will never be Lucas, Katherine but that didn't mean we couldn't try to love him the same way."* My wolf said.

✆ CHAPTER SEVEN ✆

"Efforts and courage are not enough without
purpose and direction."
—John F. Kennedy.

As much as I'd love to stay home and rest, something in me felt as if something great is going to happen today. I parked my blue mini coupé in the parking lot next to Uriel's ride. Uriel and Saraquel had just arrived as well. I turned off the engine and grabbed my bag before getting out. Alec and Isaac didn't follow me to school because I didn't need the attention, plus they look too old for high school, college maybe but not high school. As for my father, the last I saw him was when he tried to stop me from leaving. Both Uriel and Saraquel waited for me and we walked to the entrance together.

"Hi, Katherine. Good morning." Uriel said over Saraquel's side.

"Good morning, Uriel, Sara. I heard Brandon is having a party tomorrow night, I got a text from him." Brandon Spike was their cousin.

"Yeah, I was actually going to find you today about that since my baby sister over here won't give me your number." The thought of him waiting my number to ask me out as a date to Brandon's party made me blushed.

"What for?" I tried to sound as calm as possible.

"I wanted to ask if you would like to go with me. I was going to ask you directly instead of a phone call but I haven't seen you around school for weeks. So I tried bargaining with my sister over here for your number." Saraquel punched him on his shoulder, as a code to as 'leave me out of this and leave my best friend alone too'.

"What do you say, Katherine? Want to come as my date?"

The end of my lips started to creep upwards but I coughed the smirk off my face before turning to Saraquel, "Umm, yeah sure I guess if it's alright with Sara," she nodded as to approve.

"Wow, thanks sis!" He pulled Sara in for a hug but she only pulled back when the bell rang, and before I knew it I felt a hand on my wrist pulling me away from Uriel and towards the direction of my history class. Mr. Butcher, our history teacher is as mean as any teacher could get, he locks the door on anyone who comes in late no matter the excuse.

Like yeah, I could have like an asthma attack and recovered like a second after the bell rang and he would still slam the door shut. As if a wooden door could keep me from coming in.

Finally it was lunch, I went to my locker to put some of my books before meeting up with Saraquel in the cafeteria. I had my locker just a few spaces away from Uriel's. I saw him by his locker with a few of his friends, he was too busy to acknowledge my existence. I don't get why I like him, like come on! Hot she-wolf hybrid princess over here! And he is just a normal weak human, plus I don't get how I could feel this much love for him.

I opened my locker and a piece of paper fell, I picked it up and opened it to see a picture of a rose coloured in blue. It's my favourite flower in my favourite colour, how romantic was that? I turned it back to see that there was something written on it.

> *I would have put in a real rose, it's just I couldn't*
> *slide it through the locker hole now, could I? You look*
> *beautiful today by the way.*
>
> *—US*

I smiled as I read the paper over and over, I could feel my cheeks starting to cramp and it hurts. I put the paper back into my locker with my books and turned to look at Uriel once again, this time to my surprise he was staring at me with his blue eyes.

I felt myself blush and tried to look away but it was hard, how could I feel this way towards someone that isn't my mate and God towards a human of all creatures? The thought of him being a human scare me, because he wouldn't meet my father's expectations, just like Lucas being a rogue. How if my father tries to kill him, like he did to Lucas? Lucas was able to fight off a few warriors but Uriel? He wouldn't stand a chance.

"Katherine." I break the stare with Uriel and turned to see Saraquel standing beside me, "Please, don't have any sexual thoughts about my brother."

"Oi, I wasn't having any thoughts of that kind! Now come on I'm hungry, let's eat." I grabbed Saraquel by the arm and dragged her and myself away from Uriel.

"Says the girl that has been staring at a guy as if she was stripping him with her sweet Choco-cocoa brown eyes!" I rolled my eyes and kept quiet because there's clearly no way I am going to win this conversation.

Lunch went as normal I guess, we sat at our usual seat a few tables away from Uriel's with a few friends. I caught Uriel looking my way a few times, just thinking about it made me blush. The bell rang as to announce the end of lunch time, I grabbed my rubbish and threw it in the bin before going back to my locker to take my books out for the next class, I didn't see Uriel around, he must have had his books with him already or he had P.E next.

"The structure of a red blood cell and a white blood cell—" The bell rang cutting off Mr. Folk's sentence and everybody closed their books and stood up to rush for the door. "Alright, we will continue this tomorrow."

I was really tired and when I got home, I had to train as usual and by eighteen my father would announce me as his personal warrior and that I would have the same rank of a princess. Well I'll still keep my rank above from the other warriors and alphas. At least I wouldn't have to hide myself every time I go out with the guards anymore.

After everyone was out, I threw all my belongings in my bag and walked out the door. I could never be late getting home or Alec and Isaac would start to worry and they would then come and bring hell to me. I walked out the door to see Uriel leaning on the lockers opposite to the door I was standing in.

"I almost thought I waited outside the wrong class." He said, walking towards me.

"What were you waiting for?" I asked because it couldn't have been me, I wasn't his girlfriend, so why would he wait?

"For you. I want to walk you to your car and since we parked beside each other it would be on the way." I smiled and nodded. We met up with Saraquel at the main entrance and then walked over to our cars.

Uriel unlocked his ride and Saraquel got in, he gave her the key to start up the car before escorting me to my car door, "Umm, about tomorrow? Should I pick you up? Or do you want to meet up there?" He sounded nervous. Lucas, Benjamin, Victor and especially Dylan were never nervous with me, so this is an all new kind of romantic-ish for me, not that I ever did give Dylan the chance to woo me over.

"Um, I'll just meet you there. Unless you're planning on meeting my father, he is very scary." Uriel laughed and opened the door for me. I got in and he waved at me and I waved back, he then got into his ride as well.

I couldn't let him pick me up, my father would literally bite his head off! No matter if he is a human, I was only allowed to be with my mate. My car roared to life and drove back home, not in a rush, just thinking of Uriel with a crazy smile pasted on my face and to say I had the 'Cheshire' smile was an understatement. By the time I reached home Isaac and Alec were just about to put their helmets on and go searching for me.

❧ Chapter Eight ❧

*'I'd rather have roses on my table than
diamonds on my neck.'*
—Emma Goldman.

School today went as it usually did. I didn't see Uricl today though, but I spotted his car and saw Saraquel during English and Math. I wondered if he was avoiding me or something because if he was then I wasn't going to the party tonight.

I hadn't asked my father about it yet, I haven't even seen him yet but come on, I'm a five hundred and sixteen year old she-wolf, I think I am old enough to go out without permission. I parked my car at my usual place where Isaac and Alec would always wait for me. I got out of the car leaving my bag inside, "where is my father, Alec?"

Isaac doesn't talk much, so I've gotten used to asking Alec for everything.

"He is in the library as usual, thinking of a plan."

"A plan? For what? That old man needs to get a life!"

I walked to the library with Isaac and Alec by my side. I knocked on the door and waited for my father to answer before entering. "Come in, Princess." I heard my father on the other side. I opened the door to see him with a few guards and the head warrior.

"What is going on, father?"

My father nodded for everyone to clear the room. "Princess—" I raised a finger to stop him.

"Father, I'm sorry for running like that, I just—" I took a deep breath, "I was just, you know what? I don't know why I acted that way, I just got scared and I had to get away I felt as if you were going to stop me again. I—I went to the grave land, mother used to come with me. The past six years I was so focused on taking down Kevin. I—I forgot my mate." I walked over to his table, he stood up with open arms and I accepted his hug, "it wasn't your fault, you didn't know." I looked to the side of my father's table to see files on Kevin, "oh no." I murmured, "Not this crap again." I cursed.

I grabbed the file from his table, "What is this? And don't you dare say this is about Kevin? Like I said he might be dead by now, it has been six years and if he was alive you will have me to take him out like pronto, with Alec and Isaac by my side of course."

"Princess, it's just that I think if we try and figure out his whereabouts and attack him before he attacks us we could save lives here. Would you rather he goes into another pack and kill?" I shook my head. I didn't want to fight again, we had been through this a lot of times.

"I didn't come here to argue with you, I'm just here to ask for your permission. Brandon is having a party tonight and I was thinking maybe I could go?"

"And let me guess? That boy, Uriel is it? Is he going to be there? Take Isaac and Alec with you." I could always compel them to get off my back, but I won't, I'm not that evil.

Just tell him the truth and everything will be alright, "yes, Uriel will be there, so don't start with me and as much as I would like to hang out with my friends in peace. I'd rather go with Isaac and Alec than not go at all, now goodbye I have to go get ready."

As I walked out the door my father called me, "Princess, it's alright. I just wanted to see if you were going to be honest with me and you were. We haven't had that honesty in a long time. You have my permission, you may go without Alec and Isaac. I might have a men's night with them." I giggled at that and ran to tackle my father in a hug, it's a moment like this that it gets hard to hold my strength. My father patted my back, "Princess, need oxygen here, not vampire." I let him go and ran straight to my room.

I stripped off my clothes and left them on the floor, I got into the tub and just let my thoughts drift away.

Buzz! Buzz! Buzz! I heard the buzzing of my phone and got up to reach it, to see a block number calling, "Katherine Smith, Hello?" The name I used in school was Katherine Jane Smith, come on I think even the most stupid person alive could connect the dots between Katherine Claw and Balthazar Claw, it isn't as if there were many people with surname Claw.

"Katherine?" It sounded like Uriel, but how did he get my number?

"Yeah, who is speaking?"

"Um, it's me Uriel. I called to check if you're coming later?" It is him! But where did he get my number? Saraquel isn't one to give up easily. "Yeah I am, where did you get my number?"

"I gave Saraquel a hundred bucks for it." Wow! Now that is seriously 'falling in love' right there.

"A hundred bucks! Your sister sure knows how to sell but then again, I never came cheap." He laughed and I joined him. "So um, I'll see you later alright? I'm kind of taking a bath right now."

"Um yea, yeah sure. I'll be waiting, Katherine." I cut the call and kept my phone back where I got it from and got out of the bath tub. I'm sure he must have flushed after hearing what I've said, and a hundred bucks! The thought of it made me giggle, he must really like me.

After drying up, I went to put on my make-up, blue smoky eyes and lip gloss made perfect. I then went on to choose my outfit and ended up with a pair of skinny jeans and a blue sleeveless shirt with a golden owl embroidered on it. I matched my outfit my bright yellow sneakers and even the mirror fell in love looking at me.

I got out of my room to find Alec and Isaac waiting for me.

"What's up? You know that you're going to have a men's night with my father tonight, right?" Isaac nodded.

"Well good luck, you'll need it. My father doesn't come cheap on first dates." I winked.

"We're here to escort you to your car," Alec spoke up, very charming and sexy but there was a hint of jealousy in his voice.

I arrived at the party a bit late due to an accident that had occurred on the way and thank God nobody was injured, I haven't been drinking blood for a long time, I crave so much for it but I could only drink from my mate. To me the taste of blood from anyone or anything other than my mate's tasted like milk whereas my mates' tastes like fine wine.

The house was full, how was I ever going to find Uriel? And with this many people? I wasn't sure I could smell his scent, there were too many. I killed my car and got out, just as I was locking the door, I felt a presence behind me and turned to see, Uriel.

"You came, I was beginning to think you ditched me for another guy or something." I giggled.

"Shopping may be but another dude? Not going to happen." I teased.

He faked hurt and covered his hands over his chest, "It hurts to know I'm in a lower rank than shopping!" I laughed and it felt good, being able to laugh like this again, it has been long. We walked into the house. He held my hand and I could feel the sparks but they weren't that strong, not like with my mates. I guess this was just a normal human feeling, but I'm not human, then it must have been my other side, could it? But wait, how can my other side affect me this much? I wasn't born with it, I mastered it.

"Are you alright? You look worried, do you want a drink?" I shook my head. He cared for me, how sweet was that.

"It's just crowded in here I think I might be claustrophobic plus the music is too loud." I had to shout for him to hear me, he pulled me closer to him and whispered in my ear, "You want to go some place quiet?" I nodded and he led me out of the house towards the docks. The lake was wow! Amazingly beautiful! There were fishes, I could see them and it wasn't just because of my heightened sense.

☾☾☾☾ |BALTHAZAR| ☾☾☾☾☾

I watched as my daughter went off to get ready for the party. I waited for a few minutes to make sure she was in her room before I called for Isaac and Alec. They came right in, in a second, "Is something the matter, Balthazar?" Alec spoke, both he and Isaac bowed their heads.

"My daughter is going out, and I was thinking, men's night out?" Isaac nodded.

"What do you have in mind, Balthazar?" Alec had always been the one to speak, I tried to get close to Isaac, to loosen the kid up but he just won't crack.

"Well, I was thinking, night watch? I want to keep an eye on this boy. He might be human, and we can't have Katherine mating with a human."

"My king, Katherine has been alive for five hundred and sixteen years and she has mated four times, but I've never heard of her having a child or anything." The words that came from Isaac came as a shock to me. I'd never noticed it that way before. I haven't had any grandchildren, at least none that I knew of.

"I never thought of that, Isaac, and Katherine have only mated once, I've only ever seen her mark once. There is a book somewhere on these shelves, titled 'Filia' if you find it, you can read it."

"Filia? As in princess in Latin?" I nodded to answer yes. "I've heard of it, it's a rare book, only two of its kind, a book about the princess, about her early years in life." I nodded once more as to say he was correct.

"You guys may leave now. Call me when my daughter leaves." They bowed their heads and left, I stood up from my chair and walked over to the window. I've been trying to avoid her ever since she got back, I didn't know what to react to her outburst that day. Everything was going great, I thought she has finally forgiven me, but now I'm sure she has, it was a mistake. The biggest mistake of my life, if I knew he was her mate, I would have acted differently, wouldn't I? I wasn't that clouded by hate towards rogues, was I?

"My king, Katherine has just left. How will we travel? Do you want me to get the car ready?"

I turned to see Isaac and Alec. Alec calls me Balthazar, but Isaac he calls me 'my king' no matter how many times I insisted that he calls me Balthazar. It's the twenty first century, man! Not the 1980's!

"Isaac, it's Balthazar, the next time you say 'my king' or call me anything other than Balthazar, I am going to skin you alive!" His eyes widened and Alec laughs at the joke. "We're going by paws, it's supposed to be a stakeout. Oh and bring some snacks and beers, when it's about girls and if she is her mother's daughter, then I'm sure it's going to be a long night." The two boys nodded and moved to grab the snacks.

We hid behind the bushes and trees as my daughter, just parked her car and got out to lock it. A man appeared behind her, I remembered him as Uriel, I don't get what does this boy have that he has my baby girl wrap around his fingers.

"You came. I was beginning to think you ditched me for another hot dude or something."

Nice line I guess, it made my daughter giggle, "Shopping may be but another dude? Not going to happen."

He faked hurt. "It hurts to know I'm in a lower rank than shopping!" They both laughed and walked in together. I could see that he was going to attempt to hold her hand which made me let out a small growl.

"Balthazar, don't forget that your growl may sound small to you but it is massive to humans." I nodded and went back to watch my daughter, I couldn't make out what they were saying since the music was too loud and with my heightened sense it hurt a 100 times more.

A few minutes later, they both got out of the house walking towards the lake and we followed them, just not close enough for my daughter to sense me and the boys.

⫷⫷⫷⫷ |KATHERINE| ⫸⫸⫸⫸⫸

We sat on the docks and he put an arm over my shoulder, I heard a growl and I knew it was the growl of my father because it sounded in my head because if it wasn't then he must be having a death wish! Because that loud of a growl even Uriel would be able to hear it but he didn't show any signs as if he heard anything.

"Katherine, are you having fun? I'm scared that I might bore you."

I shook my head, "No it's a great night so far."

He took out a stalk of blue rose from his jacket and I looked at it in awe, I knew that it was hard to find a blue rose and even a black one, "where did you find one? It's beautiful!"

"I ordered it." What? He ordered it?

"You ordered one stalk?" He shook his head and pointed to the back, I turned to see a bouquet of blue roses on the top of my car. I was so happy that I turned back to him and hugged him, "thanks, Uriel. It's really beautiful, I love it!"

"You want to take a dip? The water's great." I turned to him and our eyes locked and I could feel him coming closer to me, coming in for a kiss but I looked away at the sound of another growl in my head again.

"Yeah, let's take a dip." He got up and opened his shirt and there was another growl.

"Uriel, if it's cold, could you hold me?" He nodded and I got up to undress, my father was going to get really pissed. But I wanted to know if his touch, if being in his arms were like being in Lucas'. Uriel jumped in and a few seconds later he appeared from under the water.

"The water is great, Katherine. Come on in, it's cold, I guess you're going to get your hug after all." I giggled and felt my cheeks flush, I backed away a bit before running along the docks and jumped in the lake. The water was cold, I was warm because of my wolf side but my vampire side was cold, but I could always change my body temperature.

"It's very cold, I think I might turn into a popsicle."

Uriel swam closer to me and I felt a hand over my waist. He pulled me closer to him and yes it felt exactly like being in Lucas' arms, the sparks that I felt was incredible. I could see that he was now staring at my lips and damn I did want his lips badly too! He came closer till our lips touched and moved in sync. He bit on my lower lip asking for entrance and I gave in, our tongues were moving in sync too, not wanting to fight for dominance.

We tore apart and it felt like my soul being ripped from my body, I craved for more of his kisses. This time all he did was staring into my eyes and hold me as if I might drown or something. "Katherine, I-I-I don't know how to say this but I really like you. I first saw you during the children's fund raiser and you were sweet and kind and I don't know, my heart just keeps skipping a beat every time I see you. Sometimes I even forget to breathe and I know this is our first date but I was thinking maybe you would like to be my girlfriend?"

What did I just hear, oh my God! I can't breathe right now, I think I'm going to faint right here and drown. Katherine! Get yourself together, he nothing but a human boy. It's so hard to hold my smile. Lucas did this for me, I don't know how but he must have slapped fate right across the face for this, for me, because he wanted this for me.

"Uriel, I-I—" he crushed his lips to mine again, it was goddamn romantic. His hold around me tightened, crushing his body to mine as sparks went through me, stronger than before, stronger than what I felt with my mate. He finally broke away and a feeling in me emerges, the feeling to be close to him again.

We got out of the lake and got dressed up when we realized that people were starting to leave the party, it must be late. I'll have to deal with my father when I get home. Uriel walked me toward my car. He was nervous, I didn't get why and then it hit me. I haven't yet answered him but I thought kissing him back earlier was already an obvious yes, I guess not.

He took the roses from the car and handed them over to me, I opened the door and turned back to kiss him on the cheeks before getting in the car. I reversed the car and Uriel waved goodbye looking sad. I remembered that I forgot to answer him so I switched the gear back into drive and drove forward till Uriel was in front of my side window. I roll the window down and smiled, "yes, Uriel. Yes,"

"Yes!" He screamed back and just like that his face lit up and he started jumping around screaming. "Yes! She said yes!" People looked at him as if he had drunk a lot, he kissed my lips once again. "I'll text you later?" I nodded and drove back home to deal with my father.

"Oh father, when I told Isaac and Alec you needed to get a life, I didn't mean mine!" I growled to him through our mind link, *"You boys are going to get it now!"*

☙ CHAPTER NINE ❧

'Victory is always possible for the person who refuses to stop fighting.'
—Napoleon Hill.

I woke up with a major headache after the fight with my father three nights ago, couldn't say he didn't deserve it. My father does not learn from his mistake and never will. I should be grateful I didn't inherit any of his stubbornness. Ok maybe not all of his stubbornness.

I'll be shocked if they have finally recovered from the beating I have given them, served them right, "men's night" he said, "stake out was all he could think of" they say. I got out of bed to get myself ready for school and let my nightgown fall to the floor as I got into the tub.

I parked the car as I reached home, got out off my vehicle ready to have a face off with my father. I busted open the door to see my father with Alec and Isaac by his side, "the field, Now!" And walked away towards the field.

"Oh boy, she is going to kill us!" I heard Alec murmured as I got out.

"Katherine, before you do something stupid, let me remind you that Isaac and I are mate less and we would actually want to meet our mates before we die and that the whole plan was your father's. Isaac didn't even want to go!" Alec tried reasoning with me. The little twat!

"Katherine! You know how I feel about humans! I don't like him and I don't want you near him and I don't want you to go out with him! And I only growl once! Alec was the one that kept growling!" My father spoke to me like I was even listening to the old man. He stopped showing his dominance over me, when he got it through his thick head that I was stronger and always will be.

"Whose head am I ripping off first? I'll let Isaac go last, since he didn't want to go. Oh and Alec, don't worry I'd be sure to glue your heads back because I still need your heir! Come on now, make a pick." I said in all my authority.

I saw my father push Alec in front of him to hide himself, "yeah, throw us to the sharks, will you, Balthazar? She is your daughter, reason with her."

"Maybe you shouldn't have kept growling like a madman!"

I smirked as I held both my father's and Alec's collar, dragging both of them into the middle of the field. I didn't have to worry about Isaac I knew he was following at the back.

"Go ahead, father. Do as Alec says, go ahead try and reason with me." Just as I let them both go my father started

talking again, inside I knew he was scared. Like come on, who wouldn't if you had a hybrid pissed off at you? "Princess—" I raised my hand to stop him.

"You know how much I hate being called 'Princess'. So the question here is, do you think that it's the right time to call me that?"

"Katherine," he corrected himself with an angry tone to scare me, "you may beat Alec as much as you like, but I still won't approve of this boy! He is human! What will people think? You! A princess of high power mating with a human? It will only downgrade your child! My grandchild! I forbid you to see this human!"

"Stop crying! You of all people should know the consequence, father! And you of all people should know that you don't have a say in who I can be with! You lost that privilege, the second you ordered your guards to kill Lucas but you know what? Let's put it this way? Think of this as training." I fell silent for a while to call all the guards outside to watch.

"Oh, spirits. She just called the guards out!" Alec cried.

"Alec! Put a sock in it!" I hissed. I turned to see Isaac so calm, he hasn't uttered a word. I didn't get how Isaac could stay so calm in this situation and Alec keeps on crying.

I waited for the audience to come out before I began torturing them, before anything happened I could already hear whispers of my men betting on who would win this and it looked like all money was on me.

When the field was finally full of warriors, I called out to them, "get armed and ready. Come on men! What would you look like? Being beaten by a girl and a vampire nevertheless, it would bring shame to you Alec and Isaac, as for you, father, I have nothing to say. The men have respect towards their king whether or not he gets beaten by a she vampire."

I winked at my father and he stepped back several steps before shifting into a huge black wolf with white paws. My wolf was like my father's. She just has blood red fur, which was not normal and her paws were white, same goes with her tail.

My father growled and Alec and Isaac too shifted, I never liked shifting and I love the clothing that I was wearing. So I did not shift, I rarely shift, I only ever shift like fifty times, give or take.

I've heard some people saying that my wolf is just breathtaking, seeing a very huge wolf, bigger than my father that has blood red fur. It had actually started out all white, but the more blood I drank the more, my fur turned to red, blood red not like brown red, like normal red wolves.

My father growled and both Isaac and Alec charged for me but all I did was smirked, they must be stupid to think they could even hurt me. I aimed a high kick on Isaac's belly had him flying away several feet, and had Alec by his neck. I punched him a few times before swinging him far, hitting a few trees before landing on the ground unconscious.

The thing about being royal blood is once you attack a normal wolf, the wounds will take weeks to heal, sometimes months or even years and possibly never.

Now that the two wolves were gone I had my father all to myself, he growled at me showing his canines and dominance. When I was a child and I couldn't shift, I was a bit frightened by him, but now that I was declared the strongest creature amongst the living and the dead, I wasn't scared of anyone.

He jumped at me in attack and I ran toward him to grab his tail. I held it really tight until my father whimpered and then slammed his body from side to side like that kid Bambam on cartoon network, The Flintstone.

The guards that were watching were suddenly howling and growling at the sight of their king hurt, some of them I'd noticed had already shifted and were ready to back up their king. Fools I thought, I am their princess.

They would never hurt me, even if I was a half vampire. One is because they wouldn't stand a chance, royal guards or not. Another is because they have respect for their princess, now that I am much scarier the before and I am after all part of their family as well, whether or not I have my loyalties straight.

I finally stopped when through my heightened hearing I heard my phone ring—it must have been Uriel—and let go of my father to sprint towards my car to grab my phone.

Uriel's name popped up which made me squeal and blush at the same time.

I got out of the bath to get ready for school, it was my first day of school as Katherine Jane Smith girlfriend of Uriel Spike, the thought of that made me giggle like a mad woman.

I didn't bump into Alec and Isaac earlier and I hadn't seen my father either. I hadn't seen them since the fight, Alec and Isaac were usually there when I got out of my room early in the morning for school. They might still be in bed I guessed, the thought of it made me smirk, they should have known better than to mess with me. I parked my car in its usual place, beside Uriel and Saraquel but it looked like they haven't arrived yet.

Just as I got out of my car, Uriel showed up behind me, which startled me. "God! Uriel, you scared me, how did you get here? Where is your car?" He came towards me and leaned in to kiss my cheeks, "I let Saraquel drive this morning and she hit a tree—"

"What? Are you ok? Is she alright? Why in the world will you let her drive? You know she failed her driving test three times!" God damn it! What is it with these men and their death wish.

Uriel grabbed my hand with his and walked me to class. "She is alright, same goes for me. She went home though because she was really freaked out. I come to school, I want to see you." I blushed and he gave me a peck on my lips. We finally made it to my class door just a minute before the bell rang.

"I'll meet you in an hour? Walk you to your next class?" I nodded and he grabbed my hand and lifted it for him to kiss. I heard gasps from behind him.

"Uriel, I did not just see what you did to her?" Liza the school slut and a popular girl, a senior, pulled Uriel by his shirt away from me and wrapped her arms around his neck. The view of this made me insane, it was like instead of me holding onto my wolf, it was my wolf holding on to me.

Seeing her made me feel scared and jealous, the feeling of jealousy I got every time I watch Victor happily with his wife. Liza kissed him, I was trying really hard to keep my eyes from changing its brown chocolate colour into red. Uriel pushed her away and she must have stumbled on her own heels because she fell on the ground, that's what you get from wearing killer heels. Liza's clique gasped and ran to help her.

"Stay away from me, Liza. I'd rather be caught dead than to be seen kissing you." Uriel grabbed my hand and pulled me close to him before putting his arms around my waist. "Katherine is my girlfriend, so just stay away."

The girls gave me nasty glares before walking away, "hey don't hate the player, hate the game." I called out to them as I motioned 'game' to Uriel, only to have him hold me even tighter. I could still picture Liza's face, it was priceless at what Uriel had said to her. The bell rang and Uriel kissed my cheeks one last time before sprinting off to class.

During lunch, Uriel asked me to sit at his table and introduced me to his friends who I got along with very well.

When class was over I offered Uriel a ride home, but he declined since Brandon his cousin had asked him over to watch a game at his house later tonight. Uriel walked me to my door though.

I reached home and there was still no sight of my father and my guards. I went to visit them at their chambers. My father will be fully healed by the next day, can't say the same for my guards, they both still looked horrible.

Just as I got into my room to get some homework done, I got a text message from Uriel saying that there was a carnival by the beach side this weekend and that he wanted to take me, I texted back 'sure, I can't wait' and went on with my homework.

⤳ Chapter Ten ⤶

*'I see nothing in space as promising as the
view from a Ferris Wheel.'*
—E. B. Wheel.

The two days passed like speeding cars, I woke up to the sound of the birds chirping. I checked my phone for the time and it was already two in the afternoon. I'd got a few new messages from Uriel saying that he'll pick me up later on at six for the carnival.

I hadn't asked my father about it and if he dared to come there for another men's night out again, I'd make sure that it would take him a century to heal, he seriously needs to get a life which doesn't include mine. Alec and Isaac were almost fully healed thanks to my extra abilities. I've decided to tell my father on my birthday next year.

I brushed my teeth before heading out to the kitchen for some lunch, I was feeling really hungry and my tummy kept making sounds. I didn't know why, but this past few days all I could think about was blood—the damn good taste of blood. Sooner or later my mate is going to show up and I'm just hoping that it's later, unless Uriel turns out to be a werewolf and you know my mate as well, but if he was, then he would already be shifting.

It was still a long way to his eighteenth birthday and my father could sense a werewolf once they reach seventeen of age. Maybe by the time Uriel reached seventeen, my father and Uriel would be nice pals and I can get my father to tell me if he is human or werewolf.

I saw my father taking his coffee and reading the newspaper out in the garden. I had one of the cooks take my lunch out and sat on the seat next to my father, "afternoon, father. How are you feeling today?"

He put his paper down and took a sip of his coffee, "I'm all healed up, can't say the same for the boys. I went to visit them earlier, they've healed faster than they are supposed to and one of the maids said you did something to them. Are you going to tell me what it was?"

I shook my head, "I'm going out tonight by the way, there is a carnival on the beach."

"Let me guess, out with that human?" He said with disapproval and disappointment.

"Yes, father and if you try and do another 'men's night out' with the other boys, I think they will decline you, so don't even bother. Don't forget that I am officially much scarier than you." My father choked on his coffee making me smirk. My food finally arrived and I ate in peace.

After lunch, I went straight for training. I'd noticed that ever since I've liked Uriel, my father had stopped worrying about Kevin and started interfering with my love life. What's wrong with being with a human? It's not like I can get pregnant, it has been five hundred years and if he hasn't figured it out then Lord help him!

I usually train for half the day, but I just went for two hours today since I had a date. I finished training as usual all covered in sweat, I took off my clothing and threw them in the laundry basket and went straight in for a hot shower. I couldn't do a bath today or I'd be late and I didn't want Uriel to wait up for me.

Wait! Crap! Uriel was going to pick me up, I forgot about that! He doesn't know where I live and he isn't supposed to. Lucky my father had bought another house—a bungalow just near here, in case I needed to like invite friends over. It wasn't like I could invite friends into a mansion full of warrior wolves. It would be awkward, especially when most of them are dominant.

I got out of the bathroom to search for my phone and texted Uriel where to pick me, he replied in a matter of seconds. I got back into the bathroom for my shower.

I showered, got dressed and finished my make up all in an hour and right now I was driving to the house where Uriel would pick me up. I was thinking that if I didn't meet my mate in this century, then maybe I could tell Uriel about my kind and he would understand.

But if he didn't, I would have to compel him to forget everything and maybe we would get married and hopefully have kids. I wasn't going to keep my hopes up though, I know I can't get pregnant, if I wanted kids I would have to adopt.

It was just 5.55 p.m. When I reached the house, got out of my car and sat on the hood. I didn't need to go in the house and get out in five minutes, I could just wait, plus I needed the fresh air anyway.

A car pulled up—a blue mustang—and Uriel was in the driver's seat. He got out of the car and walked over to me, kissed my lips first and I returned the kiss, "You didn't have to wait out for me, darling?"

I blushed, how stupid was that? "I know, but I needed the fresh air, so yeah."

He kissed me one more time before grabbing my hand, "come on now, it's our first date as a couple." He opened the door to the passenger seat and I saw a cute wolf doll on the seat, it was red like my fur, it made me look confused at him, "Saraquel told me you like wolves and your favourite colours are red and blue but I couldn't find a blue wolf so yeah, I hope you like it." He grabbed the doll and handed it to me, I took it and hugged him as a thank you.

We arrived at the beach in an hour due to traffic, and the fact that it was freaking hard to find a parking space. After we parked we went to a popcorn stall first, Uriel got popcorn and I got cotton candy. Some people from school were here too, they greeted us saying we looked cute together, that we are a perfect match.

"So umm tell me something about yourself? Your family?" He asked me and I really didn't want to lie so I tried to make it as true as possible.

"Um, they split, instead of me moving from places to places, they're the ones that move to me so that I wouldn't have the trouble of like making new friends and all those dramas you watch in movies. My mother is somewhere in Australia right now, my father came in from California six years ago, you?"

"My mother, died when Saraquel was young. She was attacked by wolves, we went camping one day, my father went hunting with Brandon's dad." My god wolves? I never thought that real wolves would hurt human unless they were like really hungry or being threatened.

"I'm sorry, I didn't know Sara—"

"It's alright." He squeezed my hand and gave me a smile, "I've heard that both your parents are pretty scary?" I nodded, "well, I can't wait to meet the man of the family. So what music do you listen to? I like rock metal, hardcore things I may not look it though."

I giggled, "me too, who is your favourite band? Bring Me the Horizon and Eyes Set to kill are mine, but the first ever song I've listened to was by Escape the fate."

He pulled me closer to him and let go of my hand to put his arm over my shoulder, "looks like we have a lot in common. I've heard that the lead singer of Suicide Silence, Mitch Lucker, died from an accident." I nodded as to answer I knew that too.

"So where to first, prince charming?" We were standing in between the Ferris wheel and the mirror of creep.

"Mirrors? Do you like the haunted house?" I should lie and say no so that he would force me there and hold me tight? "No, I get scared easily."

"Then we are definitely going to the haunted house before the mirror and then the Ferris wheel, how's that sound?"

"Sounds like a plan." He gave me a little peck before pulling me with him towards the haunted house.

The haunted house was not scary at all, I didn't even jump once, but I had to pretend and I think I was bad at it since it took me like a few seconds to react to whatever the hell the monsters were trying to do, but Uriel still held me close to him.

"I'm glad, that you acted scared." I blushed.

"That obvious huh?" He nodded, "Who the hell cares, I got hugs from you that was what I was aiming for."

He laughed and pulled me in for a hug.

"So umm why did you ask me out?" I asked a bit curious.

"Because you're my girlfriend, Katherine." He giggled and I joined him.

"No, what I meant was Brandon's party. Why did you ask me to be your date? I mean girls out there throw themselves at you and I—"

He silenced me with his lips, "that's the thing, you're different. I've never met someone like you; smart, beautiful, funny and we have a lot in common. I've liked you since your first day in high school, I've noticed you for a long time and I've tried to get you to notice me but you were like out of my league." I chuckled.

"What? Me? Too good enough for you? I've liked you since forever and I never said a thing because I couldn't beat those popular girls you hang out with."

We stopped in front of the line for the Ferris wheel, "don't think you're not good enough, babe. You're better than any of those girls and I'd like to keep it that way, don't ever change to fit in with them, alright?" I nodded.

The line took forever, I threw my hands up, screaming 'God thank you' when it was our turn. When we got on the Ferris wheel it moved in slow motion, as slow as a snail and guess what? The unbelievable happened, the power shut down for the whole area and our cart was stuck at the top. "Wow, this is like in the movies." I said with a smirk.

"Not quite yet," he pulled me to sit on his lap and he crushed his lips on mine. Damn that was hot! Our breathing began to harden, I bit on his lips to ask for entrance but he was stubborn so I bit harder making him moan at the process as well. I slid my tongue in and we moved with so much love and lust.

After a few hours the power finally came on and we stayed to play a few more games before heading home. Uriel had won me a few small dolls and at the end I went home with a red wolf and other small stuffed animals. Uriel said that I could have already opened a zoo, which made me giggle and blush. He walked me to my door and we started kissing again and it was pretty hard to pull back.

We eventually stopped and I waved for him goodbye and pretended to open the door, his car finally faded till it was no longer in sight, I threw all the dolls in the car and drove home.

❧ CHAPTER ELEVEN ❧

'I don't need a Prince to save my life.'
—Anonymous.

Our relationship got stronger with every passing day. He walks me to class everyday making me feel extra safe. Him being near, having the sparks run through me every time we touch? It used to bother me, the sparks especially when it was clear to me that he wasn't my mate and possibly not a werewolf either.

He does hang out with some of the werewolves that go to this school from nearby packs but it wasn't a shocker, it wasn't as if werewolves weren't allowed to befriend humans. I leaned over my locker as I watched Uriel walk my way with a group of friends ready to walk to our cars.

"Hey love," he leaned to kiss me. "Miss me?" I nodded with a smile, "You staying over tonight?"

"Yes, your sister and I earned ourselves a ten page essay on world war two for slacking off in class." Since Uriel's father was rarely home, I usually spent most of my nights at their place instead of mine.

I woke up in a spooned position with Uriel's body. He had his arms and legs over me like I'm one of those long pillows. He smelled really nice, just like the forest. One of my favourite scents but although the scent wasn't strong, I felt as if I could stay like this forever. I turned my body slowly trying not to wake him up and waited to watch him sleep. He was really cute, I had a really bad urge to bite his lips.

"Love the view, babe?" I jumped a bit and dropped back on the bed as I pretended to sleep, which was the stupidest thing I've ever done, "seriously? Just pretend to sleep? Now that is cute, morning Katherine." He gave me a kiss and I opened one of my eyes.

"Well, the view is great." I smirked and gave him a kiss. "You look so peaceful when you sleep, I could actually watch you sleep every night for entertainment." I raised both my brows, "if you know what I mean." I wiggled them to have that epic funny effect.

"I'm going to take a shower alright? Carry me to the shower will you? I am still too lazy to move." I begged, he nodded and carried me to his bathroom.

I got dressed and so did Uriel, we got out of his room to the smell of eggs and bacon in the kitchen. Saraquel must be cooking, though I have never seen her cook before but I haven't seen a maid in the kitchen either.

On the way to the kitchen I saw the photos on the table and the portraits on the wall. There was a woman, she was very beautiful and she was carrying a baby girl and two little boys were tugging on her dress.

"That is my mother, that's my father, my uncle and auntie and cousins," he pointed out. He must have figured that I knew that the baby girl was Saraquel and one of the boys was him and the other was Brandon, so he didn't point them out.

I saw another picture of the two boys when they were little and it looked like a mirror image of one boy, instead of Uriel and Brandon. "That's me." Uriel said over my shoulder, it must have been edited it's really nice the way the person edited it to have a mirror image of him, I almost thought he had a twin. But as far as I know it had always been Saraquel and Uriel but if he did have a twin brother, I would have already met him and Uriel would have told me.

"Morning you two love birds!" Saraquel said in a very jolly sarcastic voice, but she looked like she hadn't enough rest, I wondered what was with her.

"Are you alright?" She nodded, "yeah, I'm fine. I could have been better if I had slept in silence! But I couldn't, why? Oh I don't know because of giggles and god knows what, I don't even want to know what you guys did!"

This was really embarrassing. "Oh, sorry sis. You must be really traumatized, huh?" Saraquel gave him a deadly glare.

"Babe, want to catch a ride with us to school?" I shook my head.

"I have to go home and change first, I can't wear the same outfit." Saraquel laughed, "Silly, you could borrow mine, it's no worries. You could choose later on when we're done eating." I nodded.

"I want to take you some place later on, alright? I just found it, I wanted to show you a few days back but since it's our three month anniversary today I was thinking maybe I could surprise you." I giggled a bit then nodded and he started kissing me again, we broke the kiss to see Saraquel holding a butcher's knife. "Stop it or I swear big brother I'll chop your balls out to stop your hormones!"

"Oi!" I shouted and threw some of my eggs at her, "don't you dare threaten him, those right there are my balls too." I tried to be serious but how could I after saying what I've said, Saraquel joined in with me then Uriel.

We arrived at school just a few seconds before the bell rang, I had my first class with Saraquel and as the car was parked she got out and opened my door dragging me out with her. We ran for class, leaving Uriel alone.

I felt my phone buzz and took it out, Mr. Butcher was writing on the board which gave me time to read and reply to the text message. It was from Uriel saying that he won't be able to meet me till school was done, the whole football team was given an excuse from class to train for the game tonight.

The bell rang and I got out of the class, I had the rest of my class with Saraquel. I had other friends as well but I just got used of Uriel walking me from class to class already. Unfortunately, today I am going to have to just settle for Saraquel. School went as normal, minus Uriel by my side. I wanted to watch them practice during lunch but the coach wouldn't let any distractions during training, I could have compelled him if only Uriel wasn't standing beside me.

The bell rang again and finally the classes for the day were done. I grabbed my things in a hurry and went to my locker to grab more of my books for some homework.

"Hi, Katherine. I noticed you were alone the whole day without Uriel." I closed my locker to see Xavier leaning on the side of my locker smirking. "I don't mind staying with you if you feel lonely, Katherine. You know that." He winked.

"Back off, Xavier! I'm not in the mood." Xavier grabbed my hand as I tried to walk away and put his hands on my waist to pull me closer to him. "The hell! Let go of me jerk!!"

I couldn't fight him, I had my hands full of books. I mean, yeah I could have always kicked him where the sun doesn't shine. "Come on baby I know you want me, I'm so many ways better than Uriel." His voice was so disgusting, it was making my wolf go crazier than I already was and him being this close and calling me baby isn't helping.

"Back off, let go of me!" He shoved me to the wall and started kissing my neck. "Xavier! Get off!" I screamed and suddenly the weight of him was pulled away from me and the next thing I know he was lying on the floor holding a bloody nose.

"Don't you dare touch her again, Xavier! Or you're going to get more than a bloody nose next time!"

Uriel, he saved me. I have never been saved before, I am so strong and I've never been with a human the past century that I never fall for someone that isn't my mate. I never fall for anyone that wasn't Lucas, period. I was still in shock, my wolf was screaming at me at how a human can save me, a human that can never match my strength and speed.

Uriel pulled me away from the wall and hugged me tight, it felt really good. It showed that he really loves me.

"I'm never letting you alone again, Katherine. I'll bring you into training with me even if I have to make a deal with the coach." I blushed and he kissed me. He was so worried about me, something no man other than Lucas has been. Victor was too busy to even acknowledge me sometimes, with that wife of his and Dylan was too busy training every goddamn time. As for my father and mother, they knew my strength, they knew no man could ever hurt me and so they never worried.

We went back home to Uriel's place before going back to school for the game. Uriel got the coach to let me sit on the side beach, so that he would know that I was alright and I got Saraquel to sit with me, the girls gave us jealous glares.

We walked hand in hand to the back of the school field where the coach was talking to some of the team players before heading home, "Coach, could Katherine sit on the side bench?"

The coach frowned before looking my way, "Uriel, no, you—" Uriel finally let my hand go to walk close to the coach, "but she was attacked earlier and I need to know that she is safe or I will have a hard time concentrating on the game."

The coach lets out a deep sigh before nodding in approval.

The game started and I did what a usual girlfriend would do. I screamed for my boyfriend till the top of my lungs. Uriel was really good and half of the team too, three fifth of the football team were werewolves from the nearby pack, they didn't know me but I know them by their scent.

It was half time and the score was 5-2. I smelled the air, the other team had werewolves to play for them this time, but not as much as our team. They have only three werewolves playing, but they looked really huge.

Uriel had the ball and the three huge werewolves were running after him. Uriel was fast like the speed of a un-shifted pup, meaning the three dudes behind him were faster, all three of them jumped to tackle Uriel and as the crowd screamed, "Oh!" I stood up from my seat, then a whistle was sounded.

I just stood there in shock I couldn't see what happened to Uriel because of the three huge players standing there. I smelled blood in the air, and that's when I saw the paramedics.

"Uriel," I whispered and Saraquel stood and held my arm, I wiggled it off and started running towards where Uriel was and the sight was hurtful.

"Uriel! Uriel, baby!" I knelt beside his body.

"Miss, let us do our job," one of the men spoke. Saraquel held a hand on my shoulder then helped me get up, tears were rolling down my cheeks.

"Come on, Katherine. They're taking him to the hospital," We walked back to the bench, "where is my brother's bag?"

"It's in the locker." We both turned to Alex, one of the players and nodded. Saraquel and I walked to his locker to grab his things, his keys were in his bag.

"I should drive, Katherine." I wiped my tears off.

"No, I actually want to make it to the hospital without damaging the car!" I yelled at her, before closing my eyes and taking a deep breath as I realize my mistake, "I didn't mean it like that—" she nodded, "I know, I understand you right now. It's alright, you can drive." She gave me a hug and I hugged her back.

"Uriel Arch Spike, he was just brought in a few minutes ago? I'm his sister." Saraquel spoke to the woman, on the other side of the desk. The woman gave us a smile before typing on her computer, "the doctor is still checking him, you two ladies can wait for him over there." The woman pointed to the left.

We both sat on the waiting chair, I was freaking stressed out right now. Saraquel patted my back for comfort, "aren't you going to call your father or something?" She shook her head. "Why?" I was so confused, why would she call him? Would he not come?

"He is on a hunting trip, Katherine. He won't be back for a week, I wouldn't want to disturb him," I sighed and waited.

"Miss Spike." We both looked up to see a man in his late forties, "Me, I'm Saraquel Spike." She stood up, I was starting to feel weak for the first time, I didn't have the strength to stand. "How is my brother, Doc?"

"He is going to be alright, a few broken ribs, his left hand and leg. He'll be staying here for a week or two." Saraquel nodded and turned to me.

I stood up, "Doc, can we see him?" The doctor looked at me with a frown on his face, do I look that horrible? "Sorry but families only, are you in any way related to them?" I shook my head and pouted, he must really have taken pity on me, "Alright!" My face lit up at his answer and we went straight to his room.

I sat next to his bed, never wanting to be apart. Seeing him like this, just brought fear into me, the fear of losing someone I love again. But how could I? Feel something that is almost love for someone that isn't even my mate, let alone my kind.

"Umm-mm Kat—Katherine." Uriel murmured and I shut up in a second. "I'm here baby, don't worry I'm here, it's alright." I turned to Saraquel, "Go get someone, a doctor or the nurse!"

She nodded and headed out. Uriel's eyes finally fluttered open and I smiled down at him, tears still running down my cheeks. "Why are you crying, love?" He attempted to wipe my tears before the pain finally stopped him.

"Don't move too much. Your sister went to get someone, alright." The door opened and the doctor came in with a couple of nurses, I stood to the side with Saraquel, letting the old man do his job.

I had to bribe the doctor and nurses to let me and Saraquel stay the week with him. Alright I compelled the doctor but I gave him ten bucks that should count for something, right? I could leave his side, I would go home at some point to take a shower but went straight to his side. I wanted to be there when he woke up.

The doctor walked out a few minutes later saying that he would check up again on Uriel in the morning. I sat on the chair beside Uriel's bed, "you won't be playing for a little while, love. You scared me out there. I thought I was going to—" I couldn't finish my sentences, just the thought of almost losing him made me scared, scared that I would break down again like when I lost Lucas just like that moment it happened in front of me, that warrior biting down Lucas' neck and those three werewolves tackling Uriel.

He held my hand, "don't think about it, Katherine. I'm alright now and I'm glad that you're here. You're not going to lose me, alright?" I wiped my tears and nodded before laying my head on his hand. "I love you, Katherine Smith."

I looked up at him shocked. I even caught Saraquel's expression, her jaw dropped like she had heard him asking me for marriage. Uriel was not different from any other

111

male wolf, they had hormones that need to be dealt with and just like most man whore wolves, it's all about 'bang and gone'.

So yes, hearing Uriel say those three words were like, me submitting to an omega. Never going to happen but those words did happen. I didn't know what to say, I never really admitted loving someone other than Lucas, yeah there was that time I admitted to my wolf that I love Dylan but—but I don't know. I do love Uriel so I managed a smile, "I love you too, Uriel." And gave him a kiss.

❦ Chapter Twelve ❧

'Bullying is a terrible, terrible thing.'
—Robert Carlyle.

As months passed, Uriel finally got the hang of walking again without his crutches and only left with his cast to be taken off in a few more months. "Alright fall in!" I ordered as I waited for the group of newly recruited male wolf to fall into five lines.

"Does anyone know why I am here?" I asked out waiting for any one of them boys to raise their hands but I was left waiting, "alright, so nobody knows?" Still no answer and it was pissing me off.

"Are you all deaf? Can't any of you hear?" I growled causing them to jump. "I asked a question! And please do let me repeat myself! Does anyone know why I am here?" My words echoed.

"No, Princess." They all answered at once.

I groaned in stress, "now who in freaking hell told you that you could all call me 'Princess'? Didn't anyone brief you?" They all shook their heads as I heard giggles coming from afar, I turned to my side to see Alec laughing his ass off with a few guards making me growl. He is so going to get it now, "Alec!" I screamed with much anger.

He and the other men with him choked on their laughter, "You boys!" I pointed at all five of them, "Come here, now!" The six men stood on both my sides equally, Alec on my left of course. I put an arm over his shoulder and on the guard on my right as well, squeezing hard on them but they tried hard not to whimper. "So boys, you guys having fun?" I asked happily and they all nodded.

"So I see everyone has been getting lessons from Isaac on how to nod on my questions. Doesn't mean Isaac gets away with his 'short-not-so-real' answers does any of you will, you should have known that by now, Alec." I said still smiling as I made my fangs seen, I smelled fear from everyone.

"Now, drop!" I growled "and give me a hundred!" I looked from side to side as all six obliged. Blake, the warrior beside Alec leaned a bit to the side to whisper at Alec, "so worth it."

"Is it now, Blake?" He and Alec stared up at me, "YOLO, right?" I smiled, "so maybe after this you could clean all the toilets with a toothbrush. Preferably yours." I laughed at the expression he made and returned my focus back on the new pups. "Now, where were we? Ah! You call me, Katherine. Not 'princess', not 'your royal highness' or any of that crap, got me?" They nodded, making me growl. "I said, did you get me?"

"Yes!" They answered all at once making my frown turned into a smirk at their obedience. "Good." I nodded, "Now, all you new misfits are here because I chose you to be here. A week ago, I watched as my father trained you and picked a series of numbers and here you all are."

"One hundred!" The six wolves yelled, "Another hundred!" I ordered to punish them and they went back to doing their pushups. "If you think my father's training is, god damn horrible? Then don't expect mine to be any much similar because trust me. I bring Hell itself to my training so if you think you don't have what it takes to be a warrior? Then take a hike!" I growled.

"You want to be warriors? I'll make you warriors. You want to be wolves? I'll make you alpha wolves. I don't stand for second best, because I only train the best. So are you going to be with me?"

"Yes!" Their answered echoed, I smirked at their willingness to be trained with him, but all I am giving them is a freaking week tops before they start crawling back to my father. "Good, here are my rules, if you are going to be late? Don't come at all. If you are going to keep asking for breaks, then you will be getting another kind of break." I cracked my knuckles, "If I asked you to do something, you do it, no 'buts' 'if' or whatever excuse you all can come up with, now drop and give me a hundred!"

The second I dropped on my bed, my sweet-sweet bed, my phone went off making me jump and fell off the bed with a tug. "Oh," I groaned in pain before reaching for my phone off of my side table. Uriel's name popped up on the phone, I didn't hesitate any longer I picked it up.

"Hey, sexy." I flirted, "what's up?" I got my arse off the cold floor and back up on the bed groaning again at the feeling of relaxation, the training went on for hours.

"You alright? You sound tensed, have you been getting enough sleep?" I missed his voice, we have been really busy for the past few weeks. Saraquel got her eyes set on a brown eye hottie from her swimming class and Uriel has made it his mission to make sure that not a single chemical reaction happens between them.

"I fell from the bed, that's all. I'm alright, I missed you."

"I miss you too, you free today?"

"Yea, I guess I have some time for my boyfriend, you want to go out? Wait, no Saraquel stalking today?"

"Nah, I had a man talk with him yesterday and if I haven't scared the crap out of him yet then I make sure I do next time, just hope there won't be a next time."

"You big bully!" I teased, "What you want to do today, love?"

"Well, I followed Saraquel yesterday to her swimming class to keep an eye on her and I saw this poster that says that there is this mini zoo. They opened up just by the park, I thought maybe you'd like you go. I mean, Hye! You could even bring your dolls if you want to? You know those dolls during the carnival?"

"Yes, love. I remember those very well." I giggled. "So I'll be there in 15?"

"Yeah, sure. Drive safe, alright?"

"I will, love you, Sexy McSexy Pants." I love it calling him cute names, I didn't have that special pet name most couples have for each other or like Lucas has for me, I just kept calling him with whatever fits the sentence.

"I love you, baby." I cut the call and set the phone back where I got it and waited a few more minutes in bed before getting ready.

"There, Katherine." He pointed to the open parking space I nodded and we were finally parked after driving in circles for the past 20 minutes. I turned off the engine and opened my buckles. "Wait," Uriel ordered before walking out and taking his sweet time as he walked over to my side and opened my door.

I smiled at his attempt of being sweet, I got out and gave him a kiss. "Thanks, but you do know you don't have to, right?" He held my waist and pulled me closer to him, "I know, but I want to, Katherine. I don't want to just be romantic at first, you're my girl, I supposed to treat you like a princess." I giggled once again.

"Oh, come on now, big boy. Let's go." He let out his hands for me to take but instead of taking his hand and entwining my fingers with his, I linked my hands on his arms.

The mini zoo has been just amazing. We were allowed to pat some of the animals, I got to pat a Komodo dragon, I was scared at first I had to admit that, until its care keeper assured me that the little creature was harmless.

In fact the little lizard liked it when people carried it in the same way a mother carries her child when attempting to put it to sleep, but for this little guy it just falls asleep once in the arms of people.

We started walking around but Uriel's sudden stop made me come to a halt, "fatty! Fatty! You're so fat! What have you been eating?" I heard a little kid's voice sang and turned to see Uriel staring at something, I turned to his side to see a group of five boys picking on a girl.

"Eww, what are you? A baby?" One of the boys laughed taking the doll from the little girl's hand and throwing it to the ground. "Baby! Baby! That doll is ugly just like you! Fatty!" He called pointing at her and the boys with him followed his action.

Uriel leaned over to me, "wait here, Katherine." I nodded and let him go. I watched as he walked over to the group of children, I focused on him.

"What is going on here?" He squatted to take the doll from the ground and wiped the dirt off of it. "You boys should pick on someone your own size," he said angrily. "Now say sorry to the beautiful lady."

They all bowed before giving their apologies one by one, "Now run along." I walked over to him as he turned to the girl, held both her hands. "Hey, don't listen to them alright? They are just bullies," she nodded. "I think you're beautiful and this doll," he held out the doll examining it. "It's beautiful, just like you." She giggled.

I finally came close and gave her a smile, "That doll is beautiful, what is your name, love?"

"Elizabeth," she answered taking the doll from Uriel.

"Well, Elizabeth, you don't listen to them mean boys alright? You want to know a secret?" She nodded, "those boys tease you because they fancy you," I smiled.

"Elizabeth!" I heard her name being called causing her to turn, "my Mommy's calling me." I nodded and she ran along.

"Pick on some on your own size huh?" I quoted him raising my brows after Elizabeth ran along to her mother.

"What? I have zero tolerance for bullying," he said in his defence. "If they are men enough to bully than they are men enough to fight me." I giggled stroking his chest to calm him down. "Come on let's keep walking."

After covering every part of the park and seeing every cute little devil, we decided to go for another few grounds to pass the time because we weren't ready to leave yet. But all of a sudden I felt Uriel stiffen beside me.

I turned to see he had a very mad expression on his face, he wasn't looking at me but straight ahead and before I could try to catch what he was looking at that made him pissed, he was already brushing my hand away from his hold and started stomping to where ever the cause of his sudden anger was.

I tailed him, shoving away people that got in my way but Uriel was fast, "How the hell was he walking that fast with a cast?" I cursed as I continued to shove away people. I stopped at the sudden scream I heard but then started running towards where ever it came from, then Uriel came up to view, standing across from me holding Saraquel behind him in a protective way.

Saraquel had that expression that mirrored mine when my father's guards held Lucas away from me, I looked down to see who both Uriel and Saraquel were looking at, only to see Mike, the brown eyed boy had his lips busted.

He finally got his arse off the ground and replaced it with his feet, "Uriel stop it! He is my mate!" I was stunned by Saraquel's outburst but was brought back to reality by a few growls, I took in the environment around me as I just noticed about five werewolves.

"What is going on here?" All three of them finally acknowledged my existence when I spoke. "Did you just call him 'mate'?" I stared at Saraquel waiting for an answer.

"Yes, mate as in friend?" She reasoned but I didn't believe her one bit, "He is Australian."

"Oh and since when did you turn Australian as well?" I shot my come back like a slap against her face.

"It's none of your business, bitch!" Mike hissed, I took a step closer to him before throwing my fist at him, colliding it with his face causing him to drop back to the ground.

"It is my business, mate!" I hissed, making the 'mate' being heard clearly. "Saraquel is my friend, you mess with her! You so as much touch her, I'd make sure you would never have any other mate, mate!" I glared at him.

"Katherine!" Saraquel hissed, I looked up to see her pissed no longer behind Uriel. "I'd understand this coming from my brother but you?" She sounded so disappointed.

"What? You can't possibly be mad at me, Sara? Come on. I am a girl and he is a boy, can't he take a punch? What a chick, gosh!" She glared once more before helping Mike up and left.

I felt bad as I watched them leaving, I felt an arm crawling over my waist and instincts kicked in, I twisted the hand in a position I could break it, with a little movement, but let it go once I saw that it was Uriel.

"Sorry, I—" he held up his hand, "no. It's alright. I'm fine, I didn't know you know how to throw a punch or break an arm," he joked. He pulled me close to him, to plant a kiss on my forehead.

"She hates me, love. Your sister officially hates me, I ruined it for her and since when did she use the term 'mate'? That is just all kinds of crazy. Mike doesn't even sound like an Aussie, he sounds more of a douche."

He rubbed my back, and the sparks that went through me calmed me down. "No she doesn't, give her a few days, alright? You're her best friend, aren't girls like that? You know when you fight with your best friend, then you both will go crazy at the sudden realization that you both couldn't do anything because you guys are so used to doing things together and suddenly learn the error of your ways and make up?"

I nodded "I guess so, and it's her ways. I did nothing wrong I just lay a single punch on him for talking crap to me."

"You want to leave now? I am starving," he groaned making me laugh, boys and their foods. It's always a fun sight when Uriel gets hungry because he goes crazy, like literally crazy, he would whine like a little kid till the food is placed in front of him.

❧ Chapter Thirteen ❧

'Find a place, to call our own.'
—Anonymous.

"I'll be there in five, love." I spoke on my phone while having lunch. My father was reading his newspaper, Alec and Isaac as usual sandwiching me, on either side. Both attacking their baby back ribs like wolves, can't blame them, they are wolves.

"Are you excited?" I could hear him smile from over the phone.

"Very much. I have to get ready, see you in five. Love you." I giggled.

"I love you too."

I hung up the same time my father put his paper down, "No you don't, you are only allowed to love your mate, Princess. Don't forget that this boy is like four hundred and ninety nine years old, younger than you, darling." Alec chuckled.

"Come on now, father. I'm sure, my mate—whoever he might be would also be the same age as Uriel. Stop hating on him. I know it won't be forever. It's just a high school thing alright?" But I wasn't sure if it was just a high school thing, how if I want more? But I can't, even human have their mates and I am not his.

"Very well then, but I still don't like him one bit." My father went back to reading his paper and I swear I could hear him smirking over his paper.

"Want me to drive you, Princess?" I turned to Isaac who spoke.

"Nah, I'll have to drive him to the hospital. He will be having his cast taken off today." He nodded to answer as usual. I got so used to his nodding and shaking and shoulder rising answer that I get shocked sometimes when he talks, I took one last bite on my buttermilk chicken before standing and walked away from the table to grab my keys.

I hit the horn and Uriel came out the door with Saraquel behind him, I smiled at them both. Uriel got on the seat next to me and I rolled down his window where Saraquel was standing, "Is it alright if I join you, Katherine. My father is home and I don't have that father-daughter relationship with him."

I nodded and she got in the back seat and we drove off to the hospital. Saraquel didn't talk to me, six days tops after the Mike accident. Saraquel was really in love with him, like crazy in love. He must have been her soul mate to feel something like that, or just a normal teenage love story.

She told stories of him, their dates and all, the day after we finally made up I went to talk to Uriel, tried to change his mind a bit about Mike, but like my father, he was stubborn. "So I was thinking maybe we could go out? For dinner" I smiled.

"Where to?" I asked.

"My father is going away on a business meeting for a week again and I just remembered about that place I wanted to take you the night of the game but didn't get to because of the accident." I smiled and nodded. "So I'll pick you up later on?"

"You think you can drive?" I didn't think he could, for the past few months I had been the one picking up and dropping him home back and forth from school.

"Yes, I guess. It's a date, love. Nowhere in hell am I letting you drive" I giggled.

"Alright then, because it is so obvious that the past few months when we went out weren't dates." I giggled. "How are things going, Sara?" Saraquel was being silent, I could almost forget she was even there.

"Everything is fine. Fine. Freaking great," she faked a smile.

"What's up with her?" I asked Uriel.

"She introduced Mike to my father, and he didn't approve," he answered.

"Like father like son, huh?" I managed the joke. "What is it about your father? He is never there, you and I have been together for months now. Sara and Mike have been together not that long, and she has already introduced him to your father." I said a bit sad thinking that Uriel might not love me that much after all.

"It's not like that, Katherine. Me and my father, we don't actually have that you know, the father son thing going, well not since mum died anyway." I felt bad, I laid a hand on his shoulder and squeezed it a little as to get that I understood, he shot me a smile and everything was alright.

We arrived at the hospital in an hour and a half due to the traffic—which was starting to bug me. I am starting to get why my father doesn't have his own car. He's so used to running, I don't even think he knows how to drive, but he loves riding his bike, I think I'm getting why now.

"Alright, Mr. Spike. Have a great day." I was sitting outside in the waiting area alone, Saraquel was allowed in since she is his sister. I stood up when I heard the voice of the doctor which I officially hate when he didn't let me in the room.

"Alright, doc. Thanks again."

"Hi babe, sorry if I kept you waiting." He put his arms over my shoulder.

"It's alright, love. It wasn't that long." He kissed my forehead and we walked back to the car.

(((((|URIEL|)))))

I opened the door and got out, my sister had already walked into the house.

"I'll pick you up at seven?" I asked Katherine over her window, she nodded and I stepped back a few feet and waved as she drove off. I went in after Katherine's car finally disappeared in the drive way.

"There is a letter for you, son. It's on the counter." I walked into the house and my father was in the living room on the couch with the beta, Brandon's father watching UFC. I don't get why is he here in my house, when he has his own house, there was a reason why I moved out and that was to get the hell away from him, and now here he is acting as if he lives here.

"Alright, are you still going to meet the Alpha pack from the south tonight?"

"Yep, we'll be leaving in a few minutes. Just waiting for the rest of the members to meet up here. You going out? You haven't introduced me to her, son." He got off the couch and walked with me to the kitchen counter.

"Yep, you're always busy. Maybe when you get back or never if you're planning to embarrass me, like you did with Saraquel. She isn't my mate if that's what you're wondering. Plus it isn't as if I am future alpha for you to care whether or not I find my mate."

"How long has it been? I just got word from Zadkiel, he won't be back for your birthday and Christmas, same as for next year." I nodded.

"It has been six months, in a few weeks it'll be seven and I don't care about Zadkiel. My birthday is still months from now and it's not as if I am going to shift then."

"Less than seven months son and you'll have to join me in hunts unless you're accepted to the training academy for alpha wolves like Zadkiel."

The front door opened and a few pack members came in, I saw the letter on the counter and opened it in an instant.

The words that I was reading made me smile, "Dad, hold on." I caught up with my father just as he was making his way out.

"I applied for the academy, and they accepted me." My father's face lit up and the pack members came forward to congratulate me and patted my back.

"I'm proud of you. I guess you'll be leaving right after your birthday, huh?" I nodded.

He pulled me in for a bear hug, "I guess you're going to break the news to your girl tonight?" Katherine, damn it! I am going to be so dead. How could I forget about her?

I went into my room and slammed the door shut, I'd made my father promise not to speak a word to my sister. I wanted it to be me that tells Katherine, which I'm not planning to do anytime soon. I really like her and she might be human, but I'll choose her over my mate any day.

I really love her to death and it will kill me to leave, I could choose not to go and stay here with her but it'll only disappoint my father. I pulled out my phone and started making some calls for the date later on with Katherine.

After making the calls I took another shower thinking of a way, when and where to break the news to Katherine? What am I supposed to tell her? Should I tell her the truth? No, she is a human. She'll freak and it's not like she'll love me forever. Even humans have their own mates.

If I had just manned up and asked Katherine out since the day I first met her, then I wouldn't have sent that request and I wouldn't have been accepted. I now have to leave the woman I love, to stay at least a few years at that damn academy.

I arrived at Katherine's five minutes earlier, her car wasn't on the side way, she must have gone out I guess. I took out my phone to check for any text message from her about cancelling but there were none. I went to knock on the door and a head popped out, on the side of the house and there she was, the most beautiful girl in this whole damn world.

I couldn't stop looking at her, my wolf was howling as well. He has never complained about Katherine, people say that when you hold another girl that's not your mate, your wolf will go crazy.

"Seriously, love? Stop it or you'll start drooling like a puppy dog." She walked over to me and kissed me.

"What can I say? I'm sure that's what every man does when they see the most beautiful girl in the world. Too bad for them, you're mine." She giggled and I pulled her in for another kiss. "Are you sure you're not anyway related to Megan Fox?"

"Seriously? Megan Fox?" Ah crap now she looks pissed at me.

"Have I ever told you, how cute you look when you're mad?" She giggled again and I knew I was off the hook. Even if she does look cute, I hated it when I make her mad or sad. "You ready?" She nodded and I grabbed her hand and led her to the car.

"Come on, Uriel. I want to see it, please let go." I covered her eyes with my hands as I led her into the garden cliff.

It was on the top of a hill, flat land with low green grass that I'd had some of the pack members cut earlier, there was only one tree with beautiful flowers on it, and at the edge was the view of the whole town. The view is really breathtaking and I want this place to be our place.

"Ok! Ok! We're here."

I took off my hands and her eyes fluttered open. A smile lit up on her face, her eyes taking in everything. "It's so-so—god Uriel, where did you find this place? It's beautiful!" I pulled her back close to my chest and hugged her from behind kissing her neck.

"It's ours now, I bought it and redecorated it." I turned her to face me and as she put her hands over my shoulders I pulled her in for a kiss.

⦓⦓⦓⦓ |KATHERINE| ⦔⦔⦔⦔⦔

He finally let go of my eyes and I opened it slowly. The view was—I don't know it was too wow to have a single word to describe what it looked like. The grass looked like it had been newly cut and there was only one tree with beautiful flowers blooming.

"It's so-so—god Uriel, where did you find this place? It's beautiful!" He pulled me to him till my back was against his chest and he wrapped his arms around my waist.

"It's ours now, I bought it and redecorated it." He turned me to face him and as I put my hands over his shoulders, he pulled me in for a kiss. The kiss was longer than I thought it would be, our breaths hardened and he bit my lips asking for entrance, which I refused to give in, causing him to move his hand from my back up to my arse. I moaned giving him entrance.

We broke the kiss when I sensed that there was someone looking at us. I turned to see that there was someone and they were werewolves, "Sorry we were just leaving, we have just finished cutting the grass at the back." Uriel nodded and the two men walked away with their grass cutter.

"Hungry?" I nodded. I actually was, he held my hand and we walked to the edge of the cliff where there was a table filled with food ready for us. I smiled and gave him a peck on the cheeks.

"This is really romantic, Uriel. I don't know how you found this place and I hate to think how it looked like before you found it."

"I came here with Brandon, he had a problem at the time and so we thought of going out for a ride and found this." I nodded and we started eating.

"Uriel, are you alright? You seem uneasy, is something wrong?" He shook his head.

"Do you believe in mythical creatures?" He asked.

"What do you mean? Like the werewolves and vampires?" He nodded. "Please tell me you're not obsessed with twilight, love?" I giggled.

"I'm not, never mind. Um—college, have you thought about college yet?" He asked.

"I have another year here Uriel, can't say the same for you. You'll be leaving next year, have you chosen any college yet?" He shook his head. "Well, I'm not going to college."

"Why?" How am I going to explain this, I never thought about college before, well I went there once but I didn't stay long.

"Because I'll inherit everything my father owns and he'll just teach me how to run his business. I hate school, so yeah. I am like, trying my best to get out of high school not so that I could go to another school." He nodded. We were lying on a picnic blanket which Uriel had brought and he spread down for us to lie on.

Uriel rolled and soon he was on top of me, his elbow supported some of his weight so that he wouldn't crush me, not that he could. He started kissing me, on my lips down to my jaw the kiss was so intense, but was spoiled thanks to my freaking tummy. How could I still be hungry? I practically ate a barn full of cows, damn it what could be more embarrassing that a tummy growling? But although it was embarrassing it caused both Uriel and me to laugh.

✂ CHAPTER FOURTEEN ✂

*'I know what it's like to have my heart
broken. It is not adorable.'*
                                    —Rashida Jones.

"Katherine!" Alec called from afar. I was training my men, it actually shocked me to see that my men still came to my training after the first week. "Take five." I called before turning to see Alec with Isaac by his side, I walked over to him, meeting them half way.

"What's up?" I grabbed the water bottle Isaac was holding and drank it. "Sorry I'm thirsty." I smiled and handed it back.

"We are leaving for the east tonight for a week, Balthazar's orders."

"What for? I'm busy."

"With that human?" Alec growled earning a glare from me.

"No, training the men, douche bag." I punched him on the shoulder.

"Well, we will be leaving in five hours, get your things ready." I nodded and walked to the bench where I laid my things and went through my bag for my phone and dialed Uriel's number.

He answered after the first ring "hey, baby." He greeted making me smile.

"Hey, love. So I'm calling because my father has this thing and wants me to accompany him, it'd be for a week."

"Alright just take care, you'll call me won't you? When you get there?"

"Yeah sure, I'll miss you. Could you ask Saraquel to pick up all my home works for me?"

"Yeah yeah sure, I'll remind her."

"Alright, I have to go back now I'll call before leaving, love you."

"Love you too, baby." I cut the line and shove my phone back into my bag before standing back up and walked over to my men and started training again.

"King Balthazar." A man greeted once we reached the Dark Shadow pack, I watched as they both gave each other manly hugs. "How have you been Jasper? Long time no see old friend." My father patted the alpha's back. "This," he held out a hand for me to come forward, "is my daughter,

Katherine." I bowed my head for him not to see. "Princess," he greeted me as he let out a hand for me to take which I did for him to plant kisses on them.

"So what's the problem, Jasper? My men said you reported that rogues have been roaming around here."

"Five rogues, four males and one female." I didn't listen longer to their conversation because it got boring, though I felt strange being here and I didn't know why, I just felt uneasy ever since the alpha talked about the four rogues.

I let out a cough to interrupt them, "Princess, why I am sorry. Is there anything you would like? My men could escort you and your men to your quarters if you'd like to rest."

"Well thank you alpha that would actually be great." I heard two different footsteps coming over, "Princess, I am the Beta Kane and this is the third in command Josh. It's an honour to meet you," he said all excited, most betas I've met were always serious. "Well, it's always pleasant to meet two handsome werewolves such as yourselves." I could hear both their heart beating fast making me smirk a little. "Come on now boys lets go." I walked past them in hopes that I was going the right direction.

Once in the pack house it smelled different, as if there was a different pack in here. You see every individual has their scent and every individual in a pack has their scent like for example this pack has a more floral scent and the beta has a sweet scent so together he carried a sweet floral scent but the scent I was smelling now, was more of a bloody-ish. "Is there another pack here, beta?"

"Yes, the alpha and a few of his men from the Blood Moon pack came to visit earlier, Alpha Raphael. Could you still smell their scent? They left two hours before you and the king arrived."

"Yes I can still smell their scent." Somehow the scent bothered me so much but why I didn't know, so I just pushed the thought away. *"Alec, Isaac, can you guys hear me?"* I asked through our mind link.

"Katherine, we are just right behind you, what's up?" Alec responded.

"After settling in what are we going to do?"

"Meeting tonight on what we are going to do for tomorrow?"

"Oh alright then." I replied and shut my mind close.

"Good evening. As you all know the royals have arrived, our king and princess are here as well on the rogue matter. I know that there were only five that have been spotted but there could be a possibility that these aren't normal rogues but part of Kevin's group. Kevin to which some of you may not know had attacked almost all packs in California and has rumoured to be coming here next. So here is our king and princess to help us." The alpha nodded for my father to take the stage and the meeting soon got boring that I totally zoned out and only awaken to see Alec carried me up the stairs.

"What happened? You can put me down now, Alec." He looked as if he hesitated at first but obliged and let me down.

"You, me, Isaac and three other of our men have been grouped to do a round check in the morning. At three in the morning, it's already two, so you might as well stay up."

"Did one of them hit his head or something to be asking a princess to do a round check at three in the

135

freaking morning?" Alec left out a laugh and rubbed my hair like I am one of those little brats, messing up my hair, I slapped his hand away.

"Where is Isaac?"

"Outside, getting the men ready. Why?"

"Were you guys going to leave without me?"

"Well, kind of you fell asleep and I thought that you should just rest since you're the princess and brought you up. There are like five rogues and five of us warriors and with the strength that Isaac has, it's a definite yes that we have the upper hand with or without you."

"It's that an insult?" I punched his arm, he can be sweet and a douche at the same time but that's not a shocker almost all male werewolves have his characteristics; smart, strong, pretty and a douche. "Come let's go to Isaac. We can leave now, it's almost three anyway." He nodded and followed me outside the pack house where we were met up with Isaac and the others.

"I thought you were sending her to bed?" Isaac called out to Alec.

"She woke up and insisted on coming with us." Isaac nodded in reply and showed me on a piece of paper where the boundaries of the pack lands were.

"Ok man, it's time to set out!" Alec called and we started walking into the forest where my men shifted, I gave Alec and Isaac a nod as to say that I wasn't shifting with them. Once they were all huge wolves in different shades of brown and grey, I gave the signal and we ran together for almost an hour.

And just when we were almost done with the round check, the scent of the forest changed, it was mixed with five other scents, *"Isaac, Alec, follow me, the others go the other way. I can smell the rogues, keep your eyes open, remember we want them alive, they need to be interrogated."* With the corner of my eyes I saw my men nodded their heads, the other three went in the opposite way of mine.

With Isaac and Alec behind me we crept to where the scent got stronger, and were soon met with five wolves. Two of which had their scent mixed with each other, meaning mates. I motioned for Alec and Isaac to surround them from the side as I went to approach them.

"Rogues!" I called out startling them. They all positioned themselves in front of me ready to attack making me smirk if they thought they had a chance. "Shift!" I called out using my alpha tone, they growled a little trying to fight my request but I wasn't just anyone for them to disobey, I am their princess.

They all stared at me with fear, the male wolf held his mate close to him, protecting her from me. Looking at them all I could think of was Lucas, staring at them I imagined him protecting me like that but then instead of Lucas, it was Uriel that I imagined holding me in a protective way from Xavier. Mates, when they have finished the mating process. First process, which is first sight where they first see each other, next is the kiss or the holding hands process or anything physical where they would touch each other and feel the sparks run through them and at this stage, is when you would already have them in your head, this will make it hard to reject them if you're thinking of rejecting them, but some still managed.

The next process is the bite usually soon followed by the late stage which is mating. After the biting process a wolf not only mixes his scent with his mates but he is also open to mind linking, no matter if they are in a pack or not.

So I opened my mind just in case they were talking. *"She is the princess. We can't out run her, Daren. She is going to kill us."*

"I won't let her touch you, when we attack you run the other way alright, I'll find for you."

"No, I won't leave you. I can fight, please."

"You have to think about the pups, Aliah. On my signal you run alright, if they get you do not fight. Just follow them."

I watched as tears filled up the she wolf's eyes, she gripped her mate's hand harder. "You know what, Aliah?" I called as I walked over to them smiling at her as she looked at me with widened eyes.

"You, you know my name?" I nodded and pointed to my head as to say I heard them from their mind link and when I was almost close to Aliah, Daren growled. "Don't come any closer!" Making me let out a little laugh.

"It's not me that you should worry about Daren. It's you, your mate is pregnant and I am sure you've heard the news of rogues being hunted down. If you do love your future family you would have submitted to a pack the minute you found your mate to keep her from harm." I held out a hand to hold her tummy and images started popping in my head, of the two rogues holding their baby girl. I pulled my hand back and looked at Aliah straight in her eyes, I could see through them that mine was glowing red.

"What is your business here?" I asked Daren.

"We were just passing through." He growled back harshly, causing me to lose my last nerve at him because it was a sign that he was challenging me. I grabbed him by the throat causing the other three rogues to shift and that was when Isaac and Alec came to hold them back. I pulled Daren close to me where I whispered into his ears, "Your daughter won't do good without her father. So what I suggest Daren is that, don't!" I tightened my grip, "challenge me!" I could feel his neck about to crack and that would kill him, "Again!" I finally let him go, where he dropped to the ground causing his mate to run to his aid. "You could be stupid enough to challenge an alpha for all I care but not me."

I walked over to him and squatted to whisper one last time into Daren's ears, "Keep going west and you will find an old friend of mine deep in the woods. Tell her I sent you, tell her to give you a bag and if she asks what kind, you say 'forest'. In the bag there is money and a key to a house and an address, understood?" He nodded and I got up from my feet and walked away from them. "Alec. Isaac. Let them be." They gave a little growl before obliging, "Oh and Daren!" I didn't bother turning, "take care of them, both of them." He murmured a yes and I shimmered away.

We finally reached the pack house, I went straight up to bed and at the exact moment I closed my eyes ready to drift, my door slammed open. I got up to see Alec and Isaac half naked standing by my bed. "Explain, why you let them go?" Alec requested.

"What's there to explain, they weren't causing harm they just wanted to pass. The female was pregnant, why harm her and her unborn child?"

"What about the bag of money, with a key and an address?"

"Alec! She is a pregnant woman and a rogue, OK! They need a place to stay to raise their baby and me being the princess who is supposed to be generous and all that, helped them OK! Now get out!" They finally left at the same time, a tear ran down my cheeks. They were mates, they were rogues, wanting to have a family. I couldn't kill them, I couldn't take away what my father has taken from me. I gave them a chance, something my father didn't give me and also he wouldn't have given them. How I wished back then there was someone, anyone that could maybe save me and Lucas.

"Oh god, what am I going to tell my father tomorrow? That I let a few rogues go because they were mates? Because it was right? Because it was what I was hoping my father would have done? What was I expecting? Not as if it'd change a thing." I whispered to the ceiling.

Finally Alec parked the car in the garage. "Home sweet home," I groaned. The past week was killing. The rogues from the east finally found my old friend Olivia who was my best friend actually years back, she gave me a ring just hours before we left for home. I explained the truth to my father, can't say he was happy about my actions, but what is done is done. They weren't part of Kevin's group so why harm them?

I dragged my feet up the goddamn stairs. Shuffling them on the ground till I got to my room, Alec and Isaac had to discuss something with my father. It was past midnight when we reached home, I collapsed on my bed right away drifting off to dreamland.

I was awoken by the sound of a woman calling my name, it was like a whisper that came with the wind, but nobody was there. I got out of bed and walked over to the window to look out but saw no one other than the men on guard.

'Katherine.' The voice—I remembered that voice. Oh God! She's back!

I didn't bother putting on shoes or even a bra. I ran into the woods with my vampire speed. I heard that wolves call it shimmer, it was like running but in the speed of light, for me and my mother of course. I kept following the voice until I felt like I was in the middle of the woods and she appeared, "Long time no see, Princess." She bowed her head.

"What are you doing here, Adaka?"

Adaka is a Brazilian woman, I met her a few years back. She was a hundred and forty five years old. I didn't know how she did it but she made her aging process move slower and so now she looks like she is in the early sixties.

"My kinds are still hidden in the shadows, Princess. You made a promise and you haven't held up to it." She walked a few steps forward for me to see her face.

"I know, and I'll do it. I didn't promise when, I just promised that I'd do it, didn't I?"

"I don't want my grandchildren to grow up scared of the likes of other creatures because of our history!" She said in a fearless tone.

"I know, Adaka. No worries, in less than a year your kind won't have to fear anything from us werewolves and vampires, this I promise."

"You better see to it, Princess. Or I'll see to you."

I laughed at her attempt to threaten me, "Don't waste your energy, old woman. The next time you try your luck with me again I will make sure you're not that lucky. I can kill you before you can even attempt anything. But I won't, you know how I am, Adaka. I respect all creatures."

She bowed her head in shame, "I'm sorry, Princess. I just I don't have much time. I just want my family to live without fear." I nodded.

"I can protect them, Adaka. You know I will. I have my hands full as of now, you have to understand." She nodded before walking away to the other side.

"Until we meet again, Katherine. Don't forget what I've taught you, and don't be too cocky next time. It's the circle of life, everyone dies at the end. Even a hybrid. You might not die fully, Katherine, but you have been dead inside for over four centuries already." And like that she was gone leaving me with my thoughts of Lucas.

((((|URIEL|)))))

Today is my nine month anniversary with Katherine, still not sure where to take her. She called this morning saying she was back, so I'd told her I had made plans. I was busy thinking of ways to tell her about me leaving in five months, the past week she was away only consisted of me training, going to school and also keeping an eye on Mike. His parents are rogues and so was he, he refuses to submit to our pack making it harder for him and Saraquel to be together, because my father won't approve of any rogue, mate or not.

I got out of my room after brushing my teeth and took a quick shower. My father was on the counter having his breakfast, "Morning, son. Saraquel, I need to talk to your brother in private, please if you may?" She nodded, grabbed her shoes and walked out the door.

Seriously the man has his own house, elsewhere. Why is he here? "Good morning, father. What is it? Is something wrong?"

"Unfortunately, yes. Have you told her that you're leaving?" I shook my head.

"I'll tell her three months before I leave, Dad. I'm still thinking of a way to break it to her, nicely. I really love her."

My father sighed. "You're going to find your mate one day, son and you're not going to love her more. She is just a simple human, who won't understand our kind. Uriel, don't mess with fate, even humans have their own mates."

"Just get on with what you have to say, Dad." I don't need this, this early in the morning.

"I'm afraid that you are going to have to break the news to your girl later this afternoon, son. I'm leaving later tonight and you're going to come with me, it'll be for three months and after that you'll go straight to the academy."

"What?" I stood up from my chair, "You've never taken me with you for anything before and I refuse to go, today is a special day for us, please Dad." He shook his head and took a sip of his coffee.

"We found them. The rogues that attacked us, that killed your mother. They have a piece of land somewhere

BLESSILDA CHEONG

in the east, you're going to come with me because you're going to overthrow the bastard and take his pack. You're an alpha, Uriel. You have the right." He got up from his chair and walked away.

"But father I-I—"

"No! You're coming and that is final. Break the news and start packing," my father said with all authority, I hated it when he used his alpha tone with me. I bowed my head in respect. When my father finally left the room, I took out my phone to text Katherine, saying I'd meet her in fifteen.

Rogues with land? They must be stupid to be rogues and stay in one place. Being rogues meant that you've done something against the wolf law in a pack. Therefore there would always be some pack after you. That is why rogues don't stay in one place for long. As much as I wouldn't want to leave Katherine, I would have to. These rogues not only took my mother from me that day but also my father.

((((|KATHERINE|))))

I have just finished taking my shower when my phone buzzed. I checked to see that it was a text from Uriel saying he'll be here in fifteen minutes. I began raiding my closet for something to wear, hell I didn't know what I wanted to wear! I didn't know where we're going, so I just went with a floral dress. It was super hot outside I didn't feel wearing jeans and shirt.

I was all ready in five, I was about to start the car when one of the guards spoke to me through the mind link saying that a mustang had shown up at the house outside the woods, I had to shimmer, I remembered that there's a car at the house garage for display.

Just as I locked the door of my car, Uriel's mustang showed up. He parked his car and walked up to me, kissing me before I could say anything. He looked kind of stressed and sad today and I wondered why, he didn't even notice I was locking up a different car. I don't know if I should be grateful or worried. "Is something the matter, love? You look stressed out."

"I'll tell you later, Katherine." I looked him straight in the eyes. "I love you so much, you know that right? No matter what." I nodded.

"I love you too, silly. What's wrong? Where are we going today? Am I fit for the occasion?" He kissed my forehead and nodded.

"You better have a matching two piece under there." I giggled and he walked me to his car.

We arrived at the beach and there were two water scooters, it looked like we were the only ones on the beach.

"Why does this beach look deserted? Oh my God! Are we going to ride that? I've never ridden one before, I'm kind of scared of beaches and pools." I wasn't lying, it's true.

"It's because I had the beach cleared out for us today, it's our special day and I have to tell you something later on. Why are you scared of water?"

"When I was younger I loved the water, that's what my mother told me. I was five when it happened. My mother took me to Romania and there was a pool at the hotel where we were staying at and I was so eager to swim, I just jumped into the pool at the deep end without my floaters and drowned dead. A man dived in and saved me. Ever since that day I just hate places with lots of water. Like pools and beaches."

I really was five at the time, I was seventeen when I'd got my fangs and eighteen when I'd shifted. For the first seventeen years of my life I lived like a human. I could've died, that's what I was told.

"We don't have to go if you don't want to, Katherine. I don't want to force you to do anything that you don't want to." I shook my head.

"Are you a good swimmer?" He nodded. "Then it's alright, you'll save me if I drown, I love you, Uriel." He kissed my cheeks.

"I love you too, now come on, let's start."

"Here I got you." Uriel carried me off the scooter and let me down once we reached the sand. He was really great, I'd got over my fear of the waters.

Uriel pulled me closer to him till my chest slammed into his. "That was great, I'm having a great time Uriel, thanks! I'm so happy that you're mine and you'll always be there for me, thanks for helping me get over my fears."

He gave me a kiss, his lips tasted salty making me giggle, "What time is it, love? I'm already starving I don't think I can wait for dinner."

"I thought you'd would be." He pointed on top of the cliffs at the side and I saw a table with a flower on it, before I said anything I pretended to squint my eyes as if I was trying hard to look that far away, I was almost forgetting that he was human.

"What is that?" He gave me a smile before grabbing my hand and walking me towards the cliffs, "That is where our early dinner is."

"Wow, stairs, the one thing I love most right after you." I turned to see him smirking at me. "What? Does my house look like there is an upper level? I don't think so, carry!" He made a face which I laughed at.

"Alright, I love you so much, Katherine. That's why I'm doing this and you have to remember that alright?" I nodded before jumping on his back.

He didn't even break a sweat when he put me down, and I walked to the edge of the cliff. I closed my eyes taking in the scent of the sea and the first thing that popped up in my head was Lucas. Uriel pulled me to him till my back met with his chest, he kissed my neck and murmured an 'I love you' in my ear, and I could tell that something was wrong.

"Is something wrong, Uriel? Just spill it out, love." He looked so uneasy, what's wrong with him? It hurt me to see him like this, I wanted to take the pain away but I have to know what's wrong first.

"Katherine, I'm leaving."

The smile on my face faded as I processed the words that had just left his lips. "Leaving? You kept saying you love me for the past few hours, what the hell do you mean you're leaving?" I shouted at him, throwing my hands in the air to be dramatic. "This better not be a joke because I'm not laughing."

"My father asked me to join him for a business trip for three months and I have been accepted to an academy that my father really wants me to go to, it's really good. I'll be going there right after the business meeting."

I finally broke down into tears and sobs, I can't believe what I'm hearing. "When? When are you leaving, Uriel? For how long?"

He bowed his head, "Tonight, my father just told me this morning. I have to be home soon to pack, Katherine. I'm—"

"Don't you freaking dare! Just don't!" I shove him and made my way to his car, Uriel followed me from behind trying to reason with me. He grabbed my arm and turned me, crushing me into his chest. I tried shoving him but he just won't let go.

"Please Katherine, I don't want to leave like this."

"Then how do you want to leave, huh Uriel? Unhand me!" I kept hitting his chest. "I hate you for doing this to me, Uriel! I hate you! How could you? You made me fall in love with you from the top of my heels and now you're just going to leave! Jerk! I fell in love with a jerk! A total arse!"

He patted my back, "Sh~, I'll take you home." He kissed my forehead and carried me to his car.

The ride back was silent, and as soon as the car stopped I jumped out and ran into the house. I waited a few minutes till Uriel finally left and I shimmered to the mansion, shoving any men that came in my way. I opened the doors and slammed them shut.

"Katherine, what's up?" Alec and Isaac rose from the sofa. I saw my father coming out of the kitchen to find the cause of the noise and ran to him, burying my face on his chest and started crying.

"He's leaving, father! He's leaving me." I cried like a little girl who fell from her bike. "Why would he leave me? How could he do this to me? He said he loves me."

"Oh Katherine, you could have prevented this." I pushed him away from me, pissed at his words, his body collided with the wall behind him. I ran to my room, both Alec and Isaac followed my trail but I slammed the door shut before they could even get in. My phone kept buzzing and at the same time my father had the nerve to get in my room and I took the chance to throw my phone at him.

I buried my face in my pillow and cried my heart out, a few minutes later my father came back in with Alec and Isaac. This made me really angry and I screamed for them to get out, but they stood their ground.

"Please get out or I'll make you." My father sat on the bed beside me, "You're going to have to make us." I sat on my bed, tears rolling down my face. I stared at the door and I felt my heart break.

I said two simple words, "impetro!" Causing the three men in my room that once hand their feet on the ground to be floating on air. When Adaka taught me her ways, I was already fluent in Latin making it easier for her to teach me.

"Katherine, what is this?" My father hissed.

My hair started flying and the things on the drawers and on the side of my bed levitated too, "egressus!" And with my last word a heavy wind from out my room sucked them out and the door slammed shut.

My father started to pound on the door screaming, "Katherine! Katherine! What the hell is going on?" He went on for hours but the door stayed shut.

And just like that my secret was out, I do magic. I'm a witch, the most despicable creature alive. I started trashing my room. Throwing things and punching walls. I'd stabbed myself with wood and silver and by the time I collapsed I was all covered in my own blood and didn't have enough strength to hold the door shut.

Before I blacked out I heard the door busted open and saw six feet walking towards my body then everything went black.

⤖ Chapter Fifteen ⤖

'Nobody can hurt me without my permission.'
—Mahatma Gandhi.

I woke up with a feeling as if I had a stick up my arse, I groaned in pain at the feeling of my body. My wounds were already healed and I wasn't sure how long I have been asleep, with the damage I did to myself I'm guessing two days tops. There was a knock on my door. I didn't give any permission for the person on the other side to come in but he still did anyway.

"Katherine you're awake!" Alec ran to my side and held the back of his palm to my forehead.

"I'm alright, Alec. Get out of my room or I'll make you, I didn't even give you permission to come in." I hissed at him. He looked hurt at my words but who gives a crap,

I'm not actually in the mood. I still feel the pain of Uriel leaving, he should be gone by now.

"I'm sorry but you're going to have to make me. I hate seeing you weak, Katherine. Time to get up from bed don't you think? Your father has been waiting to talk to you, you've been out for two days."

Before I knew it, Alec was wiping the tears from my face. He came closer to hug me and I took the chance to bury my face in his chest and cry my heart out. I inhaled his scent of the forest almost like Uriel and that made me cry even more.

"Sh~" Alec patted my back, "Everything is going to be alright, I'm here. I got you, you got me and Isaac you don't need that human, Katherine."

He pulled me away from his chest and made me face him. His lips, they were coming closer and closer and soon they collided with mine. I was stunned, trying to process what was going on and just sat there with wide eyes looking at his closed ones.

He must have felt I wasn't responding so he stopped and backed away. He went toward the door but turned to say something before he left. "I'm sorry, I don't know what came over me, Katherine. Get dressed alright? I'll be back to walk you to your father. You have some serious explaining to do."

The second he left I got out of bed to take a shower still processing what had happened a while ago. But then I ended up not thinking of the kiss but crying my heart out remembering Uriel. I hate him! I hate him so much, I kept reminding myself to get over him. Maybe in a few days or so I could finally mean those three words in my head, I hate him. How could Lucas do this to me? Ask me to love only to feel the same pain of heartbreak at the end.

I got out of the shower to find Alec and Isaac in my room. I jumped a bit I didn't hear them come in, and maybe it's because of the water running or my crying. I'm not embarrassed to change in front of them, they've seen me naked a few times after runs.

I just stood there staring at Alec, finally reprocessing what happened earlier, but it broke when Isaac coughed, "Your father is waiting, princess. Get dressed and we'll walk you there." I nodded and went to my drawer for my underwear and bra.

My phone started buzzing as I got dressed and I saw it was Saraquel's name popping on my screen. I don't have time for this, I don't want anything to do with Saraquel. She will just make me cry more, and the pain, it was hard to control the pain.

I was as usual tightly sandwiched between Isaac and Alec, but Alec kept his distance from me. We were walking to the garden, my father was watering the flowers when I saw him. I nodded for Isaac and Alec to leave my side and they were gone in a blink. I walked over to my father and bowed my head, "Make it quick, father. I don't have time for this."

My father finally let go of the water spray and looked me right in the eye, "Are you going to tell me what is going on? Are you going to explain why my boys and I were suddenly sucked out of your room by a very strong wind and the door that just wouldn't budge? We tried breaking it down! We lit it on fire for freaking sake, Katherine!" Oh no! There goes my name again.

"I learned magic. Is it that hard to put the pieces together, father? Yes magic is for the living and if you've forgotten, father. I'm still half alive! The witches, they aren't as bad as we thought, father. They need our support, they need our protection. Are you going to grant it? Or do I have to wait till you die?"

"Watch your words, Katherine Rose Claw! I will not accept this! Look at you, you look like a dead panda with your eye bags! All this for a boy? You tried killing yourself! I thought I might lose you, Katherine. I almost lost my baby girl. It's not right for a parent to bury his child, I'm begging you now, Katherine. Forget this human and move on, if your mate has skipped a generation or died then get one of your kind to date you."

Is this why Alec kissed me? I turned to find Alec and Isaac, looking at us through the window and I knew they could hear our conversation since Alec was getting red in the cheeks for what he did earlier.

"I want to stop going to school and I want to train twenty-four seven and you will introduce me too packs as your personal warrior. I don't want to hide, I hate the pain I'm feeling now, father. It hurts! It hurts really bad! And all I want to do is just die!" I growled looking straight into my father's eyes to see fear, sadness and pity.

I turned to walk away, to see everything was floating except for the house. The trees and bushes and stones, everything were floating all due to my anger. It hurt to see me doing this over a man, for a human of all. I'd never felt like this with my mates not even once, not even when they died, not even Lucas. Yes, I mourned and got mad and went on a bloody spree but in time I learned to control the pain and forget, but never truly forgetting.

I hadn't realized Isaac and Alec wasn't in the house anymore, but that Alec was now in front of me, holding me close to his body really tight like he's afraid of me breaking into pieces. I could feel Isaac standing beside Alec with my father. Alec kissed my neck and I moaned and the next thing I knew everything was back in place.

"Alec, what is the meaning of this?" My father had the 'what the hell' tone. Alec let go of me and I turned to look at my father then at Alec and back to my father again.

"Explain, Alec." My father spoke once again.

"Balthazar, I know she isn't my mate but I've learned to care for her and I hate seeing her hurt. I want permission to date Katherine."

"What?" I heard myself say in a whisper but they heard me loud and clear. "Alec? I don't-. You're my guard and I-I just got out of a relationship that freaking hurts and you're declaring your undying love to me. Are you insane? Is this a phrase or something? Oh wait, maybe it's you know get what most guys don't! Maybe a freaking hybrid princess! You freaking man whore."

"That's what love can do to you, princess. And no it's not a phase, I do care for you, Katherine," I blushed. "I know you just got off a relationship and I hate that human for doing this to you. Seeing you like this, it kills me, Katherine. If you weren't so goddamn blind you would have noticed I haven't been slacking off for a long time now. I'm willing to wait and try my best until you give me a chance." I saw pureness in his eyes, he wasn't lying and he was right, if he didn't point out about him slacking off I wouldn't have noticed.

"And what happens when you meet your mate, Alec? You'll leave my daughter? You'll make her love you like that crap and leave her? She is your princess and it's a crime to hurt her, Alec. The permission you're asking is not for me to decide but Katherine; if she will have you."

So great now I am allowed to have a say in who can date me or not but when it comes to Uriel, he was ready to bite his heart out for even breathing the same air as mine.

《《《《 |ALEC| 》》》》》

I was going to check up on Katherine like I always do, seeing what happened to her a couple of days ago was killing me. I should have made my move the night, I saw her and that human in the cabin when we were at stake out but all I did was growl.

I knocked before entering to see her sitting on her bed, she must have just woken up. "Katherine, you're awake!" I walked to her side and held the back of my palm to her forehead.

"I'm alright, Alec. Get out of my room or I'll make you, I didn't even give you permission to come in." She hissed hurting me by the way she was acting for the human. I swear I'll kill him if I ever see him again.

"I'm sorry but you're going to have to make me. I hate seeing you weak, Katherine. Time to get up from bed, don't you think? Your father has been waiting to talk to you, you've been out for two days."

She was crying and my wolf was going crazy seeing our princess cry and so I wiped her tears, her lips were dry and they look so beautiful that I couldn't control myself. I hugged her body really close to mine to forget about her lips, the lips I've been dreaming and craving to kiss for years.

"Shh~" I patted her back as she cried, "everything is going to be alright, and I'm here. I got you, you got me and Isaac you don't need that human, Katherine." My wolf kept giving me images of her lips and it was getting hard to forget them and so I pulled Katherine away from my chest and stared down on her lips. When my lips touched hers I closed my eyes and kissed her.

But she wasn't responding and so I let her go and walked to the door as fast as I could, I needed to get out of here, it was really wrong, what I did. I was already at the door when I remembered something and I turned to speak my apology first.

"I'm sorry, I don't know what came over me, Katherine. Get dressed alright? I'll be back to walk you to your father, you have some serious explaining to do." And it looks like I did too.

I came back to her room with Isaac after half an hour and she was still in the shower. She got out in only her towel and my wolf was going crazy. I couldn't say a word, it's not like this was the first time I have seen her naked or anything. She was just standing there looking at me, she was making me think of what happened earlier.

The stare broke when Isaac spoke and I let out a sigh, "Your father is waiting, Princess. Get dressed and we'll walk you there," she nodded and went to get dressed.

Once we reached the door that led to the garden, Katherine nodded and Isaac and I left her side.

"Come on, Isaac I want to hear what she has to say." Isaac as usual just went with anything I say, we walked over to the nearest window and looked out on my beautiful princess with her father.

"Make it quick, father. I don't have time for this." She said in a calm tone.

"Are you going to tell me what is going on? Are you going to explain why my boys and I were suddenly sucked out of your room by a very strong wind and the door that just wouldn't budge? We tried breaking it down! We lit it on fire for freaking sake, Katherine!" Balthazar said with a lot of anger.

"I learned magic. Is it that hard to put the pieces together, father? Yes magic is for the living and if you've forgotten, father. I'm still half alive! The witches they aren't as bad as we thought, father." What she said next made me smirk, of course we all knew she had learnt magic it wasn't hard to guess after what she had done two days ago, what we wanted to know was how and why?

"They need our support, they need our protection. Are you going to grant it? Or do I have to wait till you die?" Why is she protecting witches, I'll never understand. They are not very nice creatures.

"Watch your words, Katherine Rose Claw!" She is going to get it now, it's been years since I heard her full name. Usually when Balthazar gets pissed all he does, is say her first name. "I will not accept this! Look at you, you look like a dead panda with your eye bags! All this for a boy? You tried killing yourself! I thought I might lose you, Katherine. I almost lost my baby girl. It's not right for a parent to bury their child. I'm begging you now, Katherine. Forget this human and move on, if your mate has skipped a generation or died then get one of your kind to date you."

He is letting her date her kind that lit my face in a second. I knew this was my chance and I'm going to take it, she turned to look for something until her eyes met mine and my cheeks lit up once again.

She turned back to her father and hissed, "I want to stop going to school and I want to train twenty-four seven and you will introduce me to packs as your personal warrior. I don't want to hide, I hate the pain I'm feeling now, father. It hurts! It hurts really bad! And all I want to do is just die!"

Fear was what I felt and I guessed Isaac felt the same as the trees, bushes, stones, the table outside and chairs they were all floating, Isaac kept pulling my shirt.

"Alec, come on we have to protect the king!" I nodded and we ran to them. She was looking straight at me when I ran to her and hugged her tightly to my body, I kissed her neck and her body finally relaxed and I knew that everything was going to be ok.

"Alec, what is the meaning of his?" Balthazar looks pissed at me this time so I had to let go of Katherine and my wolf howled.

"Explain, Alec." He spoke again and I answered this time. "Balthazar, I know she isn't my mate but I've learned to care for her and I hate seeing her hurt. I want permission to date, Katherine."

"What?" Katherine whispered, but I heard her and I turn to look at her.

"Alec? I don't-. You're my guard and I-I just got out of a relationship that freaking hurts and you're declaring your undying love to me. Are you insane? Is this a phase or something? Oh wait maybe it's you know get what most guys can't! Maybe a freaking hybrid princess! You freaking man whore!"

"That's what love can do to you, princess and no it's not a phase. I do care for you, Katherine. If you weren't so goddamn blind you would have noticed I haven't been slacking off for a long time now." Seeing her blushed as a reply made my wolf really happy. "I know you just got off a relationship and I hate that human for doing this to you. Seeing you like this, it kills me, Katherine. I'm willing to wait and try my best until you give me a chance."

"And what happens when you meet your mate, Alec? You'll leave my daughter? You'll make her love you like that crap and leave her? She is your princess and it's a crime to hurt her, Alec. The permission you're asking is not for me to decide but Katherine, if she will have you."

I turned to Katherine and I knelt and took one of her hands, "You better not be proposing, Alec!" Balthazar hissed and I let out a laugh my eyes not leaving hers, "Katherine, I know you're not my mate and that one day I might find her and she will understand just like one day you'll find yours and I'll understand and I'll let you go."

I kissed her hand, "I know saying this is too much but it's true, I care for you and I always will. Just give me a chance and I can show you. If you want me to work for it I will, Katherine. I'll do all that I can." With that I stood up, she smiled and before I knew it, she was already hugging me.

"Oh, Alec you don't know how tempting it is for me to say 'I will when pigs fly' but you know what? I'd actually like to see you try, Alec. My love isn't easy and it certainly doesn't come cheap." She said with her sweet tone but her eyes say otherwise.

I know I'd have to work hard, I wasn't on the blind side. I knew about her mates, about her outburst months ago. I could never live up to Lucas but if I have to die trying I will.

❧ CHAPTER SIXTEEN ❧

'I hated every minute of training, but I said 'don't quit. Suffer now and live the rest of your life as a champion."
                                        —Muhammad Ali.

The cold covered my body when someone ripped the blanket away from me, "The hell!" I sat as hissed at whoever it was.

"Rise and shine, Katherine! It's time for training again with me." Alec said in an oh-so-jolly tone, I looked over to the clock to see it was only nine in the morning.

"I thought you're trying to get me to love you, jerk, not make me hate you more! It's too early!" I grabbed my pillow and threw it at him. We were training till four in the morning yesterday and it's only nine! What part of beauty sleep don't men get?

I screamed as he carried me off from my bed and towards the bathroom. "Let me go, Alec!" I pounded my fist on his hard chest which was a turn on, I knew my eyes were black with lust right now, stupid werewolf hormones. "Please let me go, Alec, you're—"

"I know, Katherine. It's making my wolf crazy too." He let me go once I was in the shower, I stripped in front of him and got in the cold shower. "I'll wait for you outside alright, hurry up." Just as he got out I had the most evil idea of all and I couldn't wait to work it.

I got out of the shower butt naked and walked out of the bathroom to find Alec sitting on the side of my bed staring at me. This was the idea and I wasn't shy, he'd seen me naked a lot of times. Werewolves have everything heightened except for the shame I guess, sometimes werewolves female or male is forced to shift tearing their clothes and it isn't like every wolf has to run with their clothes hanging from their mouths, that'd be freaking annoying.

"What are you looking at, Alec?" I flirted.

He snapped out of his head, "I'll wait for you outside." I grabbed his hand before he could leave and pulled him closer to me. I put his hand on my waist and put mine on his chest and started kissing his neck, he kept moaning. I whispered into his ears, "You want me?" And he nodded. "I'm so cold, Alec. Hold me really tight to your body, you feel so warm." He held me tighter as I licked his neck, "Feel every part of me, Alec and make me warm." This time he growled and I knew he was keeping his wolf at bay, I laughed evilly in my head at my success.

He started kissing my neck, making me moan but I have to remember to control myself. I knew I could, "Want to make love to me, Alec?" He nodded, "You want to show me how much you love me right?" He nodded again. I patted on his chest, "Well too bad for you, jackass. That's what you get for disturbing my beauty sleep! Blue balls." I let out a little laughter and with that I got out from his arms and walked over to my drawer to dress up.

He let out a few growls as I got dressed "Didn't anyone teach you, Alec? It's rude to stare." I smirked at him "Stop raping me with your eyes, Alec because it wouldn't change a thing." I walked over to stand close, so close our lips almost touched, I managed a smile, "Let's go." I said and walked past him but stopped midway, "Oh, and pull that stunt again and not letting me have my beauty sleep? You'd be getting more than just blue balls." I hissed showing off my fangs and making my eyes glow red to scare him before I continued walking away.

After training I went for another shower. It had been a long day and I was as tired as hell after what happened earlier.

"Come on, Katherine. Keep punching till you reach the thousandth punch then we'll move on to other stuff." Alec was beside me encouraging me to keep going on, even when I couldn't anymore. Who in hell could throw one thousand punches? Especially when they only got five hours of sleep after doing the goddamn same training.

"How about we make a deal? You reach that one thousand and I'll let you rest for tomorrow, but if you don't you'll be going on a date with me tomorrow," and just like that I just kept throwing fist after fist, till one thousand in like two minutes which left Alec jaw drop and me smirking at him but I know I'd pay for it later, we then moved to another thing.

I had to kick a tree first with my right for another fifty times then my left then we got to another move. Alec's training was killing more than usual, I think this is payback for earlier, the little twat! "Come on, Katherine the same deal as before for all the moves," and again I got to another move leaving Alec's jaw dropping and pissed.

This time it was a spar and I could choose who I wanted. I chose one of the guards this time for payback. Adam, one of the guards, I could smell his fear, but I assured him that I wouldn't hurt him that much during the sparring.

He was attacking me and holding me, everywhere, and Alec had been growling from one blow to another, it's usually him that I spar with, even if its Isaac, the stronger of them both/ it had always been him instead because he always insisted on it and now I get why. It's one of his attempts to get close to me and protect me.

Adam pulled on my hair and the unthinkable happened, my wig fell off. Before I learned magic, my hair was blonde, white blonde like an old lady and I'd had to always colour it black or brown, but since my first mate my hair has started turning a faded red at the top near my scalp and when I drank from him the light red spread, every time I drank it always spread. I started wearing a wig and the more I mated and drank, my hair finally turned entirely blood red, every time I *try dying it different colour it just turns back to red, like my wolf's fur. The guard and Alec stared at me in shock.*

In a blink of an eye my father was suddenly standing in front of me, shocked as well. Alec must have called him through mind link, so I had to explain everything to him, which he understood but didn't like it and so did Alec. As for my mother she was already aware of my hair and was alright with it, we don't keep secrets from each other. Other than the 'me learning magic secret' but tell me? Which father wouldn't freak? If he saw his baby girl, colouring her hair bright red like some rebel.

I was too tired to get back up the stairs and made Adam carry me to my room. "Adam, please carry me to my room, I'm tired out." He nodded and walked towards me but Alec stopped him.

"Back away, pup. She's mine!" He growled and I rolled my eyes at him, "take a hint Alec, I'm nobody's! Adam, please?" And I held my hand up for him to sweep me off my foot bridal style and Alec stomped away.

I got out the shower once again to see Alec sitting on my bed. I smiled down at him, "What are you doing here?" I tried to go for my drawers, but he stopped me by grabbing my hand and suddenly hugging me from behind. Well thank god I was wearing a towel, then huh?

"Why? It hurts so much to see another man touch you, I know I'm not your mate but I care for you please let me, Katherine."

He turned me to face him and my wolf howled inside at seeing him crying for me. I'm a princess I'm not supposed to be mean. I held his cheeks between my hands and wiped the tears off before pulling him to bed with me. He rested on top of me, looking down at me.

"It's alright, Alec. I'm sorry if I'm giving you a hard time, I just don't want to be hurt anymore like how I am now. If I give you the chance will you promise not to hurt me? To love me and care no matter the crap I drag with me?"

He nodded and I hugged him making his body drop on me, but he was as light as a feather and I started kissing his neck again before whispering into his ears, "Stay with me tonight, Alec."

I knew I couldn't love him, I just can't but what's the harm in trying. Uriel was a mere human and I got to love him, if I could love a human, then why can't I try with my own kind? I guess this is what Lucas must have meant by 'Accept him even when it hurts.' But can I trust what Lucas' said after what happened with Uriel?

❧ CHAPTER SEVENTEEN ❧

'A whole stack of memories never
equal one little hope.'
                    —Charles M. Schulz.

I woke up to the smell of Alec's scent beside me, he had his hand on my tummy. It has been days from when I've given up and let him in, he has been sleeping in my room. He'd told my father it was to protect me more but the old man wasn't a fool, I knew that he knew what was really going on.

I watched as he slept soundlessly, one day he would find his mate and I would too but not like me, he would have a family. How I crave for a family I could never have? Even my mother hadn't guessed that I couldn't get pregnant. I had made love with Lucas, he wanted a family like me, small little pups of me and him running around but I couldn't give him any and I guess it was a blessing more than a curse.

Because I can never die and like my father said it's not right for a parent to bury their child. If my children were to be vampire then maybe they'd live forever, but what if they turned out to be werewolves? They'll eventually die. I moved Alec's arm away from my tummy and turned really slow as not to wake him.

I don't love him the way he wants me to, I couldn't because I am still in love with Uriel but I could see how he loves me so much. It has been a few days and no man has touched me, Alec just won't allow it. I couldn't train or spar with other wolves, it was cute and romantic you could say. The thought of his love for me made me blush.

I heard him growl making me jump a bit, is he awake? "Alec? You awake?" I asked as I pulled him for a short kiss which he returned and had turned into a long one.

"Carry me around the garden, Alec. Pretty please!" He turned his back to me as in motion for me to get on and I squealed, "Yay!" Before jumping on his back. He made it look like I weighed like a feather, but I knew how heavy I was. Nobody could take my feet off the ground unless I wanted them to, just thinking of that reminded me of the day Lucas kidnapped me, I felt my lips crawled in a smile at the memory.

We went down the stairs and to the garden, "Alec, I have been thinking, I want a life. Away from all these, training and father, you know. I want to feel death someday."

With my words he just stopped and let me down, then turned to face me and held my hand, "what's with this crazy talk, Katherine? You know you can't die."

"That's what you think, but now with me having magic, I might have the power to isolate my body. Like the ones you see in that movie series, Vampire Diaries? When they put a stake in an original's heart they stay dead and frozen, but not dead-dead."

He looks really worried this time, "I don't want to hear this ever again, Katherine. You of all people must live, you are our princess, don't be selfish and only think of yourself. If you die, what will happen to your kind? They will wage war."

"But, I want to die too. I want to go through the cycle of life. Maybe one day I'll love you like you love me, maybe we won't meet our mates and we'll be together and when the time comes for you to leave, I want to leave with you."

"Can we just drop the subject? This conversation is for another day, baby." I didn't argue because before I could even try he pulled me and locked my lips with his which lasted very long, we only broke apart when one of the children tugged on my dress.

"Play with us princess!" I nodded and went off with the children, they were children of warriors and guards and when they grow up they too will fight alongside with me, I'm sure I have also played with their parents when they were young like them.

(((((|ALEC|)))))

I can't believe that kid took her away from me, I frowned as she followed him to his other friends. I sat on the ground and watched my beautiful princess play, running around, reminding me of six years ago.

"Alec! Isaac! Come on, play with me!" Katherine called over from the lake.

"Katherine, Isaac and I have been training for days, we're really tired. We'll play later on." I replied as I turned back to talk to Isaac about Kevin, and in a blink, she was there standing right in front of me between Isaac and me.

"I said play with me, there is nobody else to play with. The kids are at school." She pouted but I was really tired, I wasn't lying and if I were, she would know it.

"Why would you want to play? Aren't you like five hundred years old? Playing is for kids, Katherine."

"Yes, I'm five hundred years old but the age that I take up is the age that I'll act like. It's one of the reasons why I never age myself into a one year old. So come on, Alec please!" This time she started pulling my hand and Isaac's, and boy was she strong, she was practically dragging us by our tail.

"Alright, Katherine. But if we play with you I want you to give us your word you won't force us to play Barbie dolls with you ever again?" She giggled at my words but nodded anyway.

"Katherine, I'm starving come grab your bag and I'll take you out for lunch," she looked up at me but still continued playing and so I did what every man would do, when they are hungry as hell and could eat a house full of cows and the woman they love won't listen. I walked up to her and she just smiled at me, so I smiled back before I carried her over my shoulder and walked into the house with her hitting on my back to put her down.

"Put me down, Alec!" She continued pounding and shouting curses after curses which only made me smirk.

"Oh stop struggling, you and I know you can get down if you want, plus I know for the fact that you haven't attempted to get off because you like the view behind there." I said cockily and she did the unthinkable, she slapped my arse.

CHAPTER EIGHTEEN

'Family is the most important
thing in the world.'
—*Princess Diana.*

"Katherine, get your arse down here! We're going to be late darling!" I heard Alec screaming on his way up from the ground floor. There was this party at Isaac's and Alec's old pack and I didn't want to go because he would introduce me to everyone and I don't even love him yet, it would be unfair, he has been nagging me to go for weeks. I got so annoyed I finally gave up and said yes, which I regretted the second I said it because there is no turning back with him.

Someone knocked on the door, but I ignored it, "Grant me entrance or I'll come in and I swear Katherine Rose

Claw slash Jane Smith." I giggled at his attempt to be as scary as my father when calling my full name. "I will carry you out and into the damn car! So you better be dressed!" He hissed again but unfortunately I wasn't dressed yet, I have just gotten out of the shower with only a towel to cover me and it covered very little, I've been stalling for two hours, and he is freaking pissed at me.

The door busted open and I jumped as if I thought he was joking, and there he stood in front of me staring at my body. I shut the door with my power at which he jumped and looked at the door and then back again at me. I smirked as an idea had come to me.

I let the towel go and my body was in view, my long red hair covered most of me. Alec growled which made me laugh a little, "Alright, Alec. Let's go. Come on. Carry me, you did say you were going to carry me to the car. So are you going to carry me to the party like this? I'm sure every boy will like me in an instant."

He growled once again before pinning me to the hard cold wall, "Mine!" He growled and I thought that was really romantic, so I gave him a little kiss. I started giving little kisses on his neck and went to his ears to whisper, "Mine!" Making him moan, this time he licked my shoulders and neck. He started holding every inch of me, "Oh Alec," I moaned. "We're going to be late, get off me." I said in a normal tone and patted on his shoulders to get him off me and he kept growling trying to hold his wolf in, what can I say I can be such a tease.

I chuckled when I saw how hard he was, but it didn't turn me on one bit, though the scent of him being aroused was messing with my wolf. *'Goddamn werewolf hormones!'*

I cursed in my head, "Don't get too excited." I winked and got to my drawer to get dressed.

"We are here Katherine, wake up." Alec whispered in my ears, I fluttered my eyes open to see him looking down at me with his beautiful blue eyes.

"Give me a kiss and maybe I'll wake up." I flirted, which I rarely did. He gave me a kiss and I got out of the car.

I didn't wear anything to hide my face, I was going as Alec's girlfriend. As a normal she-wolf not a princess, people here didn't know who I am, I mean how I looked like. I grabbed Alec's hand and tried to walk, since Alec was practically dragging me for being three hours late. I have never felt nervous before because my mates, they were all warriors and guards and so their parents must have already known me or I used to play with them when they were young, so I never really tried to make them like me, they just do.

An old lady came up to Alec smiling and I gave her a sweet one in return, "Is this your mate, Alec?" She asked, making my cheeks burn in the process.

"She is my girlfriend, godmother. I don't think I'll find my mate," the woman giggled before letting out her hand. "I'm Cole Margaret, Alec's godmother. It's about time my godson found someone that could tame him."

I shook her hand, "Katherine Smith. It's nice to meet you, Ms. Margaret."

"You can call me Cole, you are after all a family now, darling." She smiled and I smiled back, we chatted a little more before Alec pulled me away to meet other people. A dozen female children ran to Alec with flowers, I turned to see that a dozen went to Isaac too. I turned to Alec and giggled, "I see I'm going to have competition." It was cute that the girls giggled before running away.

After a few minutes the same girl that gave Alec flowers earlier, came back. "Warrior, I'd like to whisper something in your ears," she said with a very cute voice and Alec bent low enough for the girl to tiptoe and gave Alec a little peck on the cheeks. She ran away towards the other girls and they all giggled.

I turned to Alec and raised my brows, "I have a really good competition, huh? Cheeky little things." I faked hurt and he pulled me in for a hug and kissing my forehead, "mine!" He said possessively and I hugged him back.

"You can't be jealous, Katherine." I pulled away from him.

"You wish, Alec." I said and walked away from him and to Isaac.

I found Isaac sitting alone on the edge of the docks and I went to sit beside him.

"Is everything alright, Isaac?" I put a hand on his shoulder, "You need to speak to me, Isaac. I care for you and sometimes I feel like you hate me. You rarely talk to me and if you do it's only when it's really important."

"I don't hate you, Princes—" I put a finger to his lips to silence him.

"Call me Katherine, and if you don't then don't bother calling me princess either."

He coughed and continued, "I don't hate you, Kate. I just—" this time he stopped on his own and I think it's because I looked at him in a funny way.

"Since day one, you've been calling me 'princess' and when I finally got you to call me Katherine, you just go and decide to give me a nickname, Kate? How original of you?" I hit him in the chest.

"I'd call you beautiful but Alec might kill me."

"Nice, really nice Isaac! Nice line seriously," I patted him. "I've never seen you like this, Isaac. You smiling especially when Alec is around."

"Well you know what they say when the cat's away, the mice come out and play." He wiggled his brows to make it extra funny.

I let out a deep sigh after my laughter died out, "I'm really tired here, I want to rest. Can I lay my head on your shoulder?" He nodded, "You make a really nice pillow, Isaac." He choked on his own tongue.

"Why are you always quiet? We are here at your home village and you're sitting alone, I was hoping to finally see you mingle but I guess not. Why do you shut people out?"

"I-I-I don't do it intentionally, it just happens. I have always been a loner I guess, Alec was always the one with the mouth. I like quiet. I don't trust people well, I only ever trust my mother and Alec and Balthazar." I was hurt that he didn't say my name.

"What about me, Isaac? Don't you trust me?" I was really hurt knowing he didn't trust me. It really made me sad, I am his princess, he should know I would never stab him in the back. He laid one of his hands on mine, he was warmer than Alec.

"I-I-I have trouble trusting people, beautiful, and you being a vampire, I just don't know. It was a shock when I saw you do magic. I have more trouble trusting hybrids I guess, because you don't have loyalties, beautiful."

"I have loyalty, Isaac. To my father and mother, I would never wage war. You can trust me. I'll always have your back, can't say the same for witches though. I-I didn't know why I wanted to learn magic I just wanted to. But I hope one day I'll earn your trust, Isaac. For now I want you to know I'm not lying when I say I care for you." I put my free hand on his cheeks and caressed them, his warmth was nice.

It was so nice. I didn't realize his face coming closer to mine and by the time I did, someone had spoken.

"What's going on?" Our lips were only inches away and we both jumped, I turned to see Alec looking down at us.

⟪⟪⟪ |ISAAC| ⟫⟫⟫⟫

People welcomed me and the children danced around me giving me flowers, it was sweet but I still had to get away from the noise.

I don't get what's wrong with me, I just didn't like socializing. I walked to the edge of the dock, pulled up my pants and let my legs dip into the water.

I felt someone walk up behind me, and it had to be the princess since that person didn't have a scent, and the princess always hid her scent.

"Is everything alright, Isaac?" She put a hand on my shoulder, "You need to speak to me, Isaac. I care for you and sometimes I feel like you hate me. You rarely talk to me and if you do, it's only when it's really important."

She thinks I hate her but I don't it's just who I am.

"I don't hate you, Princess—" she silenced me by putting a finger on my lips.

"Call me Katherine, and if you don't then don't bother calling me princess either."

I didn't know what to say actually, so I coughed and then thought before speaking. "I don't hate you, Kate, I just—" what is with her? She is giving me a face, a very awkward but cute face, and I envy Alec for having her by his side. He is really a lucky man.

"Since day one, you've been calling me 'princess' and when I finally got you to call me Katherine, you just go and decide to give me a nickname, Kate? How original of you?" She hit me on my chest, I needed to think of a nice line for this and I got it.

"I'd call you beautiful but Alec might kill me."

"Nice, really nice Isaac! Nice line seriously," she rolled her eyes and patted my back. "I've never seen you like this, Isaac. You smiling especially when Alec is around."

"Well you know what they say when the cat's away, the mice come out and play." I attempted to wiggle my brows to make it extra funny.

Her laughter finally died out and she let out a deep sigh "I'm really tired here, I want to rest. Can I lay my head on your shoulder?" I nodded and she laid her head on my shoulder, my wolf was going crazy having my princess this close to me.

"You make a really nice pillow, Isaac. Why are you always quiet? We are here at your home village and you're sitting alone, I was hoping to finally see you mingle but I guess not why do you shut people out?"

"I-I-I don't do it intentionally, it just happens. I have always been a loner I guess, Alec was always the one with the mouth. I like quiet. I don't trust people well, I only ever trust my mother and Alec and Balthazar."

"What about me, Isaac? Don't you trust me?" She looked hurt by what I said and she sounded hurt too, and it hurt me as well to see my princess like this. I wondered how Alec handled her emotions. I held one of her hand to comfort her.

"I-I-I have trouble trusting people, beautiful, and you being a vampire, I just don't know. It was a shock when I saw you do magic. I have more trouble trusting hybrids I guess, because you don't have loyalties, beautiful."

"I have loyalty, Isaac. To my father and mother, I would never wage war. You can trust me. I'll always have your back, can't say the same for witches though. I-I didn't know why I wanted to learn magic I just wanted to. But I hope one day I'll earn your trust, Isaac. For now I want you to know I'm not lying when I say I care for you."

She put her free hand on my cheeks and caressed them. I was holding onto my wolf and it was really hard not to show the lust in my eyes. I wanted to kiss her, I move my face closer to her but jumped away when I heard Alec speak.

⟪⟪⟪ |ALEC| ⟫⟫⟫⟫

Katherine had wandered off earlier and now I had to look for her. I disliked it when I didn't know where she was. How am I going to protect her? A little girl came up to me again with a flower and I took it and gave her a kiss on her forehead and she went off running to her friends. I wished Katherine was like that, minus the running off, and I would kiss her lips. She doesn't blush when I kiss her, I know she doesn't have feelings for me, I'm not her mate and I am definitely not that jerk of a human.

"Aunt Cole, have you seen Katherine? I've been looking for her everywhere." My godmother looked at me confused.

"Isn't she a wolf, Alec? Can't you smell her scent?" She asked and God I didn't have an answer to that.

"Oh, I forgot sorry, excuse me." I ran off before she could say anything else.

Katherine likes hiding her scent, I never actually smelled her scent, and Balthazar said only her mate can smell it even when she hides it. She might be with Isaac, I should just start tracing his scent, which led me to the docks on the lake, and there they were, sitting side by side. Isaac was holding her hand, and my wolf growled at the sight of them.

It looked like they were going to kiss, I could see Isaac making his move and I was not going to let him. He knew that she is mine.

"What is going on here?" I asked angrily and they both jumped away from each other and Katherine turned to look at me in shock.

She stood up flushed, her cheeks were glowing, and I wasn't sure if it was because she had almost kissed my cousin or if she was embarrassed, because she got busted.

"I-I-I," my little princess stuttered.

"Well! Isaac?" I turned to look at him.

"Nothing is going on, Alec." With that he just walked past me and back into the party leaving me with Katherine, leaving her to explain herself.

"Katherine, I'm going to leave now, you can go home with Isaac later on." I turned to walk away from her.

She hugged me from behind, stopping me. I tried to take her hands off, she just kept gripping tighter, "nothing was going on, Alec. Don't leave, please? Don't leave me, don't ever walk away from me, baby."

Wait? What did she call me? I was still shocked with the particular word that came out of her lips. She let go of me and grabbed my hand to turn me to face her, which I did and she tiptoed to kiss my lips.

This kiss was different than the others, this kiss had meaning. It was passionate and hungry like she had been craving for my lips, when she parted from my lips I saw her eyes fill with lust. "Don't leave me, baby. If you leave then I want to go with you." She hugged me again.

This time I swept her off her feet and carried her bridal style to the car and we drove home.

❧ Chapter Nineteen ❧

'He is not busy being born is busy dying.'
—Bob Dylan.

As more months passed, I got closer to Alec more than I thought I would have. "Alec!" I called out from the balcony of my room, Alec was training his team of men and it was already one in the morning and I was terribly sleepy. "It's time for bed, baby! Come up and let the men rest." He nodded and wrapped up his men before coming in.

He striped into his boxers and got into the covers with me, I scooted over to him as he wrapped his arms over and we drifted to sleep.

"Attack, Rogue. Moon Water pack!" The words sounded in my head and Alec's too, causing both of us to jump out

of bed at the same time and stared at each other in fear, in fear that this might be Kevin attacking. They did say rogue.

Alec walked over to me and held both my cheeks in his hand, "You stay here, Katherine. I don't want you there. I can't fight and worry about you at the same time," he kissed my forehead but I didn't let him leave without me.

"I can help, with me there the fight will end in just a matter of seconds. I am strong, I can do this, I can't say the same for you. You can't make me wait here and wonder if you're going to come home to me or not!"

"Katherine, I don't have time to argue. Let's go but you're only going to stand on the side with Isaac." I grabbed the red hood from its hook that was nailed on the back of the door and wore it to hide my face. Once out of the house, Isaac and Alec shifted. "I'm not going to shift, I'll run with you, I'll shimmer, come on."

When we reached there, there was chaos, my father wasn't there to help anyone because he was in California. I watched them fight. I watched my men fight side by side with the fighters of the pack, with us on their side they had the chance, but people would still die unless I helped. I watched as Alec tried to handle six wolves at the same time and I stood there in fear.

He managed to kill the two but more came and bite on him and I knew that, this was my cue. I shimmered beside Alec's body, he was lying on the ground and I was not sure if he was still alive but he hadn't shifted and that was good.

All I did was stood there looking down at the ground for them not to see my face but one of them attacked me but Isaac was quick to put him down, they all started growling showing off their canines but I wasn't scared of them, I was scared for Alec. I was scared of losing him. The wolves finally had Isaac on the ground.

"Stop!" I whispered, but everybody heard me because everyone; warriors, fighters and rogue stopped and I knew all eyes were on me, but I still haven't lifted my head.

"I am Katherine, your princess and you'll all listen. I want to know who is in charge here."

"I am, princess." The werewolf pinning one of my men down spoke through mind link before shifting. I turned around to face him, I looked up a bit to see his face. He wasn't Kevin, "State your business, why do you attack?"

I could hear him smirk, "Because we're bored and wanted some fun, Princess. What are you going to do about it?"

This time it was me who smirked and lifted my hands and with that I lifted all rogues into the air, "the hell", "crap crap", "what is going on", all these words sounded from the rogues, curses after curses.

"You all will not disrespect me!" My voice echoed and they all howled in pain except for my men.

"I will not kill my kind unless by force. You rogues I will set free but you, leader." I pointed at him, "Will have to pay for the damage. Guards, take him!" I ordered but of course the rogue didn't stand his ground, he tried to run but I was faster and in a blink I was in front of him blocking his way. Every time he tried and tried but still I was in front, blocking his way. "By the law of King

Balthazar Claw, you rogue are to be captured and be given a fair trial." I nodded towards my men and they held him down.

"Beautiful." I turned to see who called, it was Isaac. He was pointing at a body, a body where Alec's wolf once laid was a human form and he was dead. Alec died on me and the anger I felt made my breath grew heavier.

"You!" I hissed, "You killed him! You killed Alec!" I pointed my finger at him and lifted him into the air.

"Princess, have mercy on me please!" He begged but I wasn't in the freaking mood. "Mercy?" I asked smirking, "I'll give you mercy, rogue! Dolour!" I hissed and he cried, "Please no princess, have mercy!"

I closed my eyes tight and when I opened them I knew they were glowing neon red, too bright for anyone to see my face and so I looked up at the rogue, "vos mos sentio dolorem!" I cursed causing him to scream again. "Vobis nocebit! Aeternum!" I hissed and he screamed louder. "If I can take your wolf I will for what you did, but this is on you! And for that! You will be nothing but a weak human, for your abilities will be stripped from you and your wolf. Every time you try to shift the pain will maximize ten times and the process will be slow!"

"Beautiful," I heard Isaac whisper and I looked back down to see me no longer on the ground, but only a few inches in the air. I let the rogue down, "Guards take him!" And they all surrounded him once more.

I looked back down because I knew my eyes weren't glowing anymore. I had already calmed, "You rogue, you will be forced to shift for a dozen times, before you will be free. That is if you survive the pain. Let you all know the pain is nothing anyone alive has ever felt but only the people in hell."

The guards took him away and I turned to the remaining rogues, "Submit." My words echoed and a few growls were heard.

"I said submit!" My voice echoed louder. I lifted my head up to see not only rogues but everybody including my men bowing their heads.

I shimmered to Alec's body and held him in my arms, "Wake up baby, please wake up." But nothing, not a single word came out. I started crying and holding him really tight to me, "Please baby wake up! Darling, please don't leave me!"

'Please please' I prayed *'Lucas what is this? Why? You asked me to love and I did love Uriel then you asked me to accept and I accepted Alec, I didn't do all that just to feel the same crap I went through with you, why?'* I cried in my head.

"Princess" I looked up and my men all surrounded me. "No!" I yelled at them and they took a step back.

"Alec. Please wake up. Pretty, please!" I buried my face in his chest and cried I felt Isaac put a hand on my shoulder for comfort. I looked up at him, "Isaac, help me! Please help me! I don't know what to do!" I cried. "There must be something I can do? Right? I know there is but I don't know what. Please Isaac! I don't know what to do."

"It's time to go home, princess. There is nothing we can do." First I hesitated but I knew my men needed to rest, so I just let go. I left his body for the men to carry him home, later to be buried. I gave him one last kiss on his lips before moving in to whisper in his ears for only him to hear, "These words are only for your ears to hear, Alec. I love you."

He deserves it, those three words. I might not love him as much as I love Lucas and Uriel but I did love him, and although I've told him that a dozen times I knew he didn't believe but maybe this time he will.

Isaac gave out his hand to help me stand and I took it and turned away from Alec's body but just as I was about to take one step I heard him, Alec.

"I love you too, Katherine." I turned to see him trying to sit and I fell to him holding him tight and crying in his arms.

"Oh, Alec! I—I thought I lost you, baby!" I cried. "Don't scare me like that again, alright?" He nodded and managed a smile. "Let's go home." I motioned for Isaac to help me with Alec.

✑ CHAPTER TWENTY ✑

'If we don't end war, war will end us.'
—H. G. Wells.

Ever since the attack months ago, my feelings for Alec grew deeper, but I never as much as what I've felt with either Lucas or Uriel. No matter what, Lucas would always be number one and for a second I almost thought Uriel was going to take his place in my heart and then he just had to go and mess things up and again there Alec was as usual to my rescue.

"Oh, father! Come on it's just a movie, and it's just going to be us. You, me, Isaac and Alec." I was pleading with my father to watch a movie with us, it was twilight and my father hated it because he thought that Bella Swan was a little bit crazy for choosing Edward, a vampire instead of Jacob a werewolf, might I add a very H.O.T one in that. Though I'm not sure if I should have told him that he chose a vampire as well.

"No, I don't want to, Princess. You just go," he rejected me for like the hundredth time in an hour. "But father!" I whined, "I'm going with Alec and Isaac won't have a date and I was thinking you'd be his date." This time I pulled the puppy dog face, "Please father it's the part two of Breaking Dawn, please! If not for me then for Isaac!"

He growled a little and nodded yes, to which I jumped and squealed and gave him a very tight hug. "Thanks you!" I gave him a kiss, "Be ready by seven."

He nodded and I went to search for Alec and Isaac at the fields to tell them the news.

"So, father how did you like the movie?" I was hugging Alec's arm for warmth. I was warm enough but just using it as a reason to hold him, I love him.

"That made your mother's kind look weak. Volturi?" He puffed, "got nothing on me." Causing all of us to laugh.

"Attack! Attack!" A warrior told through the mind link and we four stared at one another. *"Rogues! Kevin!"* The three boys that surrounded me had vanished in an instant, I wanted to fight but I didn't have my hood to cover my face. I had to go home first, but I could always go as the king's personal guard but then I'd have to shift and I think it would be clearer if they saw a blood red wolf it'd be their princess, I have to go home.

"Yes, you're going home and you'll stay there and wait for me, Katherine." Alec said through mind link.

I'm not going through this again. I can't go back home, I'd take more time. I might as well use my powers to good use, conjuring up my hood would be easy as pie. After what happened last time I'm never letting Alec alone ever again, same goes for Isaac. I closed my eyes and bowed my head to cast a spell and when I opened my eyes my face was already covered by my hood and I was standing in front of the pack's house where the attack was happening.

"Katherine." I heard a whisper of my name, not sure who it belonged to. I counted the scents that surrounded me and there were around ten different scents covering me and I knew there was no dead end and so I did what I had to, I shifted.

Once I was already in my wolf form I was bigger than the wolves in front of me, each one of them growled at me showing no fear. I stared at the one directly in front of me, I tilled my head and he followed, then I jumped at him and attacked. While in the process around two to three wolves were already biting on me. I took out two at once, my fur covered in blood, the wounds had already healed and so I kept fighting.

The fight was over and my father shifted back into his human form. One of the women had given him a pair of shorts which he put on and I walked to his side still in wolf form, Alec and Isaac walked to my side.

"Shift." My father said in all his authority and every wolf shifted except for me, "Where is Kevin?" My father asked but no one replied.

A man walked up to my father and bowed his head, "King, I am Alpha Daniel from this pack, Full Moon pack. Thank you for coming, thank you too, Princess." I nodded my wolf's head and a woman walked to the alpha's side with clothes, "This is my Luna. She has brought clothes for you, Princess." I shook my head before closing my eyes and bowing my head.

I cast a little spell, just as I shifted back into my human form all the leaves flew over to me covering my body changing into the clothes and my hood I wore earlier that had ripped when I shifted.

"Thanks, Alpha. Luna, but I'm fine," I said sweetly before running to Alec putting my hand over his waist. "Are you alright?" I asked and he nodded before planting a kiss on my forehead.

"Alpha, where is Kevin? The leader of the rogues that attacked, has he been killed?" My father asked again and this time the Alpha replied, "I'm sorry but no my king, I heard that he has a scar on his right eye, this Kevin. I was holding off a few rogues when I saw a grey wolf with a scar on his eye flee as you came."

"Damn it!" My father cursed and I went to him and put a hand over his shoulder.

"It's alright father we will be ready next time, now that we know he is still alive and finally here, we could now think about your next step. Let's go home and let the men rest and the pack too, they must be tired."

My father nodded and shifted back to his wolf form and my men too shifted and ran with my father, Alec and Isaac shifted and were waiting for me to do the same. "Alec, can I ride with you, love?" He growled at first but then nodded and I went to lick his wolf before climbing on his back and ran home.

❧ CHAPTER TWENTY ONE ❧

*'Yes, it was love at first sight. I feel
that after all these years, I have
finally found my soul mate.'*
—Barbara Hershey.

"Beautiful?" Isaac popped his head in my room while I was just getting dressed. "Oh sorry," he muttered before closing the door and walking away but I spoke before he could go far.

"It's alright Isaac come back in, it's not as if you've never seen me naked." I called out and in seconds his head popped in again, followed by his body.

"What is it, Isaac?" He looked as if he had something very important to say.

"Your father is in the library, he is planning on what to do about Kevin. Alec is there too, it's only going to be four of us, we were just waiting for you."

"Alright, I'm dressed now, let's walk together." I smiled before grabbing his arm and tugging him with me to the library.

Isaac knocked on the door and we waited for my father to answer before going in, hand in hand, causing Alec to growl. I giggled and let go of Isaac then walked over to my father to give him a kiss before making my way to Alec. I sat on his lap to calm his wolf.

"So, father. What is the plan?" I asked, I wanted this finished just the second I set foot in here, I was terribly hungry. "Come on father, I'm sure you've already thought of one or maybe a dozen. How about your plan before this happened? The one you made a few years back? Or the ones you made while obsessing Kevin for six years."

"Well if you want to use that idea then we will, I will send half the guard to protect the two closest pack that is next to the one that got attacked." My father said angrily.

He was still pissed because of the attack yesterday, we had all slacked off and thought Kevin would attack the last pack at California first before coming here, how sure my father was that he would attack the same way he did.

"If I may father, but how sure are you, that he is going to attack the way he did back in California? I think he knows that you know that he would go to the nearest pack. If this Kevin has attacked dozens of the pack and is still alive, then he is freaking good at planning things. He didn't go into hiding for six years for nothing, father. He has a plan, he called us out last night, there is something more to it than just attacking packs and wanting to be known. I can feel it, why would a freaking rogue go crazy like this?" I said while trying to stand but Alec's grip on me was strong. I couldn't decide if it was romantic that he wanted me near him or annoying for being clinging but Hye! I love him.

"That's the thing, Princess. I don't know, that's why you're here. You always think of a great plan, if we can't kill him, at least we can reduce the number of deaths," my father said sadly. He looked broken down, why wouldn't he be? He lost his people, he is after all a king. He feels the pain ten times more than the alpha would, for he loves his pack.

"Alright. How about this? We pack up half of our men and leave about two to three men in one pack, with at least two or three of our men they would have more chances of living, like come on! One of our men could hold off ten rogues, so with three they could hold about thirty more. So what do you think Father?" I said not even sure with my plan but I knew it was better than leaving half a pack in only two packs when Kevin could attack another pack.

"And you know if there is an attack then our men could contact us, also they could get more help from our men from the nearby peaks." I added and I saw my father really thought about it.

"That is a great idea." He finally smiled, pleased with me, "Isaac, wrap up our men and we will leave in an hour. How many packs are here? Twenty?" My father asked.

"Forty, sir." Isaac corrected him.

"Well, then three times forty is one hundred and twenty, that is like one tenth of our men, wrap up an extra twenty and we will leave five men to packs that are really weak and only three to packs with great fighters," my father said and Isaac stood and nodded before exiting, Alec and me following behind him.

"Are we going with my father, love?" I asked Alec who was watching the children play. I sat on his lap and laid my head on his shoulders.

"Only if you want to, darling. I think it's time to introduce you to the world. Not as the princess, of course you know what I mean, and the men would be grateful to have their princess send them off."

"Do you think our boys are ready for this?"

"Without a doubt, Katherine."

"Alright then, I guess I am going to have to take a shower, they'll be leaving in half an hour." I said sweetly as I tugged Alec up the stairs with me.

"Don't leave without me, alright?" He nodded.

"Just make it quick, alright Katherine? One thing I never understand, is why girls take forever in the shower." I giggled at his crazy talk before tip toeing to kiss his lips, "It's the hair, Alec." I gave the crazy 'you know what I mean' look, "the hair." I repeated wiggling my brows making him laugh.

After taking a shower, Alec and I met up with Isaac and my father as well as the one hundred and forty men on the field. It made me proud seeing that half of my team volunteered for this.

"Alright, men!" My father spoke, ready to give instructions on what to do. "I hope you all have been packed for months now, not just days. OK, so three men will be left at each pack with good fighters and five will be left at weaker packs. Who will choose which pack you men go to will be Katherine. Your princess will be going and will be introduced as my personal warrior and her rank is higher than any of yours, but lower than the princess, she will be known as Katherine Jane Smith, the name she uses for school in case we happen to meet any of Katherine's school mates and we wouldn't want to complicate things. So, is everything clear?" My father asked.

"Yes!" They all answered at once, my men are strong, all of them and I am proud of them.

"Princess, what do you think, should we go from pack to pack together?" My father asked and I was still thinking I wanted this to be fast.

"How about you take seventy men and head west and I'll take the other half and head east and then meet up, how about that?" My father nodded as to say yes.

"Alright then, Isaac, babe let's move. Seventy of you now follow me, I want groups of three and five so that I'll explain the situation to the alpha and leave you there at once. I don't have to choose, I want you to choose for yourself so that you feel comfortable fighting alongside your team. I'll only take seventy with me so hurry up and pair and meet us at the gate." I said with all authority and ran with Alec and Isaac by my side.

I was done with the east pack and now my men and I were running to meet up with my father at the Blood Moon pack, known as the strongest pack here. My father was still two packs away from them so by the time we reached them they would just be arriving.

My men they were running really slow, I mean slower than me what do I expect, flash?

⟪⟪⟪ |BALTHAZAR| ⟫⟫⟫⟫

We finally arrived at the Blood Moon pack, I was supposed to meet with my daughter here, but maybe her men were slowing her down, after this will be down to two more packs.

When I arrived the elders all came up to me and greeted me with respect, can't say the same for the young, they fear me and that makes me sad. I am their king they shouldn't fear me.

"Who is the Alpha here? I have business to discuss with him." I spoke out loud and waited for someone to reply, finally after minutes the lights lit up to what I presumed to be the pack house, a man in his late forties came out with a young man and a girl, I knew the girl but I could put my finger to it till I saw the young man.

"Uriel," I murmured only for my ears to hear. He isn't a human after all, the little mutt! I growled and the people took one step back. The man in his forties came up to me.

"I'm Alpha Raphael, my king. Alpha of the Blood Moon pack." He bowed and I continued to growl of the sight of Uriel.

I could already smell the scent of Alec and Isaac meaning my daughter was near, I better prepare for the worst then.

"The Rogue Kevin has finally attacked and so I'm leaving three of my men here since this is a great pack, I only leave five at weaker packs. You will welcome them for they will protect your pack, don't forget where you all stand and that is below my men." I tried to talk as fast as I could, that I hadn't realized I was being a real arse, only because Uriel belonged to this pack. I wanted this to wrap up before my daughter reached here. I nodded for three men to stay but it was too late.

I felt a chill that went behind me and I knew my darling girl had shimmered and had hidden behind me. After a few seconds two wolves came into view, Alec and Isaac I thought, then another three smaller wolf appeared. I nodded and they shifted.

"Mate!" I heard the word and a little growl and turned to see Uriel is now standing beside the alpha.

"What?" I murmured. Mate? But how can that be?

((((|ZADKIEL|)))))

The air smelled different all of a sudden and my wolf was going insane with the scent I could smell. Two huge wolves appeared from the dark, followed by another three smaller ones, none of them were female.

"Mate," I murmured and my wolf lets out a growl. I couldn't hold him in, the king turned to look at me and murmured something. I didn't know why but I think he was pissed with me, he looked so.

My wolf was bugging me to ask the king if they had a female with them and I gave up and asked.

"Do you have a female with you, my king?" I asked and bowed as of respect for speaking. The king took one step aside and a girl stood where he once stood and she was really pretty, with her red blood hair and her red blood lips. Her hair flowed down her back and had the kind of curls that didn't turn out to be a great mess but instead, her hair fell down her back like a mermaid's lock. Her eyes as beautiful as the moon above, just having her look at me, made my wolf go all kinds of crazy.

"Mate!" I spoke out loud this time, "Mine."

❧ Chapter Twenty Two ❧

*'The idea of a soul mate is beautiful and very
romantic to talk about it in a movie, or a
song, but in reality, I find it scary'*
—*Vanessa Parades*

"Mate," the one word sent shivers over my body. I could smell him, my mate and the worst isn't that Alec was standing on my right. The worst was that the voice of the guy who spoke almost sounded like Uriel. Uriel lives just near here, just a couple of houses away.

"Do you have a female with you, my king?" The man asked and my father took a couple of steps to the side revealing me behind him.

"Mate!" This time he spoke loudly and I looked up to face him. "Mine." He said and my heart broke.

"Uriel." I murmured his name. It was Uriel! I heard two growls one from my father and another from Alec.

The guy in front of me broke me but I won't show weakness, I should wrap this up since I don't think my father will, anytime soon.

"I want to know who the Alpha is," I spoke out loud.

"Watch it, Katherine. If I were you I'd speak with respect to our Alpha, you're not royalty." I turned to see Brandon, Uriel's cousin was the man who had just spoken.

"I think it's you who need to watch it, pup." I responded to him and he gave me a growl making me pissed. I walked over to him and had my hand on his throat strangling him, legs off the ground, gasping for air.

"I may not be royalty but still I am a warrior, and last I checked I'm in higher rank than you and your Alpha!" I hissed. He managed a glare I don't know how but he did, I glared back and let him go, "Now who is, Alpha?"

"Me," the man who stood beside Uriel spoke. "I'm Alpha Raphael." He bowed his head.

"Raphael?" I choked the word, "But that means—" I turned my head to search for Saraquel, who was standing beside Mike, her mate. Now I understand why she called him mate, Australian my arse. "Your Alpha female, Saraquel. Long time no see, I see Mike has finally been accepted into the family." I managed a little smile.

"And that makes you—" I turned back to Brandon, pointing at him, smirking. "Beta and still a lower rank than mine and your Alpha." I hissed to put him in his place, "And what, your future alpha, huh, Uriel?"

He chuckled and gave me a smirk, "You must have mistaken me for my twin brother I see, I'm Zadkiel. I'm older than Uriel and so I am future alpha and you babe are the future Luna." He winked and I glared at him.

"Really nice, Uriel. Change your name? Now that is a new low even for you! You're still the same Uriel, a bit taller, more muscular, I mean yeah your hair changed but your scent is still the same." I spat.

"You must be really pissed at my brother, I wonder what he did," he turned to Saraquel and she bowed her head.

"I'm not here to chat so," I turned to my men, "Three of you stay and we will be off," three men nodded and I was ready to walk away.

"Mine!" Uriel growled and was already in front of me blocking my way, "You're not going anywhere," he said possessively.

"Take a hint, pup. I don't want a mate especially a future alpha!" I hissed and walked around him but he grabbed my arm and turned me to face him.

"You are mine and you will stay, mate." He said in a possessive tone, his eyes already black from holding in his wolf.

I pulled my arm away. "Watch it! I am no normal warrior I am the king's personal guard and so being your mate!" I raised the tone of the word mate, "it's just sad, why? Because I have to lower my standards to you." I poked him in the chest causing him growl.

"I don't need a mate, because it will only weaken me!" I kept on poking and he kept growling, "I don't want a mate especially a son of an alpha, I'd rather die! And I especially don't want you, Uriel of all as a freaking mate! After the crap you put me through!" I poked him one last time and turned away from him. "Men, lets go."

"My king." The two words stopped me from walking and I turned to see the Alpha looking at my father, "May I have a word with you?"

My father nodded and they both walked away from earshot and I walked to Alec and hugged him, causing Uriel to growl. "He's my boyfriend, mutt." I said, causing Uriel to growl once more before shifting. Isaac and the other guards stood in front of me protectively as Alec pulled me closer to him. Brandon and Saraquel tried reasoning with Uriel to calm down.

Saraquel shot me a nasty to look as to say 'what the freak am I doing?' I pulled away from Alec and called out to her, "you know damn well, what he did to me, Saraquel. So don't give me that look."

(((((|BALTHAZAR|)))))

I walked with the Alpha till we were out of earshot even from my daughter and the alpha spoke.

"I see that you and your daughter have mistaken my eldest son with the youngest," he spoke calmly and I was shocked with what I'd heard.

"Is it that obvious alpha?" I said with a little laugh.

"Well I saw the way you looked at my son as if you were ready to kill him, the only way would a father look when his little girl has been hurt by a man, I've seen it in my father's eyes with my sisters and me with my only daughter. I guess it is her that Uriel left behind. You see, my king, Zadkiel is future alpha and has been away since he was ten for him to train just like me and just less than two years ago my other son Uriel had been accepted into the same academy. I forced him to go knowing that he was going to leave someone here but I didn't know at that time that it was your daughter, my princess. All I knew was that she was a human and wasn't his mate, even the more reason to go. This is the first time I've seen her." He spoke in a calm voice while I was freaking about him knowing about my daughter.

"I'm sorry for what Uriel did to her. It was my fault anyway, I forced him to leave because I thought the girl he was dating was just a human. Even human have mates, I reminded my son that when he refuses to leave and I was hoping that maybe you won't stop fate, she is a princess and my son is one of her mates and I know that this is a first. I've heard that her mate has always been warriors and my son is the first from outside of the royalty." I nodded as to say I understood, if only they knew that the only mate my daughter has ever loved was a rogue, "All I ask is that you leave Princess Katherine here as guard with two other men, she needs her mate. You yourself, my king, should know how much it pains to be away from your mate, but my son, he is only an alpha male, not royalty, he won't bear the pain."

"Alright, very well then I'll try and reason with her but you have to promise me that only you will know about Katherine until she decides to tell Zadkiel." The alpha nodded and we made our way back to the pack.

((((|KATHERINE|)))))

I could smell the scent of my father and the alpha near, Brandon had already gotten Uriel to calm down. Once my father was in eyesight I left Alec's side and went to my father's.

"Alright, Katherine, Alec and Isaac, you three will be assigned here."

"What?" I yelled in shock then bowed my head. "I'm sorry, my king but I think I heard wrong." I spoke softly.

"Father, what the hell is going on?" I spoke through the mind link but he didn't respond.

"You heard me, warrior. You and your men will be assigned here."

"But my king, I am your warrior, I fight beside you not them." I tried reasoning with him.

"Oh, father, I'm going to kill you, I can smell fear coming from you. Well you better be afraid, be very-very afraid." I hissed through mind link.

"But my men and I didn't pack for this!"

"Then Isaac will come home with me and pack both your belongings, don't argue with me, Katherine." He spoke in his alpha tone, trying to hide the smell of his fear, which made me want to smirk but knew it wasn't the right time.

"May we please speak in private, my king?" He nodded and we walked off.

Once we were out of earshot I finally screamed, "Are you insane? Did you hit your head on the way back or something? Why would you do that?"

He took a few steps away from me, knowing how I am when crossed, maybe reminding him of the time that he had the stake out with Alec and Isaac when I was with Uriel at the docks.

"Why, Princess? Why won't you stay? And saying that being with a future alpha is lowering your rank is unreasonable," he spoke with sadness and fear.

"I don't want to talk about it. It's just that it hurts to think about it, let's just go. I don't get why you want me here, years ago you hate his guts, you hated him because I tried to kill myself. You were ready to bite his heart out every time I mentioned his name even before we even dated, you know what? It's funny how you hate him more than Lucas and still there he is breathing the same air as I am." I gave a fake laugh before turning and walked back but my father halted me by grabbing my arm.

"You of all people, Katherine, should know that you can't mess with fate and this boy has been given to you by fate." He held both my cheeks up to look at him.

"I don't get it, father, I just don't. Two years ago, he was human. Werewolves that haven't shifted when they met their mates, they shift early but he only shifted when he turned eighteen."

"He is not Uriel, Princess. You know you can tell me anything, there is nothing to be ashamed of, why won't you want him as a mate?" He spoke in a sweet tone which made the tears start coming up, but how could he say that he wasn't Uriel, he looks and reeks of him.

"Oh, father, have you ever thought why you don't have any grandchildren yet?"

"I have, I have been meaning to talk to you about that but it has always crossed my mind. At first I used to think that it was because you couldn't accept your other mates the way you accepted Lucas, there's Benjamin, you two had a thing but nothing more. Victor was your best friend plus he was married and Dylan that guy is just so uptight, nothing could ever happen there, so yeah."

"I want kids, Lucas wanted kids." I replied and sighed before continuing. "We've tried lots of times but I just couldn't get pregnant and that is one reason why I don't want an alpha as a mate, I'd rather have an omega as a mate, hell I already had a rogue as a mate."

"But why?" He asked in confusion.

"Because when you're a warrior, they don't expect you to have an heir, except for the Fox and Zink of course and same goes for rogues and omega and beta but alphas? They need a child to keep the family going and me being this future alpha's mate, they will expect a child from me. One that I cannot bear and then what will happen to the pack? Even if another alpha claims it they still won't have the purity and right of the pack. I'd rather hurt and not have that man, than being with him and not being able to give him a child, with me rejecting him, he could find another she wolf."

"I-I never knew that. The alpha, he knows who you really are and maybe you could explain it to him, maybe one day if you trust your mate you will tell him the truth too and he will understand, but for now you have to try alright? You might not need him, but he is just an alpha, Katherine. Not a royal, he won't bear the pain of being away from his mate." I nodded and we walked back to the pack.

"Alright, my men and I will be leaving now. Isaac you will follow us back to the mansion to gather the belongings of Katherine and Alec." My father said once we were back with the pack. Isaac nodded and walked with my father as I walked to Alec causing Uriel to growl, the alpha bowed his head at my father and his pack followed and then they were gone, my father and his men were gone.

⚜ CHAPTER TWENTY THREE ⚜

'Let's care for the ones that we love.'
                              —Anonymous.

There was a shed in front of the pack's house, I jumped onto the roof of the shed and mind linked for Alec to come up with me. I looked back down to the Alpha who was looking at me in confusion, "Alec and I will guard from here, you and your pack may go to bed."

"What? No!" Uriel spoke up, "You are going to bed with me, mate!"

He growled and I glared, "Keep dreaming, pup. Alec is my boyfriend and I will be with him and not with you." I turned my back on him but he still spoke.

"You can't, your wolf will find for me, your wolf won't let you sleep till you're next to me."

"We'll see about that, Uriel." I glared and he chuckled.

"I'm Zadkiel, stop calling me Uriel! He is at the academy at this moment and he is not your mate, I am!" Wow he really sounds pissed, twin wolves have the same everything except scent but he smelled exactly like Uriel so there is no way I am getting fooled.

"I just can't believe it. I've known both you and Sara for years and I have never heard of a big brother, Zadkiel."

"Well, I guess you have no choice but to, mate. Because I am your mate, so I'll be seeing you in bed in five." He walked away with much confidence but I guess I'll have the last laugh. I sat beside Alec on the roof as we waited for Isaac, I fell asleep on his shoulders.

My wolf didn't bug me, she was used to being with Alec. I'm sure that the little mate of mine is waiting for me. I still don't get how Uriel can be my mate, I don't get how all of a sudden all this crap is being hurled at me. I played nice, I played by the rules and now what? As usual fate, changes the game routine every single time I got good at it. When I wanted him I couldn't have him, now that I have him, I couldn't accept him. Wait—*'hell no'* I cursed in my head, could this be what Lucas really meant? *Accept him even when it hurts?'*

The next day I woke up, in the arms of Alec. He was lying beside me with my head on his chest as he wrapped his arms around me. Isaac was standing just on the edge of the roof, dangling his legs at the end, I guess he must be on patrol. I got up and turned to the direction from where I heard a growl, to see Zadkiel on the balcony looking right at me, I glared at him.

I walked to Isaac, I didn't want to speak loudly. I wanted Alec to take his rest. "Isaac, when did you get here?" He took a look at his watch it was five in the morning.

"Around two hours ago, beautiful." I smiled at him.

"I can stand guard. You can take your rest with Alec, I'll lend you his chest." I chuckled as he made a face.

"Alright, beautiful. Wake me up if something happens." I nodded and turned to see Zadkiel still looking at me, I smiled at him as I blew him a flying kiss before jumping off the roof and landed on the ground. I walked away from the pack house, I was on patrol and so I had to check the whole land.

I got back three hours from the time I left, I didn't run or shimmer I just wanted to walk. When I got back, I saw Alec walking towards me looking pissed, he hugged me tight to his body, almost cutting my circulations. "Wow, baby where's the fire?" I joked.

"Where have you been? I woke up and you weren't there. I only saw Isaac, I woke him up and he said that you went to patrol. I almost tore the whole pack looking for you. Isaac had to get the Alpha to chain me if I didn't hold it in, can't say the same for your mate, though."

I looked at him confused, what did he mean about Uriel? "He is in his room, chained to the bed with silver. His wolf is going crazy looking for you, I think you need to see him," he said sadly. I knew he didn't want me to go see him, but it was the right thing to do, but I didn't want to hurt him.

"Would you come with me?" He shook his head.

"I think his wolf will go crazier, seeing his mate with another male wolf." I frowned and sighed before nodding and walking towards the house.

I knew which room to go to from the growls, I knew it was Uriel. My wolf was howling inside, knowing her mate was hurt. I opened the door, to see Uriel chained to the bed, his wrists were wounded by the silver that touched his skin. I remembered a few centuries ago, I asked one of my men what it felt like to touch silver, since it never did affect me not even a little when I touched it, they would say that it felt like acid going through your body but then again acid never did have an effect on me as well. Saraquel was standing beside her father, at the side of his bed.

"Can I talk to him? Alone?" The alpha nodded, taking Saraquel out with him. I sat on the bed and looked at him, my mate, I didn't want him. Why an Alpha? I'd rather have an omega, he needs an heir, something I can never give. I touched his bare chest, and his wolf purred.

"I'll give you a kiss if you calm your wolf, Uriel." He growled at me, seriously. Does he think I'd be stupid to think he is really a guy name Zadkiel? "Seriously? I am the one that is forced to kiss you and you're the one growling?" I said annoyed but smiled at him as his deep breathing finally subsided.

"Good," I leaned in to kiss him on his cheeks. His scent was nice, I haven't smelled a scent this nice since he left, I didn't realize I was already kissing him on his neck and licking him, until he let out a moan.

"Oh, sorry I got carried away," I looked away from him because I felt my cheeks blushed.

"Can you take the chains out now? My wolf wants me to hold you, Katherine." I looked at him.

"I will let the chains off but I wouldn't let you hold me."

He growled but I didn't care, I took the chains off with gloves. The silver wouldn't hurt me but I needed him to believe that it did. I opened the drawer and took out a shirt, I sat back on the bed with him, and I held his hand and licked on the wounds that were made by the silver. When a mate licks on wounds, the wounds heal faster, after they were healed I put his shirt on for him.

"Where did you go? I thought you were only going for a little walk and I didn't want to be clingy, but when you were gone for hours, my wolf just went nuts, and I need to find you. My wolf needs you beside him and I need you," he spoke weakly. He had circles under his eyes, I didn't notice them earlier.

"Did you get any sleep last night?" He shook his head.

"Well, I slept like a baby," I smirked at him weakly.

"Yeah, I know. I watched over you, it was kind of hard, with the mutt's hand over you," he managed to spit out.

"That mutt, is my boyfriend. Don't look down on him, he is a warrior and can take you out in a heartbeat."

"Whatever," he murmured. "I'm going away for a few days, I have something to do. You can stay here on my bed,

minus your two tails, I don't want their scent in this room."
It really hurt me, knowing he was going away.

"Don't worry, I won't be sleeping here because where
I go, my two tails follow me. You should be lucky there
are two instead of one so you would know that I'm not
doing anything, but then again, threesome kind of sounds
fantastic." I smiled at him as I fluttered my eyelashes,
he just returned it with a growl and I think he even
whispered, "Mine."

"When are you leaving?" I had to ask, my wolf needs
to know. Besides if he was leaving I want to leave too, I
need to talk to Lucas again. I need answers to my million
of questions.

"Tonight," he answered and my wolf howled.

"Tonight? I guess you haven't changed a bit, huh?
Always waiting for the last minute to tell me things.
Where are you going?" I waited for an answer. Some
people just never change I guess, when he left me years ago
he told me on the same day and now he is leaving again for
the freaking same day, freaking unbelievable.

"To the east, my father is going to meet with another
pack and wants me there. The daughter of the pack is really
smoking." I didn't realize I had growled at his words until I
saw the smirk on his face, I glared at him.

I got up and walked to the door, "Well, have fun. Your
father has always been going to all this trip since before,
the reason why I've never seen him before. I would be
shocked if I even bump into him while my stay here. Oh!
And I thought of going back home for a while, ever since I
spoke of a threesome, I think it's now stuck in my head. I'd

THE ALPHA OF MY EYE

send another three men to replace my post and Alec's and Isaac's as well." I smirked as he growled.

I was ready to sprint out with the last laugh but he caught me, he sniffed my neck taking in my scent before whispering to my ears, "Mine! Warriors or not, I'll rip out their heads if they touch you."

"Charming, but you'd be dead before you could even attempt that with Alec, he is a Fox, A.K.A fastest wolf alive." After me and my father of course. "So don't try your luck, you may have gotten out without a scratch from what you did two years ago but not this time." Before he could protest I got out of his grip and went into the hallway.

❧ CHAPTER TWENTY FOUR ❧

'Love cannot save you from your own fate.'
—Jim Morrison.

I watched as three black hummers drove away from the pack house, the farther they drove, the more my wolf whimpered. I took out my phone from my pocket and started to dial the number to the service line of the Auckland Airport.

"Hello, Auckland Airport service line. How may I help you?"

"Hello, I need a ticket for Italy today, back and forth."

"The next flight to Italy is in two hours."

"Alright I'll pick it up at the counter, name it under Katherine Rose Claw."

"Yes madam. Thank you for calling, hope to see you shortly." I cut the line and shove the phone back to my pocket I turned to see Alec with Isaac standing beside, I walked over to them, tiptoed to kiss Alec.

"One ticket to Italy? But there are three of us," he said waiting for me to explain.

"I have to go somewhere, Alec it is important." I replied hoping he wouldn't force to explain myself anymore.

"To the grave land?" Isaac asked, but how did he know?

"How did you know?" I asked in confusion, no normal wolf knows about it, and the only rogues that do know about it are the ones that have a death wish to think they could call me out by messing with the grave land, the reason why I got it protected.

"I read about it, in a book, Filia the title, it was in the mansion's library. A piece of land in Italy by the seaside on a cliff, home to one of the warriors, Lucas Sontoro, and also the first mate to Princess Katherine Rose Claw. After having her mate killed by her father out of anger, the princess buried her mate on the piece of land that was to be their home. Which is now called the grave land and it is to be where all her mates are to be buried." He retold me what he could recall from the book he read from, I knew it, the book I knew it very well, I felt tears coming up because of Isaac but I held it in.

"How could I forget? The great Isaac Zink. A book nerd." I joked as I faked a laugh. "I have to go pack a few shirts, my plane leaves in two hours. I'll be back in five days, excuse me." I walked away from them with a smile on my face but as I packed tears streamed down like a river.

I arrived the grave land in two days, I had to rest when I got off the plane, the ride was killing, my back ached from sitting. It was a few more miles, I decided to walk than to shimmer, as I got close I saw that there were a few people just inches away from the barrier of the force field.

The five girls were chanting words I could put a finger to, they were witches, it boiled my blood at the thought of these stupid witches thinking they were strong enough to break the barrier. I shimmered to the one in the middle.

And had her by her throat, my fangs were showing, eyes were glowing red at my anger towards them. "Who the hell are you?" I hissed.

"Princess!" Someone called, I turned to see Adaka with two more witches with her.

"What is the meaning of this, Adaka? Why are you and your coven here?" I growled really pissed, I could rip out all their heads right now.

"We found rogues roaming around here a week ago, I called out my coven to come here and help me strengthened the forced field that you already had here."

"But the spell they were chanting was to break the force field."

"Yes, we were trying to break it to make a stronger one."

"You don't have to, Adaka. The protection I made here is very powerful, even if you have a million witches, you can't break the barrier. I got the most powerful witch to put the barrier here." I heard them gasped in shocked.

"You mean?" She didn't finish her sentence I knew what she was saying, I nodded and replied, "Yes, I got Daisy Goodwood. The first true witch ever born, to put up the protection around here, you don't have to worry, you will only tire yourselves trying to break it down." Not like other witches like me and Adaka. Daisy Goodwood was born with magic, whereas like other witches they studied and master magic. "You may leave now, Adaka. I want to visit this place alone." She nodded and I waited as her coven wrapped up and I made sure they were gone before I went through the barrier.

I walked straight to the end of the cliff and sat down like the last time I was here, the wind blew in my face, "Lucas." I whispered as I close my eyes, "Come to me, I need you." I didn't keep my hopes high though in case he didn't show up.

He was the one that came to me, not me for him, well yeah technically I came to him but I wasn't expecting to see him, like really see him and talk to him. When I opened my eyes I felt a presence behind me, I turned and there he was standing behind me, I patted on the ground beside me for him to sit.

"Are you going to explain? Or are you going to wait for me to burst a tantrum?" I said calmly. He kept silent, "was that what you meant? Uriel? Did you mean accept Uriel?" He shook his head, "So what do you mean Lucas?"

"I can't tell you, mate. I've said too much the last time." Was all he said making me red with anger, I stood up and stomped away but stopped midway and turned to scream at him, "you know what? Lucas? Yes! You said too much the last time. If you didn't ask me to accept him." I raised my finger and made a quotation mark on the word him, "I wouldn't have accepted Uriel and if I didn't accept Uriel and just kept my head low, I wouldn't have to settle for Alec and now here I am, in a freaking grave land, talking to my dead mate! Talking to the only freaking guy I could ever really freaking truly love!" I hissed and threw my hand in the air with frustration.

"Accept him even when it hurts," I quoted him. "Well, screw you!" I pointed at him, "screw life! And freaking screw fate!" I shook my head, "I am done, Lucas. But loving you! Accepting you! Fighting for you! And wanting a life with you, a family, a home! That is the only thing I can never!" I sighed, "Never! Regret even if I want to."

"But this?" I motioned everything around me. "Them?" I pointed at my mates' graves, "They are not worth me feeling pain for them, they deserve better. Alec, Isaac, Uriel they all deserve better than me, I am particularly known as the girl that fate screwed over with, millions of times for centuries, and people that get involved with me apparently get screwed over as well." I turned and stomped away.

"You know what, mate?" Lucas called to me, causing me to stop in place. "You've passed the barrier, mate. If I pass it, you wouldn't be able to see me. Outside my grave land, I'd be as invisible as air, now come back and we'll talk." I turned around, to see that I have been just inches from him. He was right at the barrier and so was me, our lips practically touching if only we could feel each other. "Come back in, mate." I nodded and took a step the same time he took a step backward.

"When I first met you, you were young and fragile." He smiled and we walked side by side back to the edge of the cliff. "You didn't know how to fight well, you didn't know how to get mad, you couldn't even kill a fly."

I smiled as I remember how I used to be, "When I died, you changed. You finally felt anger, hate, everything, you started killing. But then you sobered up, you got your life together, fate didn't screw you, mate. Fate screwed me, because of me you got hurt, you felt things you've never felt. I screwed life, with my family and with you. Fate was generous enough to give you another chance with Benjamin but because you were so hurt by me, you screwed things for yourself as well."

"I want you to fight, Katherine. I need you to fight. Fate gives tasks to us, even more difficult task for people who are destined for greatness. Fate doesn't have to always win, you should know that, you're not the first that crossed fate, Katherine. But you can be the first creature to win against fate, because you have something everyone loses every time fate screwed them over. Do you know what it is, mate?" I shook my head. "Hope."

"I don't have hope, Lucas. I don't even have love by my side." I sighed.

"When you pulled your crap together, mate. That alone was hoping that everything will be alright. When Benjamin taught you to fight, that was hope to be stronger one day. When you were green with envy towards Victor and his wife that was hoping that you would be loved again. You don't only have hope for yourself, Katherine. That's what makes you strong, you have hope for others too, like your parents, Alec and Isaac, the men you've been training."

I need to think, I need to go back and think everything through. I closed my eyes and tiptoed to kiss him, but all I kissed was the thin air, he managed a smile at my attempt.

"I have to go now, Lucas." I walked away but again Lucas stopped me when he called out, "Accept him, mate. Even when it hurts." I smiled and turned, "In time, Lucas. In time. Like I always say, my love doesn't come cheap and it certainly doesn't come easy." I winked and shimmered away.

◈ CHAPTER TWENTY FIVE ◈

'The nicest thing for me is sleep
then at least I can dream.'
—Marilyn Monroe.

The week passed like a summer day, I am getting weaker without Uriel. My body is too weak to even move now, I couldn't imagine how he would be like, worst than me for sure.

Alec has taken care of me when I got back from the grave land, I really cared for him and I am scared to hurt him, me leaving him for Uriel is just not fair.

Three black hummers came up the driveway, and I could smell his scent, it was eleven in the evening. My wolf was going crazy in me as the car drove closer. I was in the arms of Alec at the moment, and got off as the door of the vehicle opened and the alpha got out followed by Uriel. I looked down at him with a smile as he looked up at me, my wolf was screaming for me to go to him but I couldn't. He did look worse than me but it looked like he could cover it better than me.

Alec walked to my side, "I think you should sleep with him tonight." I looked at him in shock and gave him a punch on the shoulder.

"I meant just sleep in a bed with him not sex, damn baby! For a girl that is going through depression, you are still one strong wolf." I glared at his joke. "Your wolf needs her mate, love. You can't keep her back, or she will die." I glared again.

"Don't forget, baby. I am no ordinary wolf, my wolf is strong and can live, with you by our side, love." I gave him a kiss.

"Katherine." I was getting frustrated. I didn't need pressure from him.

"What, love?" He just stared at me and I knew what I had to do. "Fine, give me a kiss and I'll go." He gave me a peck and I was ready to go but Alec spoke out again.

"Tomorrow, when you and Zadkicl get enough sleep I am going to round the land and I want you with me, we need to talk about this." I nodded and went to the house.

"You mean Uriel," he nodded. It was late and I thought that everybody would be sleeping but I was wrong. As I was sneaking into Uriel's room, the alpha spotted me and I knew I was busted.

"Come here a moment, princess. I want to have a word." I nodded and walked into the kitchen and sat on the chair opposite to the alpha.

226

"I know you are tired, princess," he spoke but before he could continue I cut him.

"Please call me, Katherine. I'm not used to being called princess. Only Isaac ever called me that other than my father and he is still living only because he still hasn't reproduced." I even joked when I was really weak.

"Alright Katherine, my son isn't in good shape right now and he needs you. I know you are only here for the washroom but you being here, making your scent much stronger for him, is tempting him more to kill himself for not having you near him. I know your wolf can live without Zadkiel's but Zadkiel can't, please stay with him tonight, to heal his wolf and yours. I don't like Alec and it is only because of Zadkiel." I glared at him.

"So I suppose you won't like Uriel as well, since you know, wait—I still don't get why you keep calling him Zadkiel. It's obvious that he is Uriel, I'd know if you have another son, I've known Sara for like forever. But ok fine, how about this? Let's say he is really Zadkiel and Uriel is in the academy, even if he looks exactly like Uriel as also reeks of him and also has the exact shade of blue eyes, does he know?"

He shook his head, "The twins aren't fond of each other since my mate passed and Zadkiel might kill his brother for your past." I nodded. "And how sure are you that his eyes are blue? Because last I checked, they were grey."

Grey? Well I haven't noticed them but I remember very well that Uriel's were blue, "I am really sleepy, I'll go to him now." He nodded and I got off the chair. "Wait, when I was with Uriel, he lived in another house, why is that?"

"It's actually an empty house for new pack members who already have a family. My son and Saraquel weren't close with me so they chose to live there." I nodded and went back to go to Uriel.

Wait, I remember the photo, the photo of Uriel and an image of him. I thought it was Photoshop but what if it was real? If Uriel is really at the academy and Zadkiel is really Zadkiel, then, Zadkiel will only end up hurt. "Damn it, Lucas!" I cursed.

I opened the door slowly hoping he would still be asleep, the room was dark and I felt my way to the bed. A sudden cough caused me to jump, I thought he was asleep. "You're awake?" I asked.

"Yes," he answered. "What are you doing here?" He asked me.

"I'm not feeling well and if I feel this crappy, I know you would feel crappier and my wolf won't stop bugging me."

"Oh," he spoke weakly, "So you're only here to see if I was alright?"

I was going to nod but it was dark and almost made myself feel stupid but then again he has been in this dark room longer than I have, his vision must have already adjusted but then again there's no harm in answering, "Yes." He coughed again. "Zadkiel?" He hummed as to say yes. "Can I sleep with you tonight?" I finally got to the bed and sat on the edge.

"Please do." I felt him make space for me and I lay with him, as I went under the covers.

But he didn't touch me, it was a king size bed and so he had enough space not to come into contact with me but I didn't know why I wanted him to touch me. "Good night, Katherine." He spoke again.

"Zadkiel, can you hold me please?"

"Is this a dream? I've always dreamt of holding you." I smiled at his words.

"No, it's not a dream. Can you hold me?" He came closer to me and wrapped his arms around me. I could hear his wolf purred and I kissed his neck.

"Good night, Zadkiel. Please be here when I wake up," I felt his head nodded and I was out.

I woke up four times, thanks to his snoring and every time I had to kiss his lips to shut him up, the snoring stops for a couple of minutes before sounding back up. I knew his wolf was awake and it was he, who stopped Zadkiel's snoring to help me and my wolf sleep.

It was three in the morning and I just wanted to sleep. He was sleeping in peace with me in his arms but I wasn't with his snoring. I got out of his hug and turned him slowly to lay him straight and I got on top of him, not giving all my weight though, I started rubbing his thighs as I kissed his neck and jaw.

His wolf was purring and he got too excited. I stayed like that for a while and he started moaning and I knew that he was half asleep and half awake, it made me smirk as he tried to force himself to wake up. "Are you awake, Zadkiel?" I whispered softly in his ears, he nodded his head. "Did you have a nice sleep, love?" I whispered and licked his neck more and he moaned.

"Yes." I patted him hard on his chest till he was really awake.

"Good, now let me sleep."

I got off him and he growled, "Can you just sleep like that?" He asked.

"Like what, on top of you? But your branch is sticking out." I know he was blushing even if I couldn't see it. "How about this, if you stop snoring and let me sleep? I'll sleep on top of you, since your wolf clearly loves it."

"I snore?" He asked and I could hear the confusion in his voice "Yes! Like a freaking pig! You woke me up three times and I had to kiss you to get your wolf to shut you up. I need sleep, so please."

He murmured "Alright," and I got back on him and lay on his chest, his chest was vibrating.

❧ CHAPTER TWENTY SIX ❧

*'Friendship is a single soul
dwelling in two bodies.'*

—Aristotle.

I woke still on top of Zadkiel, with his arms wrapped around me. I don't know why but I liked it, having to wake up in the morning and seeing him first before others, just like before when I slept over. I felt a rush of déjà vo with a hint of sadness. It was my turn to make the round, I searched for a clock to know the time. It was two in the afternoon so I got out of bed.

I opened the door soundlessly, I didn't want to wake Zadkiel up. He needed rest more than I do since he is a normal alpha wolf and I am a royal. I finally got my full strength back.

I bumped into Saraquel on the way out, "Katherine, good morning, did you have a nice sleep?" I nodded and tried to go to the front door again.

"I'm going for a walk, would you like to join?" This time I turned to her and smiled, "And if you heard giggles last night, it wasn't me. It was all Zadkiel's snoring, you can take out that butcher knife if you want to? I don't mind." I raised my hands up in defeat as I smirked at the memory, it has been two years.

"I've missed you, Katherine. I didn't know about my brother leaving till the minute he left. I knew you might have hated me, I kind of noticed that when you didn't call me the minute you left him at the beach, and then you started not coming to school. At first I thought you weren't feeling well, then I thought you were avoiding me. I tried going to your house but there wasn't anyone there, I figured that you transferred to another school and you moved house."

I was saddened by her words, I can't believe she thought I hated her. I was just trying to heal my heart. "Saraquel, I didn't know you felt that way. Yes I was hurt by your brother. Yes I wanted to heal, it didn't take a day or a week, I loved your brother. He was like my first love, and so the pain I felt was ten times more and I know a mate rejecting me would be a hundred times painful but I hadn't met my mate at the time. It took months to heal, even with Alec beside me, I thought of your brother. I didn't transfer school, I shifted in a young age when I was going through my healing heart. I was weak and my wolf wanted to be strong, so I shifted at a young age and I didn't want to go to school, instead I went to join the royal guards. Balthazar, he saw my strength, and at the time he was looking for a personal guard when his daughter went to live with her mother. I didn't hate you, Saraquel and I didn't blame you for what your brother did to me."

She was crying and I did what I thought was right, I pulled her for a hug to calm her down. "So where is that Australian mate of yours, huh? Mate." I emphasized the mate hoping she remembers what excuse she made at the mini zoo.

She giggled and just seconds after that, a loud sound of a door being ripped open, somewhere in the second or third floor could be heard. I let go of Saraquel and we both stared at the stairs to see who would be coming, I was already in attack mood, but then there stood Zadkiel taking deep breaths, trying to hold his wolf. I went to him and put a hand on his chest.

"Calm down, Zadkiel, what are you so worked out about?" I kissed his cheeks and he calmed down.

"You weren't in bed when I woke up," his voice still sounded a bit mad.

"It's my time to do a round check on the grounds, it's two in the afternoon. I have to go, my men need me, I'm here to protect, not mingle." I said as I turned away from him and towards the door.

"Your men don't need you but I think your boyfriend does, and I don't want him on my land!" He growled.

And I just rolled my eyes and walked out, Alec and Isaac were on the roof. "Sorry, I know it's late and—" Alec silenced me with his lips to mine.

"Shh, it's alright, you have been weak, I guess you have your strength back?" I nodded. "Good, it wasn't nice having

Isaac here to sleep with," he jerked his head to Isaac which made me giggle.

"Have you eaten, love?"

He shook his head. "I was waiting for you to wake up," I smiled at him for being sweet.

"I'm hungry, can we go on one round check and eat?" He laughed.

"Isaac and I did the ground check for you, we could just go eat." He kissed my forehead and hugged me.

The hug wasn't long, thanks to a loud growl that was coming from the house. Alec let go of me and we turned to see Zadkiel at the front door taking in deep breaths again, his eyes weren't the usual baby blue but now glowing bright yellow.

"Alec, let go of her," Isaac whispered from behind, "He looks like he isn't going to hold his wolf any longer." He whispered again and this time Alec let go of me and took a few steps away too.

I just glared at Zadkiel for doing what he did, "Go inside, pup! You're ruining my mood." I hissed as I jumped from the roof, I was shocked when I didn't land on all two legs on the ground but in the arms of Zadkiel, he caught me.

And God, that turned me on. He caught me when I was falling like literally, this guy was insane. I glared at him and punched him once and he let go of me, leaving me to fall onto the ground, butt first. When I got on my feet, both Alec and Isaac were beside me, Alec growled and Zadkiel growled back and this time Isaac growled to, I glared at all three of them.

"Alec, darling—" I was cut off by Zadkiel's growl. I punched him once again on his shoulder, "Last night, you said you wanted to talk to me about something? We could go out for lunch and you could tell me what you wanted to say."

He nodded, "Alright, I'll go take a shower first, I reek of Zadkiel." I gave one last glare to Zadkiel before making my way to the bathroom and that moment I noticed that his eyes weren't the blue eyes I used to stare into years ago, but they were grey, smoky grey exactly like Lucas'.

We went to a nearby café for lunch, we couldn't go far, and leave Isaac to take care of things alone, he might be strong but he can't take out numerous rogues at a time. We sat opposite to each other, usually we would sit together and Isaac would sit opposite to us.

We ordered our food first, I could feel that what Alec wanted to talk about wasn't going to be good since he has been acting weird, the kind of weird Uriel acted when he was leaving me or was trying to break the news that he was going to leave me. The waitress took our order.

"Is something bothering you? You've been acting funny, is this about Zadkiel? I didn't want to go with him last night." I said in my defence.

He smiled and took my hand, "Katherine, you know I love you right?" I nodded. "I care for you and to tell you the truth, it hurt having to let you go with him last night. I didn't want too but it was the right thing to do. I was hoping that your wolf would be pleased to have me, but still it wasn't."

"Go on with it, Alec. I know what the consequence of this, of us are. We both know this is bound to happen, remember? We talked about it when you were still trying to get in my pants," he choked on his steak as I joked.

"Yes, babe. We do, and this is why we are having this talk."

"Go on then Alec. Say what you came here to say, I want to hear it. How you're going to let me go. I have to say it is hurting, my wolf is howling," I forced up a smile.

"Your wolf doesn't need me anymore, it needs Zadkiel and I don't want to take you away from him because it's not right. He is your mate and soon, I'll find mine too, I was hoping you'd find yours first before mine, I didn't want to leave you to be alone."

I smiled. "Thanks, Alec. But I'm not ready to accept him yet, when I look at him I think of Uriel, I love you Alec and I always will. I care for you as you care for me. I hope you find your mate soon." He nodded.

"I hope this doesn't change anything, you're still my best friend. You and Isaac, I want to help you both find your mates. Come on, we went to half the pack and none of you found your mates, maybe when we're done with Kevin we could go search at the other half of the pack." He nodded and gave me a smile.

I know Alec is hurting now, the drive back to the pack house was quiet. Alec had told me he would try and find his mate tomorrow while he patrols. When I said I would help him he said it would be best if he would go alone, so that his mate won't think differently. If his mate is here in this pack, I would understand why she hasn't shown up because I was his girlfriend.

I was tired and wanted to go to bed with Zadkiel or maybe just lay on his bed, his scent would be there. As I was walking to the house Zadkiel was just standing there looking at me as I walked closer, I think he just had his hair done.

I glared at him as I walk past him. "Katherine," I stopped.

The way he spoke my name it wasn't like the way Zadkiel spoke, it was more like, "Uriel." I murmured his name and turned to him in shock. His blue eyes, those baby blue eyes that I remember so well stared at me, "What are you looking at Zadkiel?" I glared. I knew he was Uriel but I had to act as if I didn't know or I might break down. "I'm tired and I want to rest, nice hair cut by the way." I turned and walked away as fast as I could.

It was Uriel, and he is back.

❧ CHAPTER TWENTY SEVEN ❧

'I'm back for only you.'
—*Anonymous.*

((((|URIEL|))))

I just arrived home, it has been two years. The flight back was exhausting and my wolf kept begging me to let it out, and now I'm going to have to shift and let it have its way. As I walked out the door, a girl was walking towards me. She looked familiar, so familiar it made my wolf beg more to be let out.

Oh no, I remembered her as she walked past me and I whispered her name, "Katherine."

It was Katherine, but what is she doing here? How does she know I live here? I heard her footsteps stop as I spoke her name, I turned to see her look at me.

She looked tired, she didn't look strong. I took a deep breath, taking in her scent. She was a she-wolf, I heard her murmur my name, "Uriel."

This time she looks really pissed, "What are you looking at Zadkiel?" She glared at me. Wait—did she just call me, Zadkiel? My wolf growled at the name she spoke. I knew that she knows that it was me and not my twin brother.

"I'm tired and I want to rest, nice hair cut by the way." She turned and walked into the house and I just stood there looking at her back.

((((|KATHERINE|))))

I was trying to hold myself from breaking down, seeing Uriel just seconds ago made me want to run to him and hug him like I used to. I opened the door to Zadkiel's room to find him naked! Wet! Butt Naked! He must have just finished showering.

I hadn't realized that I was staring deeply at him until he let out a cough, "My face is here, darling." He pointed to his face.

I looked at him, our eyes locked with each other, my cheeks were burning. God! Did I seriously just stare? I looked away from him, "Sorry, I ah—I I'm tired and I wanted to just take a nap, I had a long day with Alec. We decided to break things off."

"That just made my day, love." I glared at the little jerk.

"Well it's the worst for me, because the sex was great." His growl stopped me and left me smirking, it's always fun messing with an over possessive mate. Not that Benjamin or Dylan or even Victor was ever possessive of me.

"Don't worry, pup. I was just joking." I said but was so buried in my thoughts, "Only my mate is allowed to touch me, but Uriel came close." Wait! Crap! What did I just say?

"Come again, love? I thought I heard my brother's name," he growled. His eyes turning yellow once again. I opened the button to my pants and slipped out of it, just to stall him.

"It's a hot day." I opened my shirt next, leaving me with only a two piece. "I'm going to take a nap." This time he looked at me with lust, he was practically drooling.

I walked closer to him and licked his neck causing him to moan. "Too bad, you aren't a vampire. If you were I would drag you to bed with me, since vampires are cold blooded."

He sat on the bed beside me. I heard small growls coming from him. "You're so beautiful Katherine," I chuckled.

"Thanks I guess. Could you rub my back for a while?" He didn't answer he just did what I asked, "It's getting cold, Zadkiel. Could I lay down on you like last night?"

"Sure," he murmured. I moved to give him space to lie down and I got on top of him and laid my head on his chest, his chest was vibrating, trying to hold his wolf from taking over and claiming me, I soon snoozed off.

I woke up alone that evening. Zadkiel was gone, I didn't even know how he got me off of him without waking me, my legs and arse were covered by the blanket but my upper body was covered with his shirt, my scent was mixed with his. I put on his huge shirt and very short pants, that when I went to look myself in the mirror it looked as if I weren't wearing any shorts underneath.

I got out of the room and made my way down the stairs in my own little world and was hit back into earth when my face hit a very hard back that made me growl. I looked to see Zadkiel, or was it Uriel? God please let it be Zadkiel, I just can't deal with Uriel right now.

"Going into your own little world again, Katherine? You always have since before." I glared at him trying to make a joke.

"What are you talking about, Zad? You only know me for a couple of weeks but don't worry, pup. I'll be leaving once we catch Kevin and so you could have me stop bumping into things." I glared at him and walked away.

"He lets you call him, pup? Is that his shirt? Are you two dating?" Damn it, Uriel! You have so many questions, yet I'm so guilty to answer.

"So, many questions, Uriel, so little time. I have to go back to my men." I smiled and gave one last glare.

"So you do know that it's me," he said softly, almost like a whisper. I turned back to look at him with a frown across my face.

"Please let me leave this house without crying, Uriel, you owe me that much. It's hard enough having your brother as a mate, and harder with you being back, especially when I never really got over you and him being your twin. You don't know what it's like, waking up in the morning to see him but you're the one I think of, it isn't fair to him."

"Katherine, I—" I didn't want to hear him, it would only break me down so I ran out the door. Zadkiel was standing outside with a few pack members, he caught me but I shove him away and ran.

Alec and Isaac stopped me. "Beautiful, what's wrong?" Isaac asked worried about me.

"He is back, Isaac. Uriel is back, I need to go for a walk. Alone." They both nodded.

"Katherine, come back in an hour, or I'll bring hell." I nodded, I could hear footsteps coming closer from behind me, it could either be Uriel or Zadkiel. I didn't wait to find out, I ran first, once I was far enough, I shimmered away.

I found myself in the hills, on the cliff that Uriel bought for us. It didn't look as beautiful as it used to be, the tree was still there, the grass grew as if it was being cut only once a month. I guess he got people to clean it up, I guess now it explains why the grass cutters before were werewolves, he was a male alpha.

I sat at the end and looked down at the town, it was beautiful, why did I come here of all places. Images came rushing in, I lay on the ground and closed my eyes. The images got clear, we were playing on a water scooter the day he left, and he carried me up the cliff only to let me down easily.

The kisses we shared were always amazing, and when he hugged me, I felt protected instead of protecting.

"Ergh!" I screamed as I sat up. I looked back out on the town, lights were starting to turn off, I looked at my watch for the time, it was already midnight. I woke up at seven earlier, it took about two to three hours to get here, and I hadn't shimmered all the way.

The images kept filling up my head again, and I was getting more pissed. Why is my head doing this to me? To my heart? I can't take it, I wanted to jump off the cliff. "I hate you!" I screamed as loud as I could and images of me pounding on his chest screaming the same three words the day he left.

"Why? Why did you leave me, Uriel? Why? I hate you, Uriel!"

"I hate you for making me weak! I hate you for making me love you!"

I heard a growl behind and turned to see both Uriel and Zadkiel with Isaac and Alec, and I'm guessing Zadkiel was the one who growled, "Would you care to explain, brother?" Zadkiel hissed at Uriel, eyes glowing yellow.

"How did you find me?" I asked I don't have a scent.

"You're wearing my shirt. We followed my scent," he spoke angrily.

"This was the first place I was going to look, if my brother didn't think of following your scent." Uriel spoke and Zadkiel growled.

"I'm sorry, Katherine. If you only gave me time to explain before. I didn't want to leave, I had too and now you are a wolf and I am too, you could understand why I had to leave. I am ready to choose you over my mat—" he was cut by Zadkiel's growling.

"What the hell are you talking about, Uriel!" He hissed breathing deeply. Uriel looked at me and to his brother then back to me again.

"He doesn't know? Saraquel didn't say a thing?" I shook my head.

"Well, brother. Katherine, she is the girl I told you about. The girl I love and is willing to reject my mate for!"

Zadkiel growled again but Uriel didn't care even if he growled for the hundredth time, "She is mine, brother! You are never to go near her or talk to her!" My heart was having a debate where it was romantic or plain possessive.

"Sorry brother. But I love her, and now that I am back. I am going to do everything I can, to get her back." Uriel spoke calmly. I was shocked by his words, he loves me and he is going to fight for me.

"Uriel," I whispered his name but I know they all heard me, Uriel turned to look at me and I just stared at him.

"I hate you, I hate you." I whispered and walked to him as I stood face to face with him, Zadkiel growling by his side. I slapped him across his face causing him to jerk to the side but he looked back at me, he knew he deserved it.

"I hate you." I whispered again as a tear ran down my cheeks and he wiped it off. I was going to break down but I couldn't, I turned and threw my arms around Zadkiel's waist as I buried my face in this chest.

"I hate him, Zadkiel. I hate him." I whispered this time I let my tears fall.

ᚲᚲᚲᚲ |ALEC| ᚲᚲᚲᚲᚲ

It has been hours and Katherine isn't back yet, I've been going crazy. It was getting hard to control my wolf, it was harder for Isaac to control me and my wolf and his too. Zadkiel said that we would be leaving to find her soon.

"Alright men. Let's move out, three of you go south. Another three will go west, and my brother and I will go east." Zadkiel was speaking to his men.

"We are going with you." I spoke harshly, it was hard enough holding my wolf. Zadkiel nodded and we all shifted and ran.

Once on the hill, we shifted back and wore our clothes which we carried by mouth. Uriel said she might be near the cliff, my wolf was begging me to kill him for what he made her go through. This must be their place, since he knew where she might be.

"I hate you!" I heard a scream. "Why?" I heard another and we ran.

"Why did you leave me, Uriel?" She was screaming out to the town. "Why?" It hurt me to see her like this "I hate you, Uriel!"

"I hate you for making me weak! I hate you for making me love you."

She hugged Zadkiel, burying her face in his chest and cried. "I hate him, Zad, I hate him."

My wolf was howling she didn't need me anymore, she has her mate to cry to now. I wanted to growl at the sight of them, I wanted to run but couldn't, Katherine has enough problems with the twins, I don't want to give her more. I had to man up for her and just accept this.

❧ Chapter Twenty Eight ❧

'History will be kind to me
for I intend to write it.'
—Winston Churchill.

Zadkiel carried me home, bridal style, I said I wanted him to walk instead of shifting, I wanted an excuse to be in Zadkiel's arms. He laid me on the bed and opened his shirt and jeans, he sleeps with only boxers.

"Zadkiel," I whispered. "Can you open my shorts and bra, please?" I was too tired to move, moreover I wanted to have a little fun with him. I feel like eating him, his blood would taste good, he is my mate. He opened my shorts with little growls and the growls became louder when he unclipped my bra.

"Make love to me, Zadkiel." I whispered as I looked him in the eye.

"Tempting but I won't, you're just saying it because of my brother. I'll kill him for even touching you!" He growled.

"Please, Zadkiel. You can't tell me that your wolf isn't bothering you to holding the way you are supposed to? The only way you are allowed to? Would you prefer another man hold me?"

He growled, eyes turning yellow. "No! No one can touch what is mine! I don't care is if he is a warrior or my brother or even the freaking king, you are mine!"

"Only I can please you!" And with that he tore his shirt off me and attacked my lips. His kiss made my wolf go all kinds of crazy, he then moved to my neck, licking and kissing it, leaving love bites. I pushed my body to be sitting and he's to be sitting too. I kissed his neck and licked it, I could feel my eyes glowing red, craving for his blood.

"I want you," he murmured. "I need you now." He said but I shook my head. I wanted him to beg more, he was rubbing my back to control himself.

He carried me and made me sit on him "Mine," he said as he looked at me, his eyes trailed down and back up. "You are so beautiful and you are mine!" He said possessively. "Say you're mine, Katherine." He whispered in my ears and I shook my head. He pinned my body onto the wall. "Say it, Katherine." He kissed my shoulders. "Make me!" I growled back.

I opened my eyes to see Zadkiel looking at me, smiling, boy he sure did look cute. "What are you looking at?" I flirted.

"My beautiful mate." He answered and it made me blush so I looked away. "You look cute when you blush." *Let him mark you*, my wolf begged. I rubbed my neck, but there was nothing, so he didn't mark me last night.

"Is something wrong?" He asked worried about me.

"Nothing, Zad." I whispered, my wolf was still begging. She wanted to be connected with her mate.

"I'll make breakfast," he got up and I just stared at his butt as he searched for his boxers.

"Mark me," I whispered. I was going to shut my mouth when it came out, my wolf must have done it but I was too craving. He stared at me. "Mark me, Zadkiel." I said once more, to reassure him that he heard right. I never bear Benjamin's or Dylan's mark, what more Victor's when he has already a wife that bears his marked. I only ever had Lucas' but it disappeared the moment he took his last breath.

He came back to bed still without his boxers, "I love you, Katherine." He whispered in my ears before biting me and I screamed out in pain which then turned into pleasure. He licked on his mark to heal it before cupping both my cheeks, "Thank you, Katherine." He kissed my lips and got back up to find his boxers.

"What for?" I asked.

"For letting me mark you, it made my wolf happy and for making me hold you. I've longed for that, for being with my mate, thank you." I smiled. He finally found his boxers and put them on, before going into his drawer and pulling out a pair of shirt and short and walked back to me. He put on the pair of shorts and maxi shirt on me before carrying me bridal style, down to the kitchen for breakfast.

He was tickling me as he was carrying me to the kitchen. Once he walked in, I felt eyes all over me and I didn't care I kept giggling to Zadkiel's tickle till two growls were heard. I turned to see Saraquel sitting on Mike's lap and Isaac sitting beside the Alpha but Alec and Uriel standing. I could see that they were holding their wolf.

I got out of Zadkiel's arm and he growled at them, come on I had two wolves growling and he had to be the third. I glared at him and walked to Alec and put a hand on his chest, "Calm down, Alec, it's alright." He nodded and kissed my forehead.

Again two growls were heard one from Uriel and the other from Zadkiel. I turned to Zadkiel and glared at him. "Stop it, Zad!" I hissed.

"Katherine!" Alec's voice sounded angrily and I looked at him, he was staring at my neck. "He marked you?" I nodded.

"I let him." I answered and he looked really pissed at me, he threw his chair as he tried to walk away from me, slamming the back door as he left through the back door. I could hear his clothes tearing as he shifted. I wanted to run after him, to hold him like I used to and tell him that everything was alright.

"Don't, mate! You are mine! You will stay here with me, don't argue with me. He needs to be alone," Zadkiel said possessively. I nodded and I went to him wrapping my arms around his body.

"Zadkiel, it's my turn to patrol. You want to walk with me?" I asked but Isaac was the one that spoke "It's ok, beautiful. I'll do the round check."

"Hey, warrior! Call my mate that again, and—" I crushed my lips to kiss before he could finish his sentences and start a fight with Isaac. I heard whispers and break the kiss with Zadkiel only to see Saraquel once again holding a butcher knife, we both stared at each other before bursting into laughers.

"Dear God," I wiped the tears from my eyes, "That never gets old." I turned to Zadkiel, he was looking funny at me, I turned to look at the others and they too looked funny at me. I finally fell silent, "Oh, screw you! You guys wouldn't even think Walter is funny." I wrapped my arms over Zadkiel's neck "What you say? You coming with me later?"

"Yeah sure, I have to go to the pack library later on, though. I need to find something, and you little mate will come with me, alright?" I nodded before giving him a kiss and we ate our breakfast.

I got dressed after a quick shower and jogged down the stairs, walked past the living room, to see Saraquel and Mike watching the television. "You going out?" Saraquel called.

"Yes. I'm going for a walk with your brother, bye." I called back and made my way out, Zadkiel was talking with Brandon when I walked over to him, I manage a glare before linking my arms with Zadkiel's, "you ready?"

"Yes, come on." We started walking in silence for the past half an hour, I wanted to break the silence but didn't know what to say. I was hoping he'd asked me something, anything.

"Um." I finally gave up, the silence would kill me. "How come, Uriel and Saraquel never talk about you? Aren't you close with them? I know that Uriel and Sara are close but they aren't close with your father."

"We all used to be close, but that was a very long time. A time when my mother was still alive, when my mother passed away, my father did what every mate does when they lost their mate. He broke down for the first two years leaving me to take care of all the responsibilities with my siblings while my uncle, the beta took care of the pack." I saw hurt in his eyes as he told his story.

"I got tired one day. I was seven when I started training. When I was five, I took up a lot of responsibilities because he chose to leave them. I walked up to him and said—'Father, you are letting go of your responsibilities to the pack, and I am asking you to back down and let Uncle Josh take over till I am right of age!' I was sick of my father slacking off. On the same day he got his crap together and as months passed, we grew closer. He trained me and all, but both of us were so focused on things, we forgot about Saraquel and Uriel. I was to be the next alpha, I needed to train. When I turned ten, I got accepted to the academy and I've stayed there ever since, I didn't know my brother and sister, I didn't spend my teenage life with them. I practically didn't spend my whole childhood with them because I had to grow up faster than them, then Uriel. All this, is to protect them, to ensure them a life that is safe. I don't know a thing about them but I did all of this for them. Something they won't understand, and I don't expect them too. To them I am just this guy that's acting tough because I am the 'to be alpha', but to be honest, I am jealous with the relationship Uriel has with Saraquel. Unlike my brother, I've never hugged her not even once, my sister doesn't come to me for everything, ever. She had Uriel and now she has Mike, I guess it's back to square one, huh? I did all this for them but ended up that I push them away."

"You know what, Zad? I thought you were a tough guy too, I never thought you were this soft inside, thank you for opening up to me." I smiled earning a kiss.

"The library is this way, come on." I nodded and we both raced to the library. I won the race of course, no way in hell was I going to let him win, I never let Benjamin win in any of our hunts. Just as we were walking up to the library, Zadkiel and I came across a group of four boys shoving around a smaller boy.

Zadkiel walked over to them, "Hey!" He yelled as I tailed him. He pulled on two of the boys that were shoving the smaller boy around, "You boys think it's fun bullying someone smaller than you?" He growled "Huh?!"

"No, alpha." They answered with their heads bowed. "You!" He nodded to the other boy in front of him. "Pick up his things off the ground!" He growled. "Yes alpha." The boy answered. I walked over to the boy on the ground "Hey, you alright?" He nodded, I let out my hand for him to take, I smiled as I helped him up.

I walked over to Zadkiel and laid my hands on his back to calm him down, "Next time mess with some on your own size!" He called to the four boys who were now running away from us. "You alright, man?" The boy nodded "Good, now run along."

Zadkiel turned to look at me, I smirked as I raised my brows as to ask for an explanation. "I have no tolerance for bullying." He said making me laugh as a rush of déjà vo hit me, "What?"

"Nothing, come on." I pulled him into the library. He sat on the desk, looking through something as I looked around. The books in the pack library dated way back, I've read most of them as I walked to the other end of the room I saw a huge portrait of two men, the man on the right took my breath away as I just stared at it, how can it be?

"Mate is everything alright?" I jumped the same time Zadkiel laid his hands on my waist, I nodded but still kept my eyes on the painting. "The one on the left is my great grandfather, Luke. His twin brother my great grand uncle Lucas." Oh my god, I can't believe this. "Mate, you ok?"

Did he just call me 'mate'? The pet name Lucas would call me and yet when he said it, he sounds exactly like Lucas. "I think I need to sit down." He nodded before swiping my feet off the ground and started carrying me back to the pack house. "The two men, aren't they Italian? And the one on the right, Lucas, isn't he a rogue?"

He stopped in his place "Yes, you know how packs are, mate. The beta used to tell me that this pack originated from Italy, and because of rogues we have to relocate and that's how we ended up here, but how did you know that Lucas was a rogue?"

"Back in the mansion." I replied not wanting to say more.

"Yeah, he was actually the older one of them both. Lucas just rebelled one day and took off, leaving his younger brother to take over. There was even a rumour that he was the mate of the princess." Come on Katherine pull yourself together, I mentally slapped myself.

"You mean, he was to be alpha? The true alpha of this pack?" He nodded. We finally reached the pack house, Zadkiel carried me up to his room and laid me on his bed, telling me to rest as he still had some pack business to do.

Lucas lied to me, Benjamin wasn't my second chance as well as Victor and Dylan weren't my third or fourth, Zadkiel was. They came from the same pack, both crowned to be alpha and both the older twins with smoky grey eyes. My fate was to be here, this pack was destined to have me as their Luna, long before Zadkiel. This is too much to take in, I need to rest. I closed my eyes and inhaled the scent of Zadkiel, as I fell asleep.

I woke up the next day, in bed with Zadkiel. I gave him a kiss before shimmering out to find Isaac and Alec, only to find Isaac alone, Alec has been missing since yesterday. I am worried something might have happened to him, "Come on Isaac, let's go find him." He shifted into his wolf and I got on him as we ran into the woods searching for Alec.

❧ CHAPTER TWENTY NINE ❧

'Never choose until you know it's right.'
—Anonymous.

⟪⟪⟪ |ALEC| ⟫⟫⟫

I ran out the door, if I didn't I would have tried and kill her mate. I shifted and ran as fast as I could, I hated seeing that mark on her neck. I've tried marking her twice and the mark wouldn't stay for more than a second. I heard a voice humming a song I recognize as R.I.P by Rita Ora.

I tried running towards the song and found myself at a lake and there sat a girl just at the end of the dock, dipping her legs in. *"Mate,"* my wolf growled at me, I walked to the dock and the girl turned to look at me. She just stared at me, maybe her wolf was talking to her.

"Mate," she whispered. She knew me and bowed her head, "Warrior."

I shifted. "You don't have to call me that, little mate." I said, she was totally checking me out.

"What is your name?" Her eyes were as green as the leaves on the tree, lips as pink as a new born baby.

"Katharina West," she spoke. I was shocked by her name, it was almost similar to Katherine.

"You are mine, Katharina. You belong with me." I said as I walked towards her to hold her in my arms. "I'm not going to let anyone touch what's mine, mate." She nodded and I bit down her neck, marking her as mine.

I found my mate, I finally found her. I woke up with her still in my arms, we were both naked. After marking her, we completed the mating process, we had a little fun in the woods and now it's already dark out. I played with her hair as she was sleeping. I didn't want to wake her and I couldn't carry her back butt naked.

"Alec! Alec!" I heard my name, "Alec!" I heard it again, as it got closer and closer.

"Katharina, wake up. Get dressed, darling." I shook her and she awoke and went to get dressed. I shifted and ran to where I thought I heard the voice.

I had sent a mind link to Katharina to wait where I left her, I ran to the voices that were calling me and soon met up with a brown wolf, Isaac. Katherine was with him, sitting on his back. I didn't get why she didn't like shifting, her wolf is breathtaking, and if her clothes tore she would magically re-fix them.

"Alec!" Katherine got down from Isaac's back and came running to me, hugging my wolf, making my wolf purr.

"Mine." I heard the word, it belonged to a girl but it wasn't Katherine's voice. I turned to see Katharina is standing at the back.

⟪⟪⟪⟪ |KATHERINE| ⟫⟫⟫⟫

"Who's there?" I hissed after hearing the word 'Mine', a girl came out of the back of a tree.

"Who do you think you are, mutt?" I hissed, and she glared at me, the little bitch.

"I am Katharina West, warrior." She answered while bowing her head, looked like she does have manners.

"What are you doing here?" I was rubbing Alec's fur and sniffing it, I hadn't realized his scent was mixed with another, with the girl standing in front of me. "He is your mate?" I asked and she nodded.

I felt pain coming all over me. He finally found his mate but why am I jealous? Maybe I was too used to having him be mine, I guess. I took a few steps away from Alec and stared at him.

"Don't be sad, Katherine, it doesn't mean I'm leaving, I'll still protect you." He came into my head and I nodded. I licked him causing his mate to growl.

"I'm going to head back with Isaac, you stay here with your little mate. I am happy for you, I really am, she's beautiful." I couldn't stay longer with her in my sight, Alec

nodded and I patted him on the head before giving him a kiss.

His mate growled at me, and I walked to her. My face was only inches from her, she looked at me straight in the eyes, the mutt sure had the nerve. I smirked at her, and squatted before jumping high as I shifted into my huge blood red wolf. I heard her screaming and fell to the ground as I landed back on the ground on top of her.

I snapped my canine, causing her to beg for mercy, *"She's brave at first. I think I am going to like her, love."* I turned away from her and ran as fast as I could, I knew that Isaac was behind me.

I mind linked for Isaac to go back to the pack house while I ran off to the cliff. I've lost Lucas and got Uriel, lost him as well and gained Alec and then I lost him and end up with Zadkiel my mate, can I love him? When I look at him all I think of is Uriel, the pain I've been through trying to kill myself to stop the unbearable pain in my heart.

Sometimes I wish I got to say I lost Benjamin, Dylan and Victor but no, I don't get the privilege of saying I lost three great men when I didn't even have them from the start, but it doesn't mean I didn't want to, to love them, like I love Lucas.

"I thought I'd find you here." I turned to see Uriel standing behind me shirtless, I glared at him. Why was he even here? What are you doing here Katherine? This is his land after all, he has the right to be here.

"Can I sit with you?" I hesitated for a while but nodded. "What are you thinking of, Katherine?" I turned to look at him, just to stare at him.

Looking at his eyes I remembered all the pain, I hadn't realized I had used my powers to squeeze his heart until he grabbed my hand, "Oh God, Uriel, are you alright?"

He nodded as he tried to catch his breath, "You-your eyes were glowing neon red, Katherine."

"Look at me, Uriel, look at my eyes. They are not red, how could my eyes be red?" He stared at me in confusion before shaking his head like a wet dog drying its fur. He let out a little laugh and rubs the back of his head.

"Umm, yeah for a minute there I thought they were red."

"Why would you think that?" I managed a little smile.

"Training, back at the academy, vampires they have red eyes but earlier yours were glowing really bright red or I thought it did." He let out another laugh. "Training must be catching up with me huh?" I nodded and look away from him.

"Why are you here, Uriel? What do you want?" He sighed.

"I've been trying to get you alone, I want to talk to you," he said calmly. "Isaac and Alec, they don't like me, do they? I can tell every time I walk into a room with them in it, they let out a growl." I chuckled, that's my boys for you.

"I-I it wasn't easy, Uriel. Forgetting you and pretending it didn't hurt when you left, I love you more than anyone and one day I'll explain why. I thought you were human, I was ready to leave whatever mate I have for you, but then you left me with a broken heart. I tried killing myself once, Alec and Isaac had to put up with me."

I sighed before continuing, "Alec, fell in love with me and took care of me. I soon realized he had put up with all my crap and so I tried to love him back. At first I had to admit, it was hard not thinking about you. He nearly died once in a rogue attack, that was when I realized my feelings for him. I'm not going to lie and say I stopped thinking of you because I didn't, it's just, when I think of you I don't feel like dying any more but it still hurts to remember."

Uriel held my hand but I didn't push it away, I wanted to feel his touch again, the sparks but I just—I just don't know. "I was ready to give up my mate for you too, Katherine and I still am. I love you, I never stopped. I've told Zad about you, one of the reasons why he doesn't want me near you till I find my mate."

"Are you going to fight for me, Uriel? From your brother?" He nodded.

"I had you first, Katherine," he said possessively.

"Same as you hurt me first, Uriel. I don't know if I can love you again like I used to. I don't know if my heart can take a second hit, you're not even sure you could reject your mate." I sighed and continued "You knew you were going to leave, didn't you? Like months before the day you left. Why did you choose on the day you left to be the day you announce you're leaving?"

"First of all, for you, I'll even dare reject my wolf and second, yes I did know, the day I got my cast off, I got a letter. I wanted to tell you but I just didn't know how to. I decided to tell you three months before leaving but then my father forced me to go on one of his hunts, he found the rogues that killed my mother," he said sadly and he took my face in his hands to make me look at him. "Katherine, I love you." He said calmly as he came closer to me and our lips touched, the taste of him sent sparks through my body like it used to.

I kissed him back, I've been craving for him, since the day he left. He pulled me closer to him till I was lying on him, and he only broke the kiss due to a very loud growl.

"Get off of him!" I looked up to see an angry shirtless Zadkiel with yellow eyes.

I got off Uriel and stood looking at Zadkiel, I can never love him. I can never look at him without thinking of Uriel or even Lucas, I can never be with him. It's obvious I am always going to choose Uriel from the start. I loved him first, even if it was because of Lucas. I did love him like I loved Lucas. I went to stand behind Uriel, he stood in front of me protectively.

"It's obvious brother that she has chosen me and not you."

"She is mine, Uriel! She will come around, she will come back and I won't hurt her like you did. Don't forget, that she now holds my mark. You are going to have to kill me before you can fully claim her as yours! And even if you do! It would never be pure for she is my mate! She belongs to me." He hissed at his brother before looking straight at me.

"I'll be waiting for you in bed, Katherine." And he shifted back into his wolf and ran.

Uriel turned to look at me, "Thank you, Katherine, thank you for making it me and not him." He crushed his lips to mine causing me to moan. But my wolf was screaming at me for what I did, my wolf keeps on reminding me that every wolf will love me because I'm a princess. They are supposed to love me but only my mate can love me with the kind of love that I deserve.

"Katherine, let's head back home." Uriel said, carried me bridal style before I could even answer him.

"Uriel, let me down, I want to stay here, you can go first, I want to be alone please." He nodded and shifted. I was grateful that he didn't question me.

"Oh my god. I think I finally did it, I think I finally cross fate." I called out in my head. *"But how unfortunate for you, Katherine, because fate never gets crossed."* My wolf reminded me.

Once I felt that Uriel was far enough I turned back to the cliff, I knew that there was someone there and I was right. "Adaka, what are you doing here?" I spoke to make my presence known for the witch, my mentor.

"Having trouble in paradise are we, little princess?" She spoke as she let down the hood for me to see her face, she has grown older from when I last saw her.

"My father knows about my magic and our two kinds are at peace." She nodded as to say that she knows.

"I'm here to say my goodbye, princess. It's time for me to leave but I have to tell you something about your mates," she said as she walked closer to me.

"Mates?" I asked.

"Yes, the two male Alphas are your mates." I looked at her confused.

"But, but two? At once? Ho-how?" I stuttered trying to process everything.

"They are twins and they are both your mates. Uriel, he doesn't know you're his mate. He only possesses the spark whereas his brother possesses the knowledge, it is your destiny to choose one, and the one that you choose will be the future king. One of them will be fit for a king and the other will be the end of all your kinds, and so you must choose wisely, Katherine. Who is fit and who is not . . ." Her body started to fade and I knew she was leaving, "Goodbye, princess."

"One is fit and one is not," I replayed it in my head, *"fit for a king and the other will be the end of my kind."* Why is the spirit doing this to me? I maybe five hundred years old but I am not as wise as my age.

I think I now understand why Uriel didn't shift when he met me years ago, because I have two mates, because I was supposed to choose between him and his brother. If I had known Zadkiel years ago and chose Uriel over him then he would have shifted.

I let out a loud laugh. "Looks like I didn't cross you after all, huh, fate?!" I screamed into the air. I have been destined to belong to this pack ever since Lucas, and now it looks like no matter which twin I choose I'll still be bound to this damn pack.

"I don't deserve this. I hope you know that, fate! Uriel and Zadkiel. Benjamin. Victor. Dylan. Isaac and Alec and even my parents! They don't deserve this! All this crap!" I screamed grabbing a rock from the ground and throwing it into the air, hoping somehow it'd hit fate. "What do you have to prove? That you can break me?! No! Because

I won't back down to you! I won't back down to you of all things! You might be against me! But I have hope! Just the next strongest thing to own after to you."

I let out a deep sigh and collapsed to the ground, eyes close, but then it hit me. My eyes open wide with fear, if one is to be the next king? That would mean, "No." I murmured, that would mean my father would be dead because the only time a king would step down is if it was their time too—"No." I murmured once more.

❧ CHAPTER THIRTY ❧

'Is it a crime, to fight, for what is mine?'
—Tupac Shakur.

I got back to the house a bit late. I had stayed another three hours at the cliffs, thinking about Adaka, my father and the twins. Who was I going to choose? I don't want to be the reason why my kind will crumble. I didn't know where to sleep tonight, is it with Uriel or Zadkiel? I didn't want to choose, I never like choosing, so I went to the roof and stayed with Isaac. Alec was with his mate tonight.

"Hi beautiful, had a long day?" I nodded. "Come on, my shoulder's free."

I scooted over to him and laid my head on his shoulders. "Everything is going to be alright, princess," he said softly.

"How do you know that, Isaac? I have something to tell you."

"What is it princess?" He asked with concern.

"Adaka, the name of the witch is Adaka. She's my mentor, she taught me magic in exchange that I try to get my father to make peace with her kind and I met her a few hours ago at the cliffs." I took a breath, "And she told me something."

"Do you know that when I'm with Uriel, when he touches me and kisses me I feel sparks running through me? The exact sparks that runs through me when I touch my other mates, but when I am near Zadkiel, my wolf screams 'mate' and when I touch him, I don't even feel a single tingle, not even shiver. I didn't understand why at first until Adaka came to me earlier, she told me something about the twins," I hesitated but continued.

"She said that they were both my mates that Uriel carries the sparks and Zadkiel carries the knowledge. What is worst is that, both boys are the great, great very great grand nephew's of Lucas." I took another deep breath, even managed a laugh then continued, "She told me the one I choose will be the next king meaning that my father," I sighed again "It's almost his time isn't it?"

I took my head back from this shoulder to look at him, he looked as if he knew something, "Isaac, please I need to know if this is my last century with him." He nodded and I gasped as I started crying. He pulled me in to hug, I heard a growl and backed away from Isaac to see who it was, there stood Zadkiel behind me.

"It's time for bed, Katherine." He said possessively as he took me off the roof and carried me away from Isaac, I didn't refuse him. I put my arms over his neck as he took me to the end of the roof.

"Isaac, good night." I whispered and Zadkiel jumped off, landing on both feet and continued walking back to his room.

Weeks had passed, with still no rogue attacks. I admit that it was stupid to think that there would be another attack right away, it took Kevin two to three years before another attack. I had decided to go back to the mansion to be with my father. Uriel would be taking me to the cliffs every afternoon and we would spend time together. Whereas Zadkiel would be with me every night, I'm torn between two brothers, torn between love and fate, torn between two loyalties.

I was packing my things, getting ready to leave, Alec and Isaac would follow me. Alec's mate will be coming with us as well, I've already mind linked three warriors to come and take our place. Zadkiel and Uriel were now with their father, doing some pack business.

My men and I would be gone before they would be back, I didn't tell Zadkiel or anyone about me leaving. I finally finished packing and carried my bag out, meeting Isaac and Alec with Katharina. We were going to ride in Katharina's car since I can't shimmer the whole way back with her and I didn't want to shift. Alec hasn't told her about me, and she must be stupid to not realize my wolf when she disrespected me, and me shifting into my wolf to show my dominance.

Before we could even reach the mansion a big black wolf with yellow eyes blocked our way, it was Zadkiel. Alec stopped the car making it screech as smokes were made from the tires. He was driving fast, even when the car isn't actually a sports car, I got out of the car.

"I'll go back myself. I'll call so tell Alec not to worry," I told Isaac and walked closer to Zadkiel.

He motioned for me to get on his back, I was obliged. I wasn't in the mood for arguing so I followed everything he was to ask of me. We ran for what seemed like hours, it was making me sleepy and I laid on him as he ran.

"We are here, mate. Wake up." He shook my body to get me up.

I opened my eyes to see Zadkiel leaning towards me, I got up and saw that we were in a forest, and there was a beautiful waterfall, this place—it was even more beautiful than the cliffs.

"It's beautiful, where is this?"

"This is where my father met my mother, she was a rogue that trespassed into our lands. My mother and father used to come here for dates and would bring Uriel and I." He slid his hand around my waist and I let him.

"Can we take a swim, Zadkiel?" The water looked nice, and it had been a long time since I last swam, thinking about it sent images of the day Uriel left. It was the last time I went to a beach, and it was the first of me getting over my fear with deep waters.

"Sure," he whispered into my ears and planted small kisses around my neck and shoulder from behind.

"Ah." I moaned as his hands were making their way up my body, "Undress me." He growled at my words.

My parts were screaming at me, begging me to let him take me without a fight and I was going to give in. Zadkiel bent his head, bringing his mouth closer to mine, my lips were slightly parted, mutely offering myself to him.

But he didn't kiss my lips, he just kept teasing me, making me crave for more. He's going to make be beg for it. If I was freaking love drunk right now, I'd already be on my knees begging for his lips on mine.

I arched my back, trying to bring my mouth to his. "Zadkiel, please?" I gave up and begged. "What happened to 'I am a warrior'?" He asked smirking. "You don't need a mate, right?" I glared and got off him.

"I'm going home, to Uriel. Don't forget that you two are twins and I'll be getting the same," I said just to piss him off as I walked away from him, he let out a growl, grabbing my arm and pulling me to him, it made me squeal when he pulled me to his chest.

"Mine!" He growled as he crushed his lips to mine and ripping my shirt in the process. God it was freaking hot, a real turn on. I wrapped my arms around his neck, he was playing with me, but still not leaving my lips.

He carried me, wrapping my legs on his torso. He carried me as he kissed my neck, he leaned my back against a tree before tempting to open my pants.

I was wearing skinny jeans making it hard for him to open, he was getting frustrated, making me giggle. He looked at me as I giggled and smirked at me and I knew what he was going to do but before I could protest, my jeans were already in pieces like my shirt.

He was now kissing my bottom lip, licking and sucking it, making me moan continuously. "So beautiful" he groaned, "And all mine."

His blood smelled so good I don't think I can help myself any longer. I sank my teeth in his neck, marking him as mine.

He pushed me back, away from his body, one hand putting pressure on his neck. "What the hell?" He cursed, really pissed at my action, I wiped the blood off my lips. "I can explain, please, Zadkiel." He shook his head and grabbed his pants. I shimmered in front of him.

I took the pants from his hand and toss it into the water, "Mine!" I growled at him before taking his lips with mine, he returned my kiss. I pushed down, making his body fall to the ground with me on him. But him being an alpha male didn't like me being in control.

"I love you, Katherine." He said and I felt different, I felt sparks, sparks I felt with Uriel now I felt with him.

"I love you too," I moaned. "Say it again." He whispered. "I love you, Zadkiel Arch Spike."

I woke up in his arms, still in the forest, we ended up not taking a swim. Zadkiel was still soundly asleep, I looked at him and played with his hair as he slept.

"Have you been awake for long, mate?" He said eyes still closed, it made me jump a bit.

"I just woke up, love." I answered him, he opened his eyes and pulled me in for a kiss.

"Are you going to explain why you bit me earlier?" He asked and I nodded.

"Nope not really but I am going to tell you something and I need you to understand it, alright? No interrupting, ok?" I said.

He nodded and sat up. "I am not what you think I am, or who I am. You and Uriel are my mates." He stared at me with a confused look. "You and Uriel are my mates. Uriel, he has the sparks and you mate, got the knowledge."

"But I felt it earlier, the sparks. I didn't feel it before though, my mother used to tell me stories about mates. I was curious why I couldn't feel sparks when I held you at night." I nodded.

"Me too I guess. I choose you and I think that's why we felt the sparks, and that's not all actually." He looked more confused. I guess I should have started by telling him I was his princess instead of the mate thing.

"I have a mentor, her name is Adaka. She taught me things and that night on the cliffs when I thought I chose Uriel, or I was going to choose him. She came to me and told me that I had two mates and one of them is destined for greatness while the other, not so much. I'm not sure who but it was my choice to make and I choose you."

"Will you stand by my side?" He nodded pulling me for a hug. "Zadkiel? I know it's confusing it's because I'm—" I whispered but was cut by two words.

"Kevin! Attack!" The two words came into my head and I shot up in an instant, Zadkiel just looked at me in shock as I was already fully dressed.

"Stay here I have to go, Kevin is attacking." I said and ran as fast as I could but Zadkiel caught me.

"They're attacking the next door pack." He said, "Brandon just mind linked told me they were asking for help, my men are on their way, I'll go with you." I nodded and we both shifted and ran together, he still hadn't noticed my fur, did he even know what my fur means? Didn't he notice that I am his princess?

❧ Chapter Thirty One ❧

*'We are going to have peace even
if we have to fight for it.'*
                    —Dwight D. Eisenhower.

"*Alec, Isaac, I'm on the way with Zadkiel,
updates, now!*" I mind linked them as I ran
to the attacked pack.

"*We just arrived with your father and Katherine?*" Alec
was the one who answered, Isaac doesn't like talking in
mind linking when he is fighting.

"*Yes.*" Knowing that my father is there made me run
faster, I didn't have time to run the same speed as Zadkiel,
I needed to protect my father.

"The queen is here, your mother is here. The werewolf rogues have teamed up with vampire rogues." I growled in my head and ran faster leaving Zadkiel behind.

"I have to run faster, love. The werewolves have teamed up with vampires." I ran ahead, leaving him behind.

The fight had already broken really bad when I arrived. I tried searching for both my parents and Isaac and Alec but they were nowhere in sight. The pack fighters were dying, my wolf was getting mad, forcing itself to take control of me.

I let out a loud growl and everyone near me stopped fighting. I shifted to my human form already dressed. I was then surrounded by multiple wolves, one attacked me but a wolf jumped in front of me, Alec. It was Alec, another rogue attacked me, and Isaac bit down on him.

I sniffed the air and smelled my parents close by, I knew Alec and Isaac could handle it, I shimmered to my parents and my father was in wolf form with my mother by his side. I shimmered in front of them, standing protectively.

More than twelve rogues stood before me, showing off their canines, about ten vampires, hissing their fangs. First two vampires bit down on me, the other eight followed, sucking in my blood and I let them. My blood is only meant for my mate, other than that then drinking from me turns vampires into stones. I learnt that the hard way in the process I killed a woman who has been captured by vampire rogues and wasn't fed, I offered my blood, only killing her.

Before they were even done drinking from me, they started turning into stones, screaming for help and begging for mercy but me, myself couldn't change what happened, it was part of me. My eyes were now glowing red, I could feel it. The wolf in front of me was Kevin, I could tell by his scar.

I felt pain as my blood flowed out, when two wolves attacked me but it wasn't painful as hell though. Kevin was ready to bite down on me, and I waited for the pain as he charged but another wolf blocked me and I screamed, "No!" I didn't know who it was, if it was Uriel or Zadkiel, it all happened so fast.

The wolf that took my place was my Uriel, his wolf shifted back to human. I listened as his heart stopped, making my wolf go crazy inside for losing a mate. I couldn't hold myself, I shifted into my wolf. I looked down on the ground and noticed that my paws were now red instead of black, I turned to catch a glimpse of my tail, which had also turned blood red. Soon later I felt nothing and my wolf took over everything as a way of protecting me. It was like black out, because the lost of a mate is just something that is too much to bear, especially for a royal. Just like Lucas when he was taken away from me, my wolf took over and started killing. That's what happened, some people they die soon after, others if they are strong enough they rebel.

I could feel my canines were longer than the usual and my size got bigger. I could see my eyes glowing from the reflection from one of the rogue's eyes, I was not a normal werewolf. I was a werewolf with very long fangs and red eyes, as if my whole ability just smashed into one.

Before I could even attack one, all rogues attacked me, biting me down, trying to take me out. I could feel my blood drying out of my body, and for a second I thought 'this was it' that this was what could kill me. Light flashes before my eyes and an image of two little girls playing with two other boys, and I knew what this meant.

I was pregnant, I didn't think of anything else because of it, I shook my body and the rogues were flying off of me. Alec and Isaac attacked them while they were down one by one.

More rogues tried attacking me and with one bite from me, they turned into ashes. I could smell the scent of Zadkiel near, I had to go to him to help him, killing any rogue that came at me. I lost Uriel, I won't lose Zadkiel too.

There he was, Zadkiel back to back with his cousin, Brandon. They were holding off about twenty rogues. The rogues charged at them the same way they did with me earlier, I know now that this is their tactic to take out wolves with higher rank like me, my father and alphas with betas by ganging up on them.

Howl. I heard a howl from the other side, and rushed to it, leaving Zadkiel with Brandon. I stopped to see two male wolves. Behind them were females and children, the two males were holding back about twenty rogues. A body of a man was laid beside the two male fighters, they must have been howling because of his death.

I shifted back into my human form, I raised my hands and every rogue was lifted into the air. I turned them to face me, making the wolf growl and the vampire hiss. I looked at them smirking.

"Sorry to rain on your parade boys, but you all should know better than to mess with packs," I said before turning to the vampires.

"Well, look at this. Fishes out of water," I smirked "You vampires should know not to team up with werewolves, they will only get you killed. Haven't you realized how jealous they are of our immortality?" I continued.

"You should be happy, princess." One vampire hissed. "Weren't you the one who wanted us two kinds to come together?"

I glared. "Don't mock me, rogue," I said calmly but it came out like an echo.

"Hypocrite, aren't you, Princess?" He hissed. "You don't want your people to fight but you're killing rogues yourself," he smirked at me.

"But that's where you are wrong, my little rogue. I don't kill unless it's necessary," I said calmly but still my voice echoed, I was using my princess' tone. Alphas have the same tone it's just that, only wolves below him, in the same pack would obey.

"A century ago, I gave rogues a chance to submit or be killed. They decided their own fate and a group of rogues attacked a few months ago, and I didn't kill them. In fact I even let the group go except for the leader, though. But I didn't kill him, my little rogue. I punished him. And same punishment will go for all of you."

This time he didn't smirk but I saw fear and regret in his eyes. "For the wolves, you will be forced to shift a hundred times, if you live after that then you will be let free—"

I was cut off by laughter, "I'm not finished yet, pup." I said smirking as his laugh faded. "When you shift, the process will be very slow and the pain will be a hundred times of what you felt when you first shifted and also your sons, and your sons' sons will inherit this from you." The rouge that had laughed now looked at me in shock and fear, and all I did was shot him a wink, that will teach him.

"And for the vampires, I'll give the worst punishment ever made, dehydration." Dehydration for normal vampires is really painful. They would be locked up in a room, for days or months, where on the other side of the door, out of their reach is where a blood bag would be laid for them to smell the scent of blood, making them crave every day, till the second they die.

And usually during this process, they become weak and start having hallucinations of memories they try not to remember, like a first kill or watching your loved ones die.

I walked away with pleads and begs from the rogues, they deserved it. They should know what they got themselves into, trust me. It hurts to see my children suffer but if it takes a whole rogue group to save a million pack then why not?

I heard another howl coming from where I left, Zadkiel! I panicked and I shimmered to see one huge black wolf with a human body beside it. The wolf was holding off five wolves. It was Zadkiel and the boy beside him was Brandon, dead.

The wolves attacked Zadkiel all at once biting him causing him to howl in pain. It made me mad, it could cloud my judgment, there wasn't time for mercy, they didn't deserve it so I shimmered to him ripping the rogues off of him one by one before ripping off their hearts hurling them away.

For every wolf that lost its life, I became weaker. It's a way of my mourning, Zadkiel had shifted back into his human, lying naked on the ground. I went to him and tried to wake him up but he passed out. His heart was beating really slowly that I howled to the moon, I couldn't lose two mates at once.

It just wasn't fair, but then again, fate never played fair. "Zadkiel, you better not die on us, please not you too. I won't forgive you for leaving us please! Uriel is gone, not you too. She couldn't stand losing two mates." I begged as I hugged him close, tears falling but they weren't water but blood. It shocked me at first. I couldn't stand the thought of my mate dying.

"I love you, Zadkiel Arch Spike. Please wake up, she won't be able to handle the kids alone without you!"

He started to stir before murmuring, "kids?" I smiled and nodded.

"Yes, little you and me. Pups! She's pregnant, Zad. I don't know how but she is," I cried and he got up on his own and crushed me to his chest.

"She?" He whispered and I nodded.

"I'm her wolf, I took over when she watched Uriel die taking her place." I said before another howl was heard. It was Alec, the howl belonged to Alec, then another howl sounded it was Isaac this time.

I felt something ripping inside of me. I didn't know what it was at first, till all the other wolves howled to the moon, "Father" I whispered before shimmering to where I last saw him. Alec and Isaac were standing protectively in front of my mother who was kneeling on the ground to a body, "Father." I whispered again, his heart was still beating.

Rogues tried attacking them again, "No!" I screamed and my voice echoed out loud and all the rogues turned to look at me. I felt like a feather, I looked down to see I was flying. My hair was being blown by a strong wind as my eyes glowed brighter and blood tears fell.

"This is enough! I will not take it anymore, I will not show mercy and let you all survive! All of you will be killed slowly, all of you will be cursed to shift with pain! If your king dies, your mates will be killed in front of you before you die as well! I have lost patience with all of you, and this will be the last time, you all will defy me!"

"Beautiful, calm down. You're bleeding! Your ears, nose and eyes, you're bleeding! This is enough, they will get their punishment." Isaac tried reasoning with me.

"Shift." I said calmly and all wolves were forced to shift. I lifted my hands to make a particular wolf float in air, Kevin.

"Put me down, you filthy hybrid!" He hissed at me and laughed. "Did I hurt daddy's little girl?" He said with a smirk. "Go ahead, kill me. I made my history here today, princess."

"I won't kill you, Kevin. The other rogues will be grateful for that, I will kill them but you? I'll make you live forever like me and so will your mate. She will be tortured in front of you and if you haven't finished the mating process, you will be by force, just to feel her pain as well."

The smirk on his face was gone. "Go to hell! You slut!" He hissed. Alec and Isaac let out a growl and so did Zadkiel.

"Tell me Kevin? Why? Why are you doing this? Why lead a group of rogues to kill pack alphas and betas? With your strength you could lead a pack, a real pack why settle for this?" I need to know, I need to understand why he did this.

"Don't act as if you don't know crap, princess! You are supposed to take care of the whole werewolf creature not only the ones that are obliged to the rules but the rogues as well but instead you order them to kill them! Under your orders, they killed my family! Only due to the freaking fact that you and your father couldn't control us rogues anymore! I had a family, princess. A wife and three children. She wasn't my mate but I love her and because my family and I were rogues. They killed them and I wasn't there to protect them." I saw the hurt in his eyes.

"Who killed them?" I asked but he started laughing as tears ran down his cheeks, he finally caught his breath and answered me.

"Don't act stupid, princess. It was under both you and your father's orders! It was hard times back then, rogues started acting out. You and your father decided to get all the alphas and betas to wipe out all the rogues that wouldn't agree to commit to a pack! They didn't ask them! They didn't ask them whether they wanted to join a pack or not, they just killed them in cold blood! I know they would have said yes if they had the chance, I just know."

"Wait, but that order was carried out a century ago? How could you manage to stay alive?" I am starting to understand why Kevin kills pack alphas and betas. I now understand why he is here, he is here to kill me once and for all, for killing his family but wait—if he has been alive all this years meaning—"You. You killed my mate, you killed Victor and just earlier you killed another one of my mates, Uriel. You killed two of my mates, you bastard! And the only thing you lost was a wife! You disgrace—" I hissed with much anger before I could finish I heard someone called me out.

"Princess," it was a woman's voice, I turned to see Adaka with a few friends. "Let the rogue go or we will go on a rampage," she said without a fear. Her right arm lifted pointing in the direction of my boys, I turned to see Zadkiel, Alec and Isaac being strangled by air.

"What are you doing, Adaka? You wanted peace!" I was furious but she just laughed at me. "Don't flatter yourself, princess. I waited years for you but you did nothing. Kevin here helped me kill the pack that tortured my family and I owe him a debt of gratitude, another reason why he is still alive over a century."

"That day? At the grave land? You were calling me out, weren't you? I should have known better then to trust creatures like you!"

Adaka nodded before she took out a sword from her back. "Do you know what sword this is?" She said showing it to me. It can't be, it just couldn't, I felt my feet touch the ground and I walked over to her, to see the sword more closely.

"Excalibur." I whispered and she laughed wickedly.

"The greatest wizard made this. Marlin, his name—" she spoke as she walked around me but I cut her.

"I think we all know the story, Adaka. Get on with it, you little witch!" I hissed making she smirked. Everyone was right, witches were tricky creatures to get involved with.

"Excalibur was made to kill anything!" She claimed and I laughed at her stupidity.

She slashed the sword on my tummy, letting my blood pour out. It usually takes seconds to heal little wounds like this but the cut wasn't healing, my blood flowed out, and I started to feel weak.

"Katherine," I heard Zadkiel saying my name gasping for air. She slashed me more on my legs and arm, I knew what she was doing, she won't kill me on the spot of course. She will kill me slowly like the pack killed her family, this is revenge. I whispered a chant and the boys fell back on the ground. I lifted my hand to point at my mother and the boys ran to her, just like what I hoped they would.

I prayed this time, to the spirits for forgiveness before casting another spell. I made a force field around my mother, Alec, Isaac and Zadkiel. The force field was to stop them from leaving until everything was alright and keeping the rogues and bad magic from entering.

Adaka lifted the sword as Zadkiel screamed my name trying to get to me, I was kneeling on the ground, I lifted my head to take my fate. She was smirking at me as she was about to plunge the sword to my chest. "I love you, Zadkiel," I whispered one last time.

"No!" He screamed, "I love you too." I couldn't feel the pain because everything went black for me.

❧ CHAPTER THIRTY TWO ❧

'Hope is the dream of a waking man.'
—Aristotle.

((((|ZADKIEL|)))))

She was floating on air, my wolf was screaming at me. Why was she flying? What was going on? It was weird seeing the blood running down her face. At first, I thought that she must have had cuts on her face but warriors have always had the ability to heal faster than normal wolves, her eyes were glowing red, while she was punishing the rogue. I was trying to process everything that I was seeing. Why did that rogue keep calling her princess?

Then realization hit me "Princess." A woman said. I turned to see an old Brazilian woman with her coven.

Princess, she is our princess, Zadkiel. Our mate is Princess Katherine Rose Claw. My wolf told me but it can't be, how can that be? *You've heard of the story, that the princess could only drink blood from her mate that is why she bit you.*

"Let the rogues go or we will go on a rampage." She has spoken again then looked from me, to Alec and Isaac. She lifted her hands and I was in the air, it was like someone was strangling me. I tried to push away whatever was on my neck but there was nothing. I tried to look at Alec and Isaac and they were too, having the same problem.

Katherine turned from the rogue to the witch before looking at me, "What are you doing, Adaka? You wanted peace!" She sounded furious but the old witch just laughed.

"Don't flatter yourself, princess. I waited years for you but you did nothing. Kevin here has helped me kill the pack that tortured my family and I owe him a debt of gratitude, another reason why he is still alive over a century."

"That day? At the grave land? You were calling me out, weren't you? I should have known better then to trust creatures like you!"

"Do you know what sword is this?" She said as she showed the sword off. Katherine looked at the sword in shock, she was now on the ground, walking to the old witch.

I was trying my best to fight whatever magic was on me. My eyes widened when my little princess murmured "Excalibur."

"The greatest wizard made this. Marlin, his name—" the witch tried to explain but obviously we all knew the story.

285

"I think we all know the story, Adaka. Get on with it, you little witch!" I knew this wasn't the time but Katherine looked hot when she was mad.

"Excalibur was made to kill anything!" The witch claimed and Katherine responded with a laugh.

I watched as the witch swung her sword at Katherine, cutting her tummy, letting blood pour out. I wasn't scared because I knew she would heal fast. She wouldn't even feel pain, but started to get worried and continued back struggling when the cut didn't heal. Both Alec and Isaac were trying to fight to get to her side, they must be a Zink and Fox to care that much for her. They were her personal guards their family has always been given the title.

"Katherine!" I gasped as she now looked weak.

The witch continued cutting her till she was on her knees in front of the witch. Katherine was whispering something I couldn't hear, chanting and when she was done, I fell back to the group with a tug. Katherine lifted her hands and pointed to her mother, I looked at Alec and Isaac and they nodded at me. We all ran for the queen.

Katherine bowed her head once more, chanting something like she was a few seconds before and a circle was carved on the ground around us. Which was when I knew what she was thinking, I tried getting out. Alec and Isaac as well tried, we were screaming for her to let us help but nothing.

"Katherine!" I screamed as the witch lifted the sword aiming for my mate's chest.

She lifted her head, "I love you, Zadkiel." I heard her whisper.

"No!" I gasped, please don't, please! But I knew I couldn't do anything but to tell her the words she wanted to hear, "I love you too", I whispered as I cried to the spirits to make a miracle. There is a reason why fate has given her as my mate, and I don't think she will be taken away from me just like that.

I watched as she closed her eyes ready to take it in, and I watched as the witch was about to plunge the sword in her. Just as the sword was about to touch her, a bright red light came out of my mate's body. It was too bright I had to cover my eyes.

When the light subsided, I tried to look at my princess. She was now lying on the ground with four huge blood red wolves beside her, two of them had white tails the other two had black. The wolves, they weren't solid, like a ghost you see in the cartoon movie, they were translucent that I could see through them.

The first two wolves with black tails growled as the witch tried to strike at my mate again, the other two went to attack her followers. The witch kept swinging the sword but it just went through them. The one on the right must be the oldest of them four, seeing how fast it took for it to lose its patience. It bit down on the witch, causing her to scream out in pain, but the wolf didn't stop till she was lifeless.

The rogues tried to attack them from behind but they turned showing off their long canines like they were fangs, their eyes weren't black but red, just like Katherine's. The rogues finally backed down only by the sight of the four wolves.

I was about to tremble as the two with white tails were coming over to us. I was shocked to see that they went through the force field Katherine made. Both wolves licked each of my hands and the other two with black tails came over, wrapping me with their body as a hug.

The wolves then walked back to Katherine, all lying beside her, soon a red light appeared again but I forced myself to see it. The wolves were being sucked into Katherine's tummy. Oh my god, I think I got a glimpse of my four children.

Katherine started to stir, I was still trying to fight the force field to let me out because she needed me. "Katherine! Katherine!" I screamed.

☾☾☾☾ |KATHERINE| ☽☽☽☽

"Katherine! Katherine!" I heard my name being screamed by my mate. Was he in trouble? I quickly got up and shimmered to the circle I left them in, "Zadkiel," I whispered weakly.

"Katherine, open the circle," he said quickly. I crossed my feet over the line breaking the circle before I passed out again.

I woke up in somewhere dark. "Hello?" I shouted. My eyes were still trying to adjust to the darkness when suddenly the lights came on. I saw Isaac and Alec with Katharina in hand, my mother and Zadkiel.

"Uriel." I whispered as I remembered that he died saving me. He should have known that a little bite wouldn't kill me. My wolf was going crazy in me because of his death, I wanted him beside me now.

I hadn't realized that I was in a cell till I saw the smirk on Zadkiel's face. "What the hell is going on? Why am I in a cell? Where is Uriel? I need to see him I can save him, I know I can! You know this won't lock me up, right, Zadkiel?" I glared at him, trying to break it open, I just felt so pissed at him right now, and I wanted Uriel.

"I know love, but the queen here can. I made a deal with your mother, you know when you lost a mate you go crazy? Well for a royal you go extra crazy, but we have mourned enough, Katherine. You've been sleeping for months. You've just woken and you must be looking for my brother," he said smirking.

"Why thank you, Zadkiel. For reminding me about how I went on a bloody spree when your great uncle died! How thoughtful of you!" I growled glaring at him, I turned to my mother ready to burst a tantrum at her. "What is the meaning of this mother?" I hissed at her, not liking what was about to come to me.

"Darling, I get why you are acting like this. When Lucas died you went on a bloody spree because he was your first mate, and Uriel is no different from him. You love him, something you couldn't have done with your other mates but this? It's nothing personal, darling." She said still daring to smile.

I watched as Zadkiel dug his hands in his pocket and took out a little red box, making my eyes wide just looking at it. He came closer to the silver cell not close enough to touch it, he got on one knee, "Will you, Katherine Jane Claw, do the honour of marrying me?"

I just stared down at him, he is to be king. He is to be my husband. My other mates, never asked me to marry them, except for Lucas, but we didn't actually get the chance now, did we? I glared at his stupid attempt. What did he think? I won't go out till I say yes? I may have accepted him but I want Uriel now. I had to make sure he is alright, I really have to. I wasn't thinking straight, my wolf kept telling me to forget Uriel, but I couldn't. If he wasn't my mate, he was still the man I love so much and my wolf is just pissing me off. How could she just ask me to let it go? He is also our mate.

"Let me out, Zadkiel," I said flirting.

"I would listen to her if I were you, Zadkiel. Beautiful over here is best known for getting what she wants and if she wants out she'll get go. Don't fall for her act, she may act as if she wants a hug, but she will do more. If you're not going to take my word for it, take Alec's." Isaac said calmly beside Alec, he of all people knows I don't get pissed off easily but I do get freaking furious.

I looked at him and managed a smile, even if he almost ruined my plan to rip Zadkiel's heart out. "Come on love, let me out. I really do want to give you a hug. I want to hold you close to me." I said calmly before lashing out. "So tight you run out of breath! Now let me out! I want my mate! I want Uriel!"

"Oh darling, we didn't want to do this the hard way," a voice came from the back of them. Father! It was my father he is alive.

"What are you going to do, Father? Take away my Barbie doll?" I hissed.

Isaac opened the cell with gloves, my mother and father walked in and both held my side, my father on the left and mother at the right. Isaac shut the door back, and opened the cell opposite to mine and Zadkiel got in. What is going on, the stupid moron is going into a cell?

Isaac and Alec disappeared a moment only to come back with silver chains and went into Zadkiel's cell, I don't like this one bit. I stared deadly at Zadkiel, my breath had deepened. Alec and Isaac wrapped the silver around Zadkiel, making him scream. His eyes were turning yellow as he tried his best to keep his wolf in.

"What are you doing? Stop!" I tried to pull away from my mother and father ready to kill my two boys, do they have a death wish or something? Zadkiel kept screaming in pain, making me weak. I could feel the pain he felt, only because we have already mated.

I turned my head weakly to look at my father, sadly. "Why?" He didn't answer, he just looked back at me and I only cut the stare when Zadkiel screamed again. "Father please! Don't. Please not again, don't take another mate from me. Please," I pleaded crying.

"Please stop," I begged. "Please, Zadkiel. Why are you letting them do this?" Alec soon took out a knife from behind him. I could tell he was enjoying it, if he hadn't met his mate he would be alone.

"Don't you remember what happened before you passed out, Katherine?" My father asked and I shook my head. I don't remember much.

"I just remember a war and Uriel. He saved me, he tried to save me, that stupid mate. I couldn't die with only a bite, Father. I couldn't!" I wept. "Zadkiel." I whispered,

I can't do this anymore, I can't see him hurt. I bowed my head ready to give in when Zadkiel went in my head.

"Marry me, Katherine and they'll stop. If I can't marry you, if I can't have you with me, if I can't show that you're mine then, I'd rather die."

His words finally did it, I was officially pissed. He did this to get a yes out of me. The little pup, my eyes was now literally glowing red with anger, I pushed my father to the side knowing my mother will go to his aid.

I busted the cell door open before going on to Zadkiel's and breaking it too, I tilted my head at Alec and Isaac and they knew it was their cue to leave. I would never hurt them, I may not always be in control, but my wolf recognizes who Alec and Isaac were to us. I ripped the silver from Zadkiel's body and he dropped only to have me catch him.

I kissed his lips, down to his jaw lower to his neck and back up till I whispered in his ears, "I'll marry you, Zadkiel Arch Spike." I could hear him purr as I licked his wounds.

"Say it, Katherine. Say it," he whispered. At first I didn't understand until images popped up in my head, me telling him I love him, me choosing him. My wolf, she must have blocked everything after Uriel died, she must have blocked every moment I had with Zadkiel just like when Lucas left.

I'm pregnant with Zadkiel's baby, as the images came back I had a smile on my face "I love you Zadkiel Arch Spike, I love you."

❧ EPILOGUE ❧

I gaze out through the window from the attic, watching two of my little boys being trained by my father. Well I don't think you could call it training, when the teacher is the one on the ground and the students are on both feet with a sword aiming at you.

"How the mighty have fallen," I thought making me smirk.

Kevin escaped that day with a few rogues, my boys have been training for years to take him down. Nobody will sleep in peace until he is found, dead or alive. There were rumours that he died because Adaka was gone as well, he needed her to live longer. It was after all because of her, that he had lived many centuries. But unless his body is lying in front of me will I not believe that he is really gone.

I steal my eyes away from them for a moment and look up at the sky, watching the flock of birds pass by. I smiled as I remembered just a few years ago, I was in a cellar kneeling down by Zadkiel's side, telling him I'd marry him and a few weeks later there I was in my room standing in front of a mirror, admiring my wedding dress. My father knocked on the door telling me it was time and walked me down the aisle. I remembered the way Zadkiel stared at me in awe as the pianist played the wedding song.

"I was destined for this," I told myself then, sometimes I thought of me being there, walking down the aisle, would be the same feeling I would get with Lucas. Either way, this was what I wanted. This is the life I wanted, the life I craved for, the life I've chosen and the life I was destined for. I was about to get what I wanted, what I have been fighting for. I was about to make a family, to have a family.

I remember as he said his vows and I said mine, when he said I do and I did too. When the priest announced us man and wife, when we had our first kiss one more time.

Now it had been five years from when we were wed and here I am in the attic starting out at two of four of my angels. I wondered where my girls could be, but I needed not worry much, Zadkiel, Alec and Isaac would never leave their side.

We were now the new king and queen, Zadkiel and I. Both my parents had retired from their throne. Just after the day we came back from our honeymoon. Every month I would be away just to keep things in both vampire and werewolf world sane. When I am away, my babies would come with me, and we would be leaving Zadkiel to deal with things here. No vampire would obey any werewolf, well, unless you're a hybrid.

My father, he is now immortal, and he has forever to spend with my mother. I'm sure you'd love to know how my father turned into immortal, well just like my mother he could be a little too cocky as well, one thing they have in common I guess, also one thing I've inherited from them both. My father was taking care of my little angels one day as Zadkiel and I went out on a date, we came back to find my father on the floor, all four angels of mine biting down on him for being too cocky and saying that he is the strongest werewolf that has ever lived and could take them head on. I know it's really mature for a dozen century year old wolf, huh? Well, the bite somehow did something to him, it made him immortal, I don't know how but I just knew he was going to have forever now. Forever with his mate, they are both happy, I rarely see them happy and that has been what I've always wanted as well for them, to be happy, they lived most of their life in pain and now fate has found pity in them, enough to let them be happy.

As for my angels, I have four magical children, my first born is a boy whom we named Rayzac Jace Spike, right after was another boy by the name Rayyan Jaden Spike, then my girls, Amaranth Hope and Accalia Fate Spike.

My babies, they are truly magic, they were born immortals, they were born with fangs. Zadkiel freaked out at first, I remember that night, when Zadkiel took me out for dinner, Saraqael took care of my little pups, when we got home and asked if they were asleep, she nodded her head and we made our way up to kiss them good night, only to find four baby wolves, sleeping in their crib. It was first in history, they were youngest wolf that shifted, at first I was scared of course, it would be unimaginable that they could be each other's mates. But my fear has been kept at rest when I visited Lucas, he explained that they were powerful and had to shift. As for Alec and Katharina, they are soon to be parents as well and I am happy for them.

With my heightened sense of hearing I could hear footsteps running up the stairs to me, making me steal my gaze away from the window and watch the door for who was coming. Alec suddenly busted in with deep breath, "Wow, where is the fire?" I joked as he tried to take his breath.

"It's Zadkiel," he said catching breaths, my eyes widened as I waited for him to say more. "He and Isaac are at it again."

I laughed at this, they have been at it for more times than I could already count, "What happened this time? Zadkiel asked Isaac to go home again?"

I watched as Alec shook his head, "Fate and Hope, were playing tag with a few children. One of them might have just tagged a little too hard, Fate fell and Isaac is threatening to rip the child's head off. Zadkiel came soon after, now stop laughing and stop them."

I laughed a little again as I made my way to them, Isaac, he has been having problems. Zadkiel has been keeping an eye on him since my baby Fate was born, who would have thought that, when Zadkiel showed Isaac Fate, the first word he would say was, "Mate."